Time to Fly

Time to Fly

LYN ASQUITH

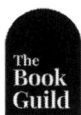

The
Book
Guild

First published in Great Britain in 2025 by
The Book Guild Ltd
Unit E2 Airfield Business Park,
Harrison Road, Market Harborough,
Leicestershire. LE16 7UL
Tel: 0116 2792299
www.bookguild.co.uk
Email: info@bookguild.co.uk

The manufacturer's authorised representative in the EU
for product safety is Authorised Rep Compliance Ltd,
71 Lower Baggot Street, Dublin D02 P593 Ireland (www.arccompliance.com)

This work is entirely fictitious and bears no resemblance to any persons living or dead.

Typeset in 11pt Minion Pro

Printed and bound in Great Britain by 4edge Limited

ISBN 978 1835742 846

British Library Cataloguing in Publication Data.
A catalogue record for this book is available from the British Library.

1

Helen wandered into the kitchen to make a cup of tea. Her attention was immediately drawn to the bowl with the crusty remains of the lasagna she'd recently eaten, along with the stack of washing up from earlier piled erratically in the sink. Her mum had constantly told her 'Always put dishes in to soak' but, as usual, she hadn't followed the practical advice given. How she regretted that now, knowing baked-on pasta was going to be very difficult to shift. She was also aware there was at least a full load of washing to deal with. To make matters worse, at the bottom of the basket were her soggy, smelly socks, which she had worn on a walk earlier in the week. Every time she had put more washing into the basket, the strong, musty odour of the socks hit her nostrils. She shuddered.

Deciding she didn't want to face either job and finding no clean mugs in the cupboard, she grabbed a glass of wine instead and headed back into the living room. She could hear the rain lashing against the window, and feeling the draft blowing into the room from the gap under the front door caused her to shiver. She lay on the settee, pulling the duvet she had grabbed from the bedroom tightly around her.

'I really need to do something about that,' she said to herself, dreading the thought of another awful job to get round to when she had the money and energy.

It was Saturday night, and she was bored.

Life was far from a riot of activity at the best of times, but usually at weekends, she was out with her best friend, Ana, either at The Top Hat tavern (especially if there was a band or quiz night on) or another local pub. Ana had gone out for a meal with work colleagues late afternoon and said it was unlikely she would want to go out in the evening if she'd had a few drinks. So tonight, Helen was on her own.

Flicking through the TV channels, there was nothing much on, not even a good (old) film. So, with limited options, she did something she wouldn't normally do and decided to watch the lottery show. It wasn't usually on, but a brief show had been added to the TV schedule, as it was the largest lottery rollover. Feeling herself drifting to sleep, she hung in there because Ed Sheeran was due to sing his latest single and give details of his forthcoming UK tour. She sighed. Ed Sheeran's gigs were always sold out quickly and the tickets were so expensive. She didn't have the money to go to a concert, but if she closed her eyes, she could imagine she was there, watching him 'live'.

He confirmed that as part of The +-=÷x Tour, he would shortly be performing at Wembley Stadium, and although most locations were sold out, a couple of extra dates had been added, and there were still a few tickets available. Then it was time for the lottery to be drawn. She was mildly interested, as the lottery hadn't been won the previous week, and it was a massive rollover. However, that soon changed when she recognised the number of the first ball, and then the second, were both hers. She sat up and immediately paid more attention.

Her first thought was, *Well, this looks good. I have probably won a fiver or maybe a lucky dip.* By the fourth number there were dreams of a holiday in the Bahamas and some new clothes. And by the fifth, her heart was beating fast. What the hell?

And then the sixth ball…

Sitting there for a moment, there was so much to process. This must be some kind of joke. Her immediate thought was, *Where are the hidden cameras?* Were Ant and Dec going to pop out from behind the settee and say it was a prank for an episode of *Saturday Night Takeaway*? It would be the kind of 'surprise' Ana would play on her, as she had jokingly talked about it in the past.

Get a grip and think logically, Helen told herself. Had she really seen the right numbers or been too sleepy to take them in and made them fit hers?

Trembling, and in what felt like slow motion, she turned on her laptop. Going on to The National Lottery website, she discovered the numbers were not available yet. How long would it take to put the information on to their site?

Not to worry, she thought to herself, *at least go and get your ticket and check the numbers.* Then, she panicked. *Where* was the ticket? Was it even still in date? Normally, she bought four weeks at a time, but occasionally she had missed the odd week when she had forgotten to check if the ticket was still valid. How she wished she had listened to friends who had constantly said 'Why don't you just put it on direct debit if you play every week, Helen? Saves you having to mess about.'

They had a point. But she remembered buying it, as she had also splurged on a nice bottle of white wine and a three-pack of Turkish Delight (her guilty pleasure), either last week or the week before, after finishing an awful temp job.

She breathed a sigh of relief when she saw the ticket on the fridge door, showing there were two more weeks left on it.

Frowning, she wondered if the remaining two weeks would still be valid, if she had actually won this week?

She laughed. Why was she worrying about continuing to play the lottery if she had won the 'Big One'?

With the ticket in front of her, Helen frantically tried to recall the numbers from earlier. In her head, they seemed to be the same as those on her ticket. She always played the same numbers every week: five (her birth date); nine (her flat number); twelve (Ana's birth date); twenty-five (her brother's age); forty-four (her lucky number); and fifty-six (the age her mum was when she died).

This is crazy, she thought. She couldn't just sit at home, waiting for confirmation of the numbers. This was important! She decided to ring Ana. The phone seemed to ring for ages. Assuming Ana wasn't back from the meal yet, she put the phone down.

Had she won? No, it was unlikely. She had obviously made a mistake.

Of course, Ana rang straight back.

"Why did you hang up? Have you had a drink? Or had a better offer in the last ten seconds?" she asked.

There was laughter in her voice, as the chance of a better offer was very slim and she knew it.

"Sorry," Helen replied, not knowing quite what to say.

Ana could read her like a book. She immediately knew something wasn't quite right.

With no response, Ana became worried.

"Are you OK?"

Her voice was gentle and full of concern.

Feeling nervous, confused, and excited, Helen was unsure how to respond. All she knew was, she had to go and see Ana.

"Can I come over?"

"Of course, you idiot, but just promise me you haven't had a drink or are emotional, because if you are, get a cab."

"Give me ten minutes," Helen replied.

This was crazy. What if she was wrong? Should she wait until the morning and check the website when the numbers were available, just to be certain? It was probably all a big mix up, and Helen had just seen what she had wanted to see, following half a glass of wine. Some sort of 'projection' to make a boring Saturday night more fun.

It was imperative she saw Ana. With her calm and practical approach to life, she was sure to be able to make sense of it all.

The girls had been friends since the first day of high school. Helen had been determined, moving from primary, that she already had all the friends she needed and didn't want to make any others at a new school. She would stay with all her primary friends in their own little bubble. Unfortunately, when it was discovered where everyone was going, Helen quickly realised she had got into her third choice, and none of her friends were going to the school she would be attending. Distraught, she begged her mum to appeal. She did, but the decision was upheld. So, there she was, on her first day with no friends, feeling so alone and on the verge of crying, but trying her hardest to be brave. Sitting on the floor in the hall, waiting to find out which class she would be in, she was suddenly conscious of someone sitting next to her. In fact, they were sitting *very* close to her.

Then someone whispered in her ear.

"Are you on your own too? Scary, isn't it? Perhaps we should stick together."

Helen felt the person squeezing her hand. *That* was her introduction to Ana. Half Portuguese, with beautiful long dark hair, olive skin, tall, slim, and pretty, she was the complete opposite of Helen; wavy, mousey brown hair, short, glasses, and wrapped up in so many insecurities. The pair of them soon discovered, however, they shared the same wicked sense of humour. Ana could always make Helen laugh, and over the years, they often laughed until they cried. Ana would always have to be a part of Helen's life – she knew too much about her!

Helen had never had such a deep and meaningful friendship. They could read each other like a book and were always aware of the other's moods; offering comfort when it was needed or keeping a low profile when one of them wanted some space. They experienced the joy and excitement of boyfriends and were there to console each other during the inevitable heartbreak when relationships finished.

They also shared all the major events in each other's lives. Ana had never known her dad, as he left when she was a baby. And when Ana was only twenty, her mum had died of cancer. Helen lost both of her parents in a car crash on their way back from a holiday when she was twenty-four. During those particularly difficult periods, the pair's friendship was more important than ever. They really didn't need anyone else. Despite having a younger brother, Sam, Helen couldn't tell him her concerns about finances or when things were going wrong in her life, as she always felt she had to be strong for him. As a result, Ana and Helen were their own powerful, invincible team, always there for the other to offer support, guidance, and (occasionally) common sense.

They both knew their friendship would last forever. However, 'forever' can be relatively short. Just seven months ago, Ana had been diagnosed with cancer. She'd had various tests, but it took well over a year for the diagnosis, and they knew it was serious. The day and time would never be forgotten, as it changed their lives in such a cruel and devastating way.

As the consultant was giving Ana the results, Helen's world stopped in an instant. Selfishly, all she could think about was how she would cope without her best friend. She soon snapped out of it, knowing she couldn't let Ana down, as she needed to be strong for *her*. They had handled difficult situations before and would get through it again, as Helen felt confident Ana would fight it and come back even more resilient than ever.

During the appointment, they both tried to be strong and hold it together to take in all the facts, but when they got outside the hospital, they just cried, hugging each other so tightly, for what seemed like forever.

They agreed there would be no discussions about the cancer unless it was in preparation for an appointment or going for treatment, as that was what Ana wanted. Generally, Helen went with her to every appointment, including chemo. Having been made redundant from her secretarial job six months earlier, Helen was currently temping. In a way, this made it easier to get the time off, but it also meant any absence from work was unpaid. Ana was conscious of this and offered to pay for her time, but Helen wouldn't hear of it. This was her best friend, and she said she could manage. However, where possible, appointments were scheduled at the start or end of the day, to make it easier to take time off work.

Fortunately, Helen's mortgage was small, as house prices were reasonably cheap when she'd bought her flat in Luton eight years ago. It had desperately needed a considerable amount of renovation work and lots of tender loving care. Luckily, her dad had been able to help with most of the major repairs before he died.

Ana had a well-paid job as a regional account manager for a worldwide finance company, and luckily for her, one of the benefits of the job was a good sickness scheme. Fortunately, she didn't have a mortgage, as her lovely little cottage had been paid for with the inheritance she received when her mum died.

From what the consultants had said, it was assumed Ana's treatment and aftercare would be complete within a year, so the financial impact would be minimal.

Following an operation to remove the cancer, the

doctors felt it had been successful. The consultant explained it would be necessary for this to be followed by a course of chemo and then hopefully, Ana would be OK.

With Helen's phobia of needles and hospitals generally, they had discussed whether she should attend Ana's chemo sessions. The idea of sitting with her best friend during chemo filled her with dread. However, it was important she was there, so it was a no-brainer really.

Helen would never forget the first time they went. Ana guided her into the room as she had her eyes shut, not wanting to see the needle. Helen began to feel very sick while they fixed Ana up with the drip, as she could hear the nurses explaining what was happening.

As a result, during those sessions, Ana and the nurses were more worried about *Helen*! However, their bond was so strong, she would always be there to support her best friend, however difficult it was.

As usual, Ana took it all in her stride, and there was soon a routine; Helen would sit the other side of Ana, so the needle wasn't visible. Then, they would talk, laugh, play games, and just be their 'normal' selves. This meant they were often being told off by the nurses for making too much noise. On one occasion, they were playing Which Would You Rather Be, a Bear or a Gorilla and Why? A nurse came in just as Helen was leaping around the room making gorilla noises. She then had to try to justify what she was doing. Another time while waiting with some other patients for chemo, they all started a hearty rendition of 'Always Look on the Bright Side of Life.' It made everyone laugh, and the nurses could see it lightened the mood.

As Ana responded well to the chemo, it looked like the cancer had been beaten. But it was not to be, as it returned soon after, and this time much more aggressively. The consultants discussed various options to try to keep it at bay, which the pair of them clung on to in the belief the doctors would eventually find a way to treat it.

Getting ready for the appointments or just after, was always the worst. Privately, both Ana and Helen cried bucketloads of tears, hiding their sorrow so they could be brave for the other. It seemed cruel, wondering if the treatments would work, and if not, how long they would have together. Outwardly, it was a united belief Ana would recover, and everything would go back to normal, as doctors did say there was a fair chance the cancer could be treated. Helen hung on to that 'chance' like a big thick rope. If anyone could beat this, Ana could.

Cancer is a horrible thing, as you don't know what the treatments will be like or how you will feel during those times. Also, if the prognosis isn't good, you are left wondering how much time you have and how bad the ending will be. Ana, like so many other people who have had cancer, seemed to gain an amazing inner-strength. Helen knew Ana was scared and how hard it must be for her, but she never complained or asked 'Why me?'

Her attitude was 'Why *not* me? It could happen to any of us.'

Helen was so proud of her.

It helped that her consultant, Carl Peters, was so great. During Ana's first appointment, Helen was holding her hand as they walked in, and she continued to do so to show her support while Ana occasionally rested her head on Helen's shoulder. Mr Peters asked how Helen, as Ana's partner, was coping with it all? Both girls looked at each other and laughed.

Ana replied, "Well, Mr Peters, I don't know what makes you think I fancy Helen! However, if you said *you* were single…"

After initially looking embarrassed and not knowing quite what to say, he soon began to understand the girls' sense of humour as they sought to deal with the cancer.

It meant appointments with Mr Peters were very relaxed most of the time, and Ana encouraged him to be completely honest with her about everything. No pussyfooting around or trying to sugar-coat everything. Initially, some of the nurses found her behaviour a little odd as she could be very blunt, but when they got to know her, they ended up loving her and her strength of spirit.

A ritual developed on appointment days; get it out of the way, then off to Jasper's Cafe for a cup of tea and cake. The more calories the better. Not good though for someone like Helen, who always seemed to be fighting with her weight. They never talked about the earlier appointments during their visits to the cafe, as this was their way to de-stress and forget about it for a while. A treat away from the madness of it all.

The only time they didn't go to Jasper's after an appointment was when the consultant told them the treatments hadn't worked, and their worst fears were realised – 'incurable' and 'not sure how long' were the only words that registered. Shrugging her shoulders, Ana refused to talk about it, saying when the time was right, she would discuss it further, but not until then.

So, on that particular Saturday evening, with the lottery the only thing on Helen's mind, she arrived at Ana's cottage in Lilley in a daze. She remained in her clapped-out, old Escort for a while, wondering how the hell to explain what had happened. Ana had obviously picked up that something wasn't right, as she was looking out of the window, waiting expectantly for Helen. As she remained in the car, Ana rushed out of the door and started banging on the passenger window.

"Get in here right now!" she ordered. "What's so urgent that you need to come round at this time of night? Is Sam OK? Have you met someone? Have you won the lottery?"

Ah, so there it was. 'Have you won the lottery?' It *was* a joke. She was obviously in on it; there were probably cameras following Helen's every move, and any minute now...

"OK, very funny, where's Ant and Dec? You can come out now!" Helen shouted, feeling really disappointed and humiliated at such a sick joke. She got out of her car and locked it, heading slowly towards the front door.

"What are you going on about?" Ana asked, sounding cross as they walked into the living room. "Sit down and tell me what the hell is going on."

Helen did as she was instructed while Ana disappeared into the kitchen to get her a glass of wine. Helen was clearly shaking as it was handed to her.

"Oh my God, you are scaring me now," Ana said, sitting on the sofa. "What's happened? Just tell me what's wrong. You know I won't judge."

Then, with a look of panic on her face, she gasped and said, "Oh no, you're not pregnant, are you?"

Laughing at the absurdity of it all, Helen then began to cry.

Unable to bear the suspense, Ana shouted at her best friend.

"For goodness sake, tell me!"

Babbling and hoping it made sense, Helen began to explain how the evening had panned out.

"Well," Ana said brightly, "by the sound of it, you can treat us to a mini break somewhere. What about Brighton?"

Taking a minute to compose herself, Helen continued. "No, I don't think I have a *few* numbers, I think I have them *all*. I think I have *won* the lottery!"

Ana looked rather confused.

"What?"

Helen knew she must have made a mistake but tried to explain as clearly as she could about watching the lottery show, seeing Ed Sheeran, and then the subsequent draw of the numbers.

Ana laughed at first, but looking at her friend's face, she realised it was no joke.

"Come on, let's check again. Did you bring your ticket with you?" Ana asked in her typical, logical manner.

"No," came the dazed reply. "I didn't think to bring it. I know it is safe, but—"

"Oh, Helen! We should check it properly. Hang on, let me grab my coat. We need to go back to yours. I'll pack my pyjamas and stay the night."

Full of nervous excitement, Ana bounded off to her bedroom to pack while Helen's glass of wine remained untouched on the table.

Arriving back at Helen's flat, neither of them was sure what to do. Helen topped up the half glass of wine, which was still on the table where she had left it before going to Ana's and poured her friend an orange juice.

Checking the website, the numbers were still not listed.

Ana looked thoughtful as she sat down.

"So, if you *have* actually won the lottery, what will you do with all that money?"

Although it was highly unlikely Helen *had* won, it hadn't stopped her wondering how she would spend her winnings.

"First things first, I would move out of this little flat and buy a nice big house with its own grounds. It would have to be a minimum of five bedrooms, all en-suite. Obviously a huge one for me with a walk-in wardrobe, one for you, another for Sam – if he wanted to come and live with me – and another two for any other friends who wanted to come and stay. I'd like a gym, indoor swimming pool and some land so I can have a vegetable patch and a typical English garden. Maybe some chickens too."

"You don't go to the gym, you hate getting your hair wet as it goes frizzy, you know nothing about gardening, and you are afraid of chickens!" Ana said, laughing.

"Well, I'll hire a personal trainer and get a swimming cap. Monty Don or Alan Titchmarsh can design the garden and teach me how to look after it, and maybe I'll give the chickens a miss! Then you and I need to do some serious clothes shopping and go on a cruise while Monty or Alan work on my garden. Now, where are we going?"

They spent the next few hours making lots of amazing plans: road trips, cruises, hiring private jets, as well as visiting exotic locations.

And to top it all, there would have to be a private concert by Ed Sheeran in Helen's new (huge) back garden. To hell with the cost!

2

Helen couldn't remember what time they finished making all their grand plans, but she awoke the following morning, still on the settee, to the smell of bacon and eggs. Raising a very sore head from all the wine from the night before, she realised it was eleven o'clock. Ana came through to the living room with the food and a very welcome cup of tea.

"I knew the smell of bacon would wake you up," she said. "Now, let's have some breakfast and see if we can find out if you really have won anything, or if you just had some sort of meltdown that affected your judgement last night."

Ana grabbed Helen's laptop and waited for it to whirr up, before checking if Helen had, in fact, lost her marbles.

Ten minutes later, they sat there in shock, neither of them saying a word. There, in front of them, was confirmation Helen's numbers were correct. As it was a rollover, it was one of the largest UK National Lottery

Jackpots since it had started. An estimated £18 million!

The most she had ever won was £25 and that had only happened once.

"What now?" she asked, finally breaking the silence.

"How the hell do I know," Ana replied, laughing nervously.

Helen continued, "I don't even know who to ring. As I bought the ticket at ASDA, should I let them know and ask their advice?"

Ana punched her friend's arm, causing her to yell out in pain.

"No, you idiot. Do you want everyone to know you have potentially won a fortune? You'll get people knocking on your door begging for money, or you'll find you suddenly have lots of new best friends!"

Ana was right as usual.

Helen had stupidly imagined someone would come knocking on her door to confirm the win. Thinking logically, having bought the ticket from the local supermarket, no one would know who had the winning ticket.

Ana suggested they take time to think about what the next step should be. It wasn't as though there was an immediate time limit on claiming the money. Helen was sure it was something like six months. With neither woman generally impulsive, it seemed sensible to leave it a few days to think it through.

Because of the size of the win, the media carried stories stating there was only one jackpot winner on the Saturday night. There was also an indication the ticket had been purchased 'somewhere in the South-East', but nothing more.

Looking at the ticket regularly, and continually checking the lottery website, Helen knew it wasn't a mistake. For the rest of the day, Ana kept trying to be helpful by coming up with ideas for the money; the wilder the better! Before long, they had a whole year of travelling planned, including safaris, a trip to Iceland, an Asian Temples tour, and a trip to India to include the Darjeeling Himalayan Railway. This was a dream of Helen's dad, so she felt it would be nice to do it, in memory of him. While in India, they would also need to visit the Taj Mahal and many of the interesting, colourful markets.

Helen was finding it hard. How, when you believe you have won the lottery, do you manage to keep quiet about it? It's not as though you can just carry on as normal, especially with all these mad, wonderful ideas floating around in your head.

On the Monday morning, sitting at her desk in yet another new temp job, surrounded by people she didn't know and with an awful manager who obviously had no respect for casual staff, Helen had trouble mastering one of their computerised systems. The screen had gone blank. She tried vainly to get back into the files, but to no avail. After twenty-five minutes, she asked one of the other girls in the office for help. The young woman sighed, reluctantly got up from her desk, pressed two buttons, and retrieved the document.

When presented with the updated paperwork, the manager was clearly annoyed it had taken so long to correct something which he considered to be straightforward. Helen felt like getting up and walking out, saying as she went "Do you know how much I am worth?"

For the remainder of the day, she regularly found herself daydreaming about spending the money.

Although still not fully convinced she had the winning ticket, despite the evidence suggesting otherwise, the one thing clear in her mind was that she didn't want any publicity.

Helen remembered seeing the newspapers full of horror stories over the years, about how people's lives had changed when they had won, and often not in a good way. After a big win, relationships with partners, friends, and family members were often tested to the limit.

What would Helen even do if it was confirmed she had won? You can't exactly go back to 'normal' living after a huge win, can you? And why would you want to? Change would obviously happen, and as much as it was exciting, it was also very scary. How do you manage such a phenomenal amount of money? Where do you put it? Into your normal bank or a special savings account? That was another reason for putting off contacting the lottery. It would then become real, and the enormity of it all would have to be faced head on.

Over the next few days, life for Helen continued as normal. The media, however, were very keen to find the winner. The net was closing in on the area where the ticket had been bought.

Watching the local news one evening, the owner of a small convenience store in Lilley said he was sure the winning ticket had been purchased in his shop. He went even further by claiming he thought he knew which customer had the winning ticket. Whether he genuinely believed the ticket had been purchased there or not, it was a great publicity opportunity for the store. Journalists from all over the country popped down there to find out what the shop owner knew.

In a way, it took the pressure off Helen, who was completely aware of where the ticket had been purchased. But there was still a constant niggle in the back of her mind. Maybe she hadn't won or perhaps someone else would come forward.

It was then the nightmares began.

The first was that someone had found out Helen had won. They broke into her flat, took the ticket off the fridge, and claimed the win for themselves.

In the second, Helen had gone into the bank, and when she got to the desk to pay some bills, the cashier screamed at her.

"Oh, you are the lottery winner, aren't you? I can see all the money in your account."

Everyone in the queue immediately surrounded her, begging for help paying their bills, etc. She awoke in a cold sweat; it felt so real.

Reliving the nightmares to Ana, she advised Helen to take the lottery ticket off the fridge and put it somewhere safe. Not knowing where else to put it, Helen hid it in an old sock in her underwear drawer. *No one* would go in there!

Just over a week after the 'possible' win and unable to cope with the uncertainty any longer, Helen went round to Ana's with the ticket. They went onto the lottery website again, just to see what the procedure was if you thought you may have won.

On the website there was a number to ring. Helen sat there for a minute, thinking.

"Well, go on, ring it," Ana said excitedly.

"But what if I haven't won? I am going to look really stupid."

"Don't be silly! You have the ticket, and we can see the numbers are the same. *Of course* you have won!"

It was so good to have Ana's voice of reason. Despite the evidence, Helen was still unsure if this was either a mistake or a joke.

"Give me the phone," yelled Ana. The next minute she was dialling the number.

Helen panicked and tried to stop her.

"Hang on. Do you think it is a good idea to ring yet? I think you have something like six months to claim. And what if they want a big press conference or something? I don't want that."

"Look, there's nothing wrong with ringing them and being careful about what you say. You don't even have to give them your name. You can just say you *think* you may have won something, and can they give you some advice. Come on, I am right here."

Ana handed the phone over, before grabbing Helen's other hand, placing it firmly in hers for reassurance.

Suddenly, there was someone on the other end of the line.

"Good morning, National Lottery Helpline. How can I help you?"

With that, Helen took a deep breath… and it was out of her hands.

3

The woman on the other end of the phone was polite, but from her tone, it sounded as though she probably had lots of calls from people who rang as a joke, or others who thought they had won big, but were disappointed to find they had only won a few pounds. She began with some simple questions, including Helen's full name and confirmation of the number on the ticket.

"And where did you purchase this ticket?" she enquired.

Once Helen had provided the information requested, she was asked if she could hold for a minute.

It seemed ages before the woman came back to her, and when she did, she asked for Helen's mobile number, stating someone would have to call her back. Then, with a polite "thank you", she was gone.

Helen sat there, listening to the dial tone for a moment.

"What's happening? Why didn't she pass you on to someone?" Ana asked anxiously.

"I don't know, she just said someone will ring me back," was the simple reply.

Ana's patience was wearing thin.

"There must have been someone you could have spoken to about your win. I mean, if you have won the lottery, you should be seen as a top priority. Does she think it's a joke?"

"I don't know, Ana!"

Helen was feeling nervous and totally out of control. Would they ring her back? And more importantly, did they even believe her?

Twenty minutes later, perhaps the longest time in her life, Helen's phone rang.

"Hello, Miss Pond? This is Stuart from the National Lottery."

Ana dug Helen in the ribs as she didn't immediately respond, causing her to yell out in pain.

"Sorry, Miss Pond? Is everything all right? I am just ringing regarding the phone call you made a short while ago."

"Yes, it is me, Miss Pond. I mean, please call me Helen. Um, I think I may have won the lottery, but I am not sure. It could be a mistake, or someone playing a cruel joke on me, I just don't know..."

Was she making sense? She couldn't be sure.

"Don't worry, let's start from the beginning," Stuart said.

"Right, can you give me the ticket number?"

Once again going through all the questions she had been asked earlier, Helen began to calm down a little.

There was a slight pause from Stuart, as he seemed to have asked all his questions.

She hated pauses and immediately jumped in.

"I've made a mistake, haven't I? I knew I couldn't have won."

Stuart was very composed.

"I haven't said there was a mistake. Can we just go through the ticket details one more time?"

As well as answering all his questions relating to the ticket, he also took a few personal details. He asked if she could email him a copy of the ticket and her passport for verification purposes.

Writing down the email address he provided, she confirmed everything would be sent through as soon as the call ended. Stuart explained that once all the documentation had been checked, he would get back to her. He also suggested writing her name on the back of the ticket to confirm it was hers.

Putting the phone down, Ana asked a flurry of questions, despite having listened to the whole conversation on speaker phone!

"Well, it wasn't a 'no', was it?" Ana squealed.

"Agreed, but it wasn't a 'yes' either!" Helen replied. "I'd better go and get my passport so I can scan it."

She then began to panic. Where *was* her passport?

After an hour of frantic searching, the flat looked as though it had been burgled, but the passport was nowhere to be found. As someone who was normally good at keeping important documents together, she became agitated.

"So, when did you last have it?" Ana asked.

"Stop being the voice of flipping reason," Helen responded, angrily. "If I knew, I would be able to find it, wouldn't I?"

Then she remembered. A couple of weeks ago, she had missed a parcel delivery, and the note through the door said she had to pick it up from the post office. She had needed to verify her identity and had taken her passport. While there, she had also bought some stamps. Moving over to the drawer where she kept the stamps, the passport was underneath the book of second class she had purchased.

She ran around the room, waving it in the air.

"Got it!"

Turning on the printer, she scanned the passport and lottery ticket and sent it to the email address Stuart had provided.

"Well, we'll soon know if your life is going to change," Ana said.

Now, there was nothing further to be done until there was a call back, confirming one way or the other.

Not knowing when someone would ring, they didn't dare move out of the apartment for the rest of the day, so by half past one they were starving and, as usual, there wasn't much food in the flat. There was nothing in the fridge, as Helen hadn't been shopping for a few days, but she managed to find a small can of sardines in the back of the cupboard. She had bought them a while ago for a diet she had tried, so lunch consisted of sardines on toast.

Ana pulled a face as the plate was passed to her. "Urgh, I hate sardines. They don't even look or smell very nice."

"Don't worry. If I have won the lottery, you can choose whatever you like in future," Helen replied.

The National Lottery office called back at quarter past four, the time forever after deeply ingrained on her brain.

"Hi, is that Helen Pond? It's Stuart here. We spoke earlier."

As if it was possible to forget!

"Are you sitting down?"

She gulped and nodded, which wasn't very helpful to Stuart.

Not receiving any response, he continued.

"Congratulations, I can confirm you have won the lottery, and a very significant amount, too. My advice is not to mention it to anyone else at this stage. Better to wait until our representatives have had a meeting with you to go through everything properly. A couple of our advisors could see you at two o'clock on Tuesday, if that's convenient?"

"But that's two days away! Can't we just have a chat about it now?" she asked naively.

Having already had over a week to think the win was a possibility, she was keen to talk to someone to get things sorted.

"I'm sorry. We need to prepare our paperwork and then come and see you, just to clarify everything and check your documents, so I am afraid the earliest will be Tuesday. Or I can make it another time, if you prefer?"

Well, what could she say? She confirmed Tuesday would be fine to see their representatives and hung up the phone.

Ana pulled her friend up from the settee and started to whirl her around the room, shrieking with excitement.

Helen was more subdued. Two days is a long time when you are waiting for something so important. When Ana had calmed down, they started to talk more about what the win would mean.

Helen wondered if she should tell Sam. She was close to her brother, but as Ana quite rightly pointed out, he was the worst person to keep a secret.

"Do you remember when you tried to spring a surprise birthday party for me two years ago?" she asked. "Sam started quizzing me about what theme I wanted for my surprise birthday party, then put his hand over his mouth. I reminded him the clue had been in the word 'surprise'. I love Sam, but honestly, you know he can't keep a secret to save his life!"

Helen smiled and nodded, knowing Ana was right. If Helen *had* won a lot of money, and it sounded as though she *might* have done, the last thing she needed was unwanted publicity, and Sam definitely wouldn't be able to keep it to himself. So no, telling Sam probably wasn't the best idea at this stage.

Also, Stuart had advised her not to mention it to anyone until his team had been round to confirm the win and talk it through in more detail. She explained she had told Ana, but being her best friend, she didn't count as they had no secrets, and she trusted her implicitly.

Helen thought it was a good idea to take the Tuesday off work to meet the representatives, as she knew it would be impossible to concentrate.

Going into work on the Monday and telling her manager where she was temping that she wouldn't be in the following day, he told her in no uncertain terms not to bother going back, as they needed someone more committed. It wasn't surprising, as she had already taken a day off the previous week for Ana's hospital appointment.

Ringing the temping agency, they were also unhappy, saying they needed 'reliable' temps. Apologising, she explained there was a lot going on in her life, so maybe it was best not to find her any other bookings for now. They didn't sound disappointed.

On Tuesday morning, she was up very early, not having had much sleep the night before due to the excitement and trepidation of what was to come.

Her first thoughts were about what to wear to meet the representatives of the National Lottery. Smart or casual? What was appropriate in this situation?

Having thrown half the wardrobe onto her bed looking for something suitable, she finally settled on a black and white patterned top and black trousers.

Having given the flat a good clean too, hoovering and dusting like a woman possessed, she remained nervous, not knowing what to expect. The time seemed to go so slowly, and she couldn't face lunch, so a banana and a cup of tea bridged the gap. Ana turned up at one o'clock with an expensive packet of chocolate biscuits, ready to offer moral support.

At exactly two o'clock, a black Mercedes parked outside the flat. Two people emerged; a man wearing a very expensive-looking black suit, and a woman impeccably dressed in a beautiful blue trouser suit, her blonde hair swept up in a very neat bun. The thing Helen remembered most, was how lovely they both smelt as they walked past her into the flat.

"That's the smell of money," Ana whispered.

It was quite a squash, four people in the living room of the tiny flat, with the two representatives on the little old settee, looking extremely 'cosy'. Ana sat in the armchair while Helen grabbed one of the stools from the kitchen.

"I am Penny, and this is Mike. We are representatives from the National Lottery. Which of you is Helen, please?"

Helen introduced herself and then Ana.

Ana was amazing with the representatives, making small talk with them while Helen made a pot of tea. She managed to find a plate which wasn't chipped and arranged the chocolate biscuits in what she hoped looked like a pretty pattern, trying to create a good impression.

Penny opened her expensive-looking briefcase and pulled out a folder with a copy of all the paperwork inside. She also took out a laptop and asked to see Helen's passport, despite having had the scanned copy.

She went through all the details again and asked to see the lottery ticket. Handling it very carefully, she studied it intently.

"Was it yourself who bought the ticket?" Mike asked. He hadn't said much up to that point.

"Yes, I had popped into the supermarket as I knew my favourite wine was on special, so I grabbed that first, plus I treated myself to a pack of Turkish Delight, then went and bought my lottery ticket. I was caught in a queue for ages, and nearly decided to give up…"

"But it was *you* who bought the ticket?" Mike interrupted, obviously not really interested in her shopping activities.

"Yes, yes, of course," she replied.

"And you bought it solely for yourself, not as part of a syndicate?"

"Just for me," she confirmed.

Penny nodded at Mike, and he got up.

"Excuse me for one minute," Mike said, as he pulled out his mobile phone and headed towards the door.

Helen sat there awkwardly, while Ana asked if Penny would like a cup of tea, as it had been brewing for quite a while, before passing her the plate of biscuits.

Helen wondered why Mike had left and was slightly worried there had been a mistake or that they thought it was a fraudulent ticket.

"So, what do you think you will do with the money?" Penny asked.

"I really don't know," came Helen's reply. She then realised, having processed Penny's exact words, she had definitely won something.

Mike came back.

"Well, congratulations, you have indeed won the lottery!"

Penny beamed at Helen.

Mike opened his briefcase and produced a bottle of champagne. It was hard to believe someone would have a bottle of champagne in there, but it also seemed equally appropriate under the circumstances.

Smiling, Helen wondered if there were glasses in there too, but she soon got her answer, as he enquired, "Do you have any glasses?"

Ana headed to the kitchen, as the tea, now stewed, was forgotten.

"Dare I ask how much?" Helen stammered.

"Of course!"

Penny peered at her laptop. "Just over £18.25 million."

Gripping the stool tightly, Helen sat there open-mouthed, not knowing what to say.

Trying to get her head around the win, the rest of the conversation was a blur, but she did pick up that the money would be paid into whichever account she wanted and would be accessible within a few days. Mike recommended going to the bank and letting them know there would be a substantial amount of money going into the account.

Penny seemed amazingly composed, but she was probably used to this situation, Helen thought to herself.

Penny continued. "We'll go at your pace, as I know it is a lot to process. Some people start spending straight away, which is fine if you want to clear debts, for example. Others want to take their time to get their heads around it first. This is just the beginning of an exciting journey for you. Obviously not many people win the kind of money you have, so it is important to make sure you know we are here to support you every step of the way. I will arrange for a few meetings to be set up with our lottery advisors to help you with everything initially, then when you have all the facts, you can decide who you want to assist you. We will also initially provide you with a financial advisor and a life coach, who can help you adjust to the changes this money will bring to your life. These people can also help you with any big decisions you want to make going forward. It is up to you whether you use our people, or in the future, arrange to use your own. Now, is the telephone number you originally gave us the best one to contact you on?"

Trying to process everything that had been discussed, she nodded. Penny confirmed she would be in touch with times and dates to arrange the meetings.

"As the money will be paid into your nominated bank account in the next few days, why not take some time out? Perhaps you would like to go away, just to relax and take it all in?" Mike suggested. "In the meantime, if you have any queries, just give me a call. Here's my number." He passed her his card.

With that, Penny and Mike got up, shook Helen's hand, and Ana showed them out. Helen continued to sit there, dumbfounded.

When Ana returned, she was smiling.

"I need a very strong drink," Helen said, as she sat there trembling, the enormity of it all suddenly hitting her.

Ana laughed.

"You've had two glasses of champagne, both gulped down at tremendous speed, so I don't think you need another! I'll put the kettle on again. You need a clear head."

She came back with tea and gave her friend an enormous hug before adding, "I can't believe it. Nobody deserves this more than you."

Helen's mind was already whirring with ideas of what to do with the money, and top priority wasn't holidays or expensive cars, but what the money may be able to do in the way of possible treatments to help Ana. However, for the time being, she would keep those thoughts to herself.

She knew she would need Ana, with her common-sense approach more than ever to help her process everything.

"Can I come and stay with you for a couple of days, Ana, so I can get my head around all this, and then maybe we can go away? Wherever you like, my treat, obviously!" She laughed.

Ana hesitated.

"I am sorry, I've got some appointments coming up in the next few days. Maybe leave it 'til later in the week? Nothing to worry about, but I won't be around. Can I let you know?"

Helen nodded but was a little confused by Ana's reaction and the odd tone in her voice. It felt like Ana didn't want her to question what she was up to. This made Helen upset, as now was the time she needed her best friend and there was no one else she could speak to about her win.

"OK, let me know when you are free, and we can make some plans then," she replied, sounding more irritated than she had hoped.

She was still trying to take it all in long after Ana left. It just didn't seem real, and any minute now, it felt like she was going to wake up from a very strange dream.

The next morning, she was up early. For the second night in a row, she hadn't had much sleep. Thoughts kept going through her head about what she may want to spend the money on. Perhaps a trip to London to hit some exclusive boutiques and have a Julia Roberts *Pretty Woman* moment, especially if she turned up in her old jeans and staff didn't want to serve her. Or maybe some expensive jewellery?

While she was thinking, she cleaned the flat again from top to bottom, despite only doing it the day before. It was important to keep occupied, she thought. Looking around, it was obvious so many things in the flat needed to be replaced, including the old settee. In fact, all the furniture had been second hand when she had moved into the flat. The wallpaper also needed to be changed. But what was the point? She would hopefully be moving out in the near future into somewhere much bigger, so it made sense to wait and buy furniture that would suit her new home instead.

It was only half past ten in the morning when the cleaning was finished. As Ana wasn't around, she decided to pop into town to Jasper's Cafe for a slice of carrot cake. Julian was serving. He always had a smile for everyone.

"What can I get you today? A nice mini slice?" He smiled.

Julian was being tactful. Helen and Ana had been going to the cafe for years, and he knew it was approaching the end of the month, when neither of the girls generally had much money, so he would find a couple of smaller cakes or something that was a little crushed, which he could sell to them at a discounted price. Wording it as a 'mini slice' meant other customers wouldn't know, saving awkwardness or embarrassment.

"No thank you, Julian. I would like the biggest slice of your lovely carrot cake and a big pot of tea, please!" she replied, beaming.

"Did you win the lottery or something?" he asked.

Her face froze. How did he know?

Then she realised. Of course he didn't know. People often joked about winning the lottery when they spent more than normal, didn't they?

"Well, wouldn't that be lovely!" she replied, laughing nervously.

"Go and sit down, I'll bring it over to you."

She made her way to the corner table by the window, which was where she usually sat if it was free. Both girls liked to watch everyone as they dashed past the window, getting on with their busy lives. The pair of them would often try and guess where they were off to or what they had been doing. Taking out a notebook and pen from her bag, her plan was to spend the rest of the day working out what to spend the money on.

She had started working on the list the night before:

1. Holidays

   A holiday to St Lucia was a must. It was somewhere both girls had talked about visiting for years. When they were at school learning about different countries, they had seen pictures of St Lucia and had always vowed to visit one day.

   She immediately added New York. She smiled. Well, what female didn't want to go shopping there?

   In addition, the pair had also discussed going on a cruise. They would have to think about what towns or cities they would like to visit. Oh, and a trip to Australia was a must, to see relatives Helen had never met.

2. New house

   The dream had been that when she could afford it, she would move from her tiny flat into a small house, but up to this point, it had always been a pipe dream. Now, she could afford a mansion!

She liked the idea of moving to a nice property in a village. Somewhere reasonably close to ensure she was still near Sam and Ana, but also big enough for them to stay if they wanted to.

3. Buy Sam a house and a car?
    Sam. Hmm, now *this* was a tricky one. Helen had always been careful with money. Sam was the complete opposite – the big spender. If he had five pence left in his pocket, he would feel he had to spend it. As the responsible one, she had tried so hard over the years to encourage him to save, and as he had got older, he had managed to put aside a few pounds. The problem was, he liked enjoying himself with the lads too much to have enough put by for a rainy day. It was important news of the win didn't get out (and it certainly would, if she gave Sam a large amount of money), so helping him would be tricky. She knew this would require a great deal of thought.

    She then realised it would be the same if *she* suddenly bought a house, as he would wonder, with her currently only temping, how she could afford it.

    It would be possible to get away with an expensive holiday, as she could claim she had found a cheap deal to Spain. But buying a big house… This was proving much more difficult than she had initially imagined if she wanted to keep her win a secret.

Just then, Julian interrupted her thoughts by bringing over the tea and cake.

"No Ana today?" he asked.

"No, she had a better offer." Helen realised how bitter she sounded.

"I thought you two were joined at the hip!" He laughed. "Oh well, looks like it has given you time to catch up on your list." He pointed to her notebook, which she quickly snapped shut.

Surprised by the reaction, Julian pulled out a chair from the next table and sat down beside her, looking concerned.

"Hey, is everything OK?"

It would be so easy and exciting to tell him what was going on, as having visited Jasper's Cafe for many years, it was getting harder to keep the news to herself. The shop was owned by Julian's dad, Jasper. Julian had initially started working at the cafe after school and at weekends as a young boy and now worked shifts when he wasn't at university, to help fund his studies. Both Helen and Ana had got to know him well, and it was lovely seeing how his confidence had grown over the years.

Instead, she kept her reply short and was keen to change the subject.

"Yes, yes, everything's fine. And you? How's university?"

Shrugging his shoulders, he said, "Hard, but nothing in life is easy, is it? I really want to continue, but I know Dad's finding it a struggle to help fund my medical degree. People aren't spending so much in the cafe these days. They are all watching the pennies I suppose, so I may have to settle and be a GP rather than carrying on for a few more years to specialise like I wanted."

She was saddened by his news.

"That's terrible!" she exclaimed. "Can't you apply for a grant or something?"

"I already have a huge student loan, which will hang over me for years, as well as Dad helping me. I don't know. I haven't got to make any decisions just yet."

As he could see a customer at the till, he got up and touched her arm.

"Enjoy your cake."

She watched him deal with another customer, making polite conversation and being patient while she constantly changed her mind about which cake she wanted. Julian was great. He had time for everyone and had such a lovely manner, which would make him perfect for dealing with patients. Such a shame he was worrying about money to achieve his dream.

He seemed a perfect candidate for the list:

4. Help Julian with his university fees
    Helen would need to *discreetly* find out how much he would need to fund further specialist studies.

    Finishing her tea and cake, she decided against another piece, as having checked her bank account a short while ago, there was only £89 in there until the lottery money came through. She waved goodbye to Julian and headed back to the flat.

When she reached home, she went to ring Ana, as she had not heard from her all morning. It was unusual for more than a couple of hours to go by without one of them ringing or texting the other. She hesitated, then decided not to make the call. Ana had made it perfectly clear she wanted a couple of days on her own. *Why?* she pondered. Was she jealous of the lottery money? She immediately pushed those thoughts out of her head and was cross with herself for thinking such a thing. Ana was one of the kindest people in the world, and it wasn't in her nature to be like that. But equally, her behaviour had been a little odd recently.

The phone rang, and thinking it was Ana, she picked it up, jumping in before Ana had a chance to speak.

"Hi, you silly old bat, what are you up to?"

There was a slight silence, before a male voice said, "Miss Pond? I think you might be expecting a call from me?"

She immediately felt embarrassed, wondering who she was speaking to, hoping it was just a sales call she could end quickly.

"Who is this? What do you want?" she asked a little abruptly.

"My name is Ben Kelsey. Penny and Mike suggested I call you. I am a life coach and work with people like yourself."

It took a moment to realise what he was talking about, but then it dawned on her. He was probably being cautious in case he had the wrong person or because she may be with other people and couldn't talk.

Ben put her at ease immediately. He explained that as a life coach, he was there to make the transition into newfound wealth as easy as possible.

It seemed an odd thing to say really, because how

difficult would it be, going from having nothing, to being able to have everything you could ever dream of?

He must have read her mind.

"It might seem as though all your Christmas's have come at once. If you take advice, are sensible, calm, and don't make rash decisions, you'll be fine, and you can enjoy everything the money can bring."

"Sounds rather boring," she replied flatly.

"Believe me, I have worked with quite a few people who have come into money," Ben continued. "It can be a godsend or a curse, depending on how you manage it."

Ben suggested meeting him and his colleague George, one of the National Lottery's legal and financial advisors, at one of the company's offices. She said she would like to bring her friend Ana, and he confirmed that would be fine, but suggested it might be better not to mention the win to other people until after the meeting. He said he would get back in touch with a date for the meeting as soon as he could.

"It's been lovely talking with you. If you think of any other questions, write them down, and we can discuss them in the meeting."

With that, he hung up.

Helen's mind was racing. All this was becoming real and a little frightening as well as exciting. The guy on the other end of the phone had sounded lovely. She felt a little flutter in the pit of her stomach. What did he look like? He was probably old and married, a couple of kids in tow, but it was worth having a daydream in the meantime!

The enormity of the situation then began to hit her, especially thinking about the disadvantages of having lots of money. What kind of people would she now attract? Would they only be interested in her for the money? How would she know? These were the kind of questions she would need to have answered, so she decided to write them down.

Ben was on the phone the very next day. "Can you come to the office on Monday? Or we can meet at your house? George Bolan, who I have worked with before, is a great financial and legal expert, and he has a space at eleven o'clock. Would that be good for you? The sooner you get to grips with all this, the better. I appreciate it is probably a lot to take in."

Remembering how cramped it had been when Penny and Mike had visited the flat, it seemed sensible to meet at the company's offices. Ben said the company would arrange for a taxi to collect the girls. She quickly wrote down Ben's mobile number too, as, rather stupidly, she hadn't taken it the day before.

Having calmed down, she rang Ana. She seemed very quiet, but Helen didn't take much notice as she filled her in on all the news. She asked her again if she fancied going away for a few days.

"When?" she enquired.

"How about Friday? By the sound of it, the money will definitely be in my account by then. Unless you have something else planned? Just for a couple of days, as obviously I must be back for the meeting?"

Ana's mood seemed to lift as she replied, "I've heard St Tropez is nice at this time of year. We could take a private jet!"

They decided to talk some more after Helen had been to the bank. She was conscious this was more than a 'little windfall' and had hoped Ana would accompany her to the bank. However, she declined, saying she had one more appointment she needed to go to before the weekend, and as a result, she would be too tired. Helen said she hoped it went well, expecting her to elaborate or ask her to go with her, but she didn't, so nothing else was said.

She then rang the bank to make an appointment to see someone. The person at the bank asked what the reason was for the appointment. This caused her to panic, making her say the first thing that came into her head.

"I need to discuss a loan."

The girl said she could set it up over the phone, but Helen told her it was a complicated situation. She insisted she could help, but she stuck to her guns, saying she really needed to see someone in person. Reluctantly, the bank advisor booked her in for the following day, as they'd had a cancellation.

The next morning, she found herself once again looking through the wardrobe, this time for a suitable outfit to visit the bank manager. Initially she had thought about keeping it casual and wearing jeans and a nice, fluffy pink jumper, but then she changed her mind. It was important to have a look that stated 'I am a professional and have just won the lottery'. In the end, she opted for her trusty interview outfit; a black suit with a smart white blouse.

Arriving ten minutes early, she queued at customer services before explaining she had an appointment. She was told to take a seat. She was annoyed they were making her wait, as they obviously didn't realise how important her meeting was. She then scolded herself for being so irrational and full of herself.

Before long, a young man, probably in his very early twenties, came up to her.

"Miss Pond? My name is Paul Swift, and I am one of the financial advisors here at the bank. Do you want to come through?" He took her into a little side room.

Was this some sort of joke? She couldn't discuss the win with him! He might work for the bank, but she needed someone who could be discreet, had authority, and much more experience! She was probably being totally irrational but didn't feel comfortable with Paul Swift.

"I am really sorry, but I would like to discuss this with a manager if I may," she stuttered.

"The manager isn't available at the moment," he countered. He looked a little confused, but then a thought seemed to cross his mind.

"I have all my financial qualifications, and although I am young, I really can give you good advice on loans."

She felt awful and tried to explain.

"I am sorry, I am sure you are very good at your job, but I really do need to see someone a little more senior. It has nothing to do with your age, and I am sure with most things you are more than capable of handling them brilliantly. It is just, well, it's a delicate situation. I know I said I wanted to talk about a loan when I rang, but I don't want a loan. I have, um, er…"

She was struggling to think what she could say that wouldn't disclose her win. Taking a deep breath, she leant over, trying to whisper, just in case anyone else could hear, despite them being in an enclosed room.

"I have come into a significant amount of money and would really like to speak to someone more senior about it. *Please*?"

He looked at her, perhaps wondering if she was a complete lunatic or telling the truth. He must have believed her (or decided he didn't want to deal with the mad woman in front of him), as he said, "I'll see what I can do."

He disappeared, and sitting there, Helen wondered what he was saying to the manager, half expecting him to come back and tell her there was no one more senior available. She also knew that if he checked her bank account, it was likely he would accuse her of wasting his time. However, before long, he returned with another man who was much older. He didn't look very happy about being forced to come to see her. She stood up as he entered the room. He held out his hand, which she shook.

"My name is Timothy Grainger; I am one of the deputy managers here. I understand you want to see someone more senior than young Swift here?"

She nodded. 'Young Swift' was still standing with him.

"Mr Grainger," she began nervously, "I hope I am not putting you to any inconvenience, but could I just have a very quick word with you on your own? It is a rather delicate matter."

It was obvious Mr Grainger didn't appreciate being called, probably feeling this was likely to be a total waste of his valuable time. But equally, he was slightly intrigued by what this woman may have to say, so he waved the young man away, saying, "Leave this one to me."

He closed the door and gestured for her to sit down again, seating himself on the opposite side of the desk.

"Now young lady, how can I help you?"

He sat back in his chair, looking at her suspiciously.

She took a deep breath, feeling quite flustered.

"I know this may seem strange. To be honest, I am finding it very hard to get my head around it…"

She paused, not really knowing what to say.

"Um, before I continue, I trust any conversation I have with you is completely confidential and you are bound by banking secrecy rules?"

He nodded and waved his hand, as if to encourage her to continue.

"Well, I have won the lottery, and it's quite a lot of money."

Mr Grainger's face broke into a grin, before he said, "Congratulations, well done! So, you would like to deposit your little win into your bank account then?"

It was obvious he was humouring her.

"Yes, that's right," she replied.

He looked pleased with himself, but she knew he wouldn't be prepared for what came next.

"For the time being, I'd like the amount to go into my current account, just until I decide what I want to do with it all."

He signed into the computer on the desk and asked for her bank details so he could check the account. With the small amount in there, it was clear he thought she was wasting his time.

"How much are we talking about?" he asked.

"Just over £18 million," was her reply.

He immediately looked up, held her gaze for a second, and then began to laugh. It was evident he thought she was pulling his leg.

"£18 million? Yes, of course!"

Now he was actually belly laughing!

She became angry with his attitude but remained composed. She didn't want to be in the bank any longer than necessary.

"Good, because I have given the lottery representatives details of my bank account. However, I was unsure if the money needed to go into a different account, what with it being such a large sum."

Sitting back in her chair, it was a relief to have it all out in the open.

He looked at her, then looked again more closely, gulping as he did so.

"You're not serious, are you?"

He replied with more than a degree of scepticism, but he continued to watch her intently to gauge her reaction.

She was beginning to relax and enjoy this now.

"Yes, I am. Do you remember the big lottery win recently? Well, that was *me*. I can give you the name of someone at the National Lottery offices, if you would like to ring them for confirmation. I am afraid it has taken a little while to get my head around it, so I delayed ringing them. When I saw them the other day, they explained I would need to provide them with my bank details so the money could be paid into an account. They also suggested I talk to someone in the bank. But obviously I wanted to deal with someone senior here, as I am trying to keep it secret."

Timothy was now sitting bolt upright in his chair. He looked a little dumbfounded at first, wondering what to make of the crazy woman in front of him. Then he started to laugh, before asking, "OK, where are the cameras? Who's put you up to this? Was it Graham in marketing?"

He began to look around the room, then at the door, as if waiting for someone to burst in at any second.

She continued.

"Your reaction isn't surprising. In fact, it is very similar to my own when I realised that I had won. However, I can assure you, it is no joke. Now, please can we get serious for a moment and talk about whether my current account is the best place to keep this money for the short term? I am waiting for an appointment with a financial advisor from the lottery, but I do want to make sure my money is in the best place for now."

Beads of sweat were beginning to appear on Timothy's forehead. He leant forward. He was seriously wondering if this could, in fact, be real. The woman in front of him did not appear to be bluffing.

Before long, Timothy was her 'new best friend'. Tea and coffee were ordered, and after well over an hour, she left his office with six or seven different brochures about bonds, ISAs, and stocks and shares. Timothy also suggested that if she wished to discuss any options, to ask for him personally. *Amazing how attitudes change when you have money*, she thought, smiling to herself.

4

For their break away, the girls decided on a few days in Clacton! Hardly the first place that would spring to mind when you have just over £18 million in the bank. However, Helen had spent many family holidays there when she was little, and some happy, cheap (and often slightly wild) weekends away with Ana there, too. The other advantage was, with Ana's cancer, it was a relatively short distance for her to travel, and it was easy to get back quickly if there was the need to.

For over twenty years, she had always stayed at the same bed and breakfast. It was OK as B & Bs go, but basic and most definitely not the smartest in Clacton. Paint was peeling off the external walls, and it was very dated; the internal décor hailed from the 1960s and there were lots of ornaments on every available surface. It was relatively cheap, but the main reason for returning was because of the owners – Alice and Dick. A couple in their early seventies, they had owned Sea Breeze B & B for many years, long before Helen and Sam had started to visit with their parents. There was always a warm and friendly welcome; it was like going to visit family. She had rung Alice to check there were vacancies, but she needn't have worried. As the girls had suspected, because it was low season and out of school holidays, the B & B wasn't busy, and Alice was pleased to hear they would be visiting.

Helen hoped spending some quality time together would help them to get their relationship back on track and bring some much-needed colour to Ana's cheeks. She looked so pale. The last round of treatment seemed to have taken a lot out of her, much more than she was letting on.

Alice opened the door and gathered them both up in a welcome hug.

"So great to have you both back!"

She looked past them, as if expecting someone else.

"No one else with you? When are you two going to find yourselves a couple of nice young men?"

She laughed at her own joke.

"I'll put the kettle on and see whether Dick has left any of the lemon drizzle cake I made yesterday. Bloody man! He forgets I make it for the guests, not him!"

It was great to come somewhere where everything felt 'normal', and they could just be themselves for a while.

After a cup of tea and cake, the girls unpacked, and Ana said she could do with a quick nap. Helen read a book, and when Ana awoke, she suggested walking over to the beach.

They sat on their favourite bench overlooking the sea with fish and chips from the cafe by the pier. This was a ritual that was *always* observed on breaks down to Clacton.

It was a little windy and cold, but it was great to see the palm trees that had been planted on the beach, put there to probably offer a 'Mediterranean' feel to the location, and to hear the waves crashing against the rocks.

"Fish is a lot smaller this time, isn't it?" Helen queried, prodding at it.

Ana agreed.

"I know, you could buy a fish and chip shop with your winnings!" exclaimed Ana suddenly, and they both laughed.

They were then silent for a while, enjoying the food and the view.

Turning to Ana, Helen said, "Seriously, what the hell am I going to do with all this money?"

Ana thought long and hard for a moment.

"It's up to you, but if it were me, I would be finding myself a good-looking rich man so we could pool our money, travel the world, and do whatever makes us happy."

Turning to her friend, she decided now was the time to discuss the idea which had been at the forefront of her mind since the win.

"Ana, I've been thinking. I want to find out if there is a treatment for you. There must be something that can be done, some new medical breakthrough or trial. I don't care how much it costs, if we can find a cure. Let's start to look when we get back, maybe some pioneering treatment in America to speed up your recovery..."

Tears began welling up in Ana's eyes. It was horrible, seeing her so sad.

She kept her gaze firmly fixed out to sea. She took a deep breath, before she replied.

"Stop, please. There is nothing more that can be done. They have already made it very clear, so I just want to make the most of the remaining few months I have left, savouring each day and enjoying every moment."

Helen paused, taking in the enormity of what she had just been told.

"Hang on, you don't know it is only a few months."

Ana didn't reply.

Feeling sick, completely thrown by what she was hinting at, Helen waited for a response. Nothing was forthcoming.

"Why are you saying it's only a few months? What's going on? Talk to me, Ana."

Tears were now pricking her eyes. This wasn't how the conversation was meant to be going.

Ana reached over to grasp her friend's hand, as she hung her head. She still wouldn't look at her.

"I couldn't tell you. I didn't want you to come. I saw the specialist a few days ago. I knew it wouldn't be good news. I didn't want to ruin things for you, so I went on my own. It looks as though I only have a limited time, so I'm not going to have any more treatment. I don't want drugs that *prolong* my life but don't give me any *quality* of life."

Casting a quick glance at her best friend, Ana broke down.

Helen was hurt and angry. Why hadn't she known about this appointment and the discussions she'd had? She felt like screaming at her friend. Ana had been so selfish not allowing her to go to the appointment or telling her what was going on, keeping it all to herself. But looking at her, almost broken, she knew the only reason she hadn't told her was to protect her from everything she'd been through.

Fighting back the tears, she hugged Ana and said, "It will be longer than that, and we will make damn sure we make the most of the time we have."

When they had both stopped crying, Ana said she didn't want to talk about the cancer anymore, and they should just enjoy the break away. It made sense. It was a waste of time, and Helen knew better than to argue. They both knew there was nothing they could do to change the situation, so that was that. But her heart had been shattered into a thousand pieces.

She knew she would have to take a positive approach and stay strong, for both of their sakes. She would make sure the time Ana had left was enjoyable, and she now had the means to do whatever it took for that to happen.

Trying to sound positive, she continued.

"Right, let's start planning. Where do you want to go first and what do you want to do?"

Before long, the mood lifted, and they were soon laughing and joking, coming up with silly ideas of how to spend the money.

It was getting colder, and the sun had gone down. They slowly walked back, and as they approached the drive, Ana noticed Alice sitting on the little rusty bench outside the front of the B & B. It looked like she had been crying.

Had Ana already told her about her diagnosis?

Obviously not, because Ana was the first to rush over to her and say, "Alice, what's wrong?"

Alice looked up. She hadn't realised anyone was there.

Seeing their concern, she immediately planted a smile on her face.

"I'm fine, nothing for you youngsters to worry about. Just not sure how much longer we can keep this place going. Bills have gone up phenomenally over the past couple of years. Also, people want to stay in brand new, expensive-looking hotels or those multi-national cheap chains that can afford to make budget rooms look really fancy. Now money is being invested in the area, we can't afford to compete with the big boys who are moving in. They have what people want and can offer low prices, so why would people come and stay here? The days of the traditional B & B are probably numbered. It's not proving financially viable for us. If we were to stand a chance, we would need to smarten this place up, and we just don't have the money."

It was obvious Alice was trying so hard to hold it together. The girls knew how much the B & B meant to her and Dick.

For Helen, it was the second big shock in under an hour. It would be heartbreaking to lose the place that held so many childhood memories for her, and the additional ones she had made since with Ana.

"Oh, I am so sorry to hear that," Helen replied, not knowing what else to say.

"No worries, love, it's not your problem. Just ignore me."

Alice dug a tissue out of her apron pocket to mop up the tears. She straightened herself up.

"Now, time to get on with making some more cake," she said brusquely, and she was off.

Thinking about what Alice had said, the girls returned to their room. The B & B was in a prime location – on the opposite side of the road to the beach – and with the bedrooms having big sash windows and all facing out to sea, there were wonderful views. Yes, the external paintwork was faded and peeling and the general décor was a little old fashioned, but it was built in 1926, and many would view it as 'quaint'. However, what Alice was saying was quite right.

Several large hotel chains had moved in over the past few years and knocked down many of the traditional B & Bs to make way for more modern hotel accommodation with smaller rooms, while others had been renovated and changed into flats. Probably more revenue in that, Helen reasoned. Alice and Dick didn't have the kind of money to plough into refurbishing, which was what the place needed.

It would be such a shame for them to give up their home as well as their business.

"I can't believe they may have to leave this place," Helen said sadly to Ana as they sat on their beds. "How many years have we been coming here? And obviously it is where I came when I was a child. I know it's not upmarket, but where else would you get a personalised English breakfast with unlimited tea, toast and home-made jam, and such a warm welcome when you arrive?"

The girls knew if they did sell, it would probably be taken over by a national hotel chain, and then it would lose its identity and charm; in fact, everything that made the place so special.

Helen looked at Ana, and she could see she was thinking, trying to come up with an answer. Suddenly, her eyes widened as she casually said, "Well, you could always buy it."

"Are you mad? Why would I want to buy a B & B in Clacton, and how will that help Alice and Dick?"

As usual, Ana had it all worked out.

"Well, you could pay for it to be renovated. If you wanted, they could continue to run it, and you could take a small share of the profits."

"I really would love to help them," Helen replied, "but I don't want a B & B business hanging round my neck."

However, an idea had begun to form in her head. Inspired, she turned to Ana.

"Why don't I just *give* them some money to do the place up, make it more attractive, and therefore more competitive against the big chains? What do you think?"

Ana frowned.

"They would never accept the money or your help, they are too proud. Anyway, they would want to know how you could afford it. If you tell them about the win, it may get out, and you then get the publicity you don't want."

Helen had a brainwave.

"OK, what if I did it anonymously? The money could possibly be from someone who had stayed here in the past, and had left the money in their will, asking for Alice and Dick to spruce the place up, to help give other people wonderful holiday memories?"

Ana's eyes lit up. "Do you think that's possible? It would be amazing!"

"Well," she replied, "there's only one way to find out. We'll raise it at the meeting with Ben and the financial guy."

The break passed by without further incident, but it was impossible to stop thinking about Ana's bombshell, or the potential plight of the B & B.

5

On the day of the meeting, Ben had arranged for a taxi to collect the girls.

After half an hour, they pulled into an unassuming industrial estate and parked outside a non-descript, two-storey building. It was a complete surprise, as nothing about the place screamed it was a National Lottery office. The only detail that gave any indication it was the right place was a small Crossed Fingers lottery logo in the window. The girls had assumed the offices would be housed in a large and imposing building, with lots of glass windows and a grand reception area.

However, walking past reception and taking the lift to the floor above, it was a little more what they had expected, including nice, thick carpets with the lottery logo on it.

Looking around the walls, there were photographs of people who had won the lottery, all looking radiant, holding their oversized cheques and big bottles of champagne.

How their lives would have changed; some for the better, some for the worse. Helen began to wonder if there was a way to ensure she could have such a vast amount of money, be happy, and protect her anonymity? It seemed impossible.

The girls were shown to one of the side rooms and advised that someone would be with them shortly. Sitting down in the plush swivel chairs, Helen felt slightly underdressed in jeans and a jumper.

"These chairs are much nicer than the ones I get to sit in when I temp," she exclaimed, and she started to spin around in the one she was sitting on. While she was having fun whizzing along the length of the room, a man walked through the door. She stopped immediately, feeling like a naughty schoolgirl who had been caught doing something she shouldn't.

"You must be Ben. I'm Helen," she said, blushing.

The expensive tailor-made suit with matching waistcoat and handkerchief in the pocket were exactly what she had expected, but he was older than he had sounded on the phone.

'Ben' looked at her.

"Hi there. Sorry to disappoint. I am George Bolan, legal and financial advisor. Ben has asked me to apologise on his behalf, as he is running a few minutes late."

He strode towards her shaking her hand, ignoring the previous antics.

"Pleased to meet you."

"Lovely to meet you too, Mr Bolan."

He had a very firm grip. She warmed to George straight away as he reminded her of Uncle Jack, who was kind to everyone and very funny. Although he wasn't really her uncle, he had always been like a second dad to her, especially when her own passed away. Uncle Jack was her dad's oldest and closest friend. He had met his girlfriend a couple of years ago and moved to Wales, so he wasn't around as much, but he did keep in contact by phone. If George was anything like him, she would feel totally comfortable, and she felt reassured he would give great advice.

He looked at Ana, and she introduced herself.

"Please call me George," he said with a smile and a twinkle in his eyes.

George organised tea and coffee and pulled out a laptop from his briefcase. He continued.

"While we are waiting for Ben, I'll tell you a little about myself. As you know, I work for the lottery, and I am here to talk about your win – congratulations, by the way. I am here to help you think about how to manage the money, if you want me to, or you can appoint your own advisor."

Just then, a young lady came in with tea, coffee and cakes, and Ana was straight in there with the Danish pastries. Typical!

Just then, a man who looked to be in his mid-thirties entered the room. He looked a little out of breath.

"Hi, ladies. George." He nodded in acknowledgement. "Apologies, traffic was terrible on the M25. I hope I haven't kept you waiting too long. I'm Ben, by the way."

Wow! Now *that* was more like it! Dark brown hair, brown eyes, about six feet tall, at a guess, and again, very smartly dressed. Handsome but not overly so. He was quietly spoken and seemed a little clumsy, as he knocked over a cup and saucer as he got out his laptop.

George immediately remarked, "At least you didn't break that one, Ben." It sounded like it happened on a regular basis!

George made sure everyone was settled, then began with some basic questions.

Who was aware of her win? Did she already have a financial advisor? She informed him about her recent trip to the bank, which made everyone laugh.

He explained the lottery offered advice and support to all their major winners because they knew it would probably take time to get used to a big win and 'grow into' the wealth. She didn't understand what that meant but felt sure it would become apparent at some stage. In a way, it seemed such an odd thing to say, because how difficult can it be to get used to having a large sum of money?

George gave a rundown of his credentials, explaining what types of jobs he'd had previously as a legal and financial advisor and the current work he did with the lottery team. He mentioned he had worked with quite a few other lottery winners, but only one of those clients had won a substantial amount, though still not as much as Helen. He also said that after the initial shock of winning, people usually appreciated the support, both financial and emotional, that the lottery could provide.

He offered some good advice on how to make the most of the money, one of which was to invest most of it and live off the interest.

It was very evident he had worked with Ben before, as they were very much at ease with each other, which provided her with a great deal of confidence in them both. He asked if she had thought about what she may want to spend some of the money on?

He smiled when she told him they had 'celebrated' with a weekend in Clacton.

And then the big question. What were her thoughts about publicity regarding the win, or did she want to keep her anonymity?

Up to that point, much of what had been said had gone completely over her head as there was so much to take in. But the one thing she was very sure about was there should be no publicity. She explained that whatever happened, she didn't want anyone to know she had won anything and understood she would need a great deal of advice on how to spend the money yet retain her anonymity. George and Ben nodded, acknowledging her decision.

Then it was Ben's turn. He explained that he had been working as a life coach for the National Lottery for the past five years. As well as managing the financial side, the lottery believed it was incredibly important to support winners with their mental wellbeing and the adjustment of a win. Obviously, it was an unbelievable amount, and it was important to know how to deal with everything the money could bring – both good and bad.

Ben continued.

"Winning the lottery gives you the opportunity to do so many fantastic things, but it takes a bit of getting used to. Also, as you can appreciate, if you did go public with your win, or if your anonymity is compromised, there can be demands from people with requests for money, which can be difficult to cope with. Along with George, I can help to take away a lot of the stresses and strains the win may bring. We can give you a great deal of advice, and you can then decide what *you* would like to do. If you want it, the lottery gives you our services for the rest of your life, to help you enjoy what you have won."

She could feel herself drifting away, listening to his voice and looking at those lovely brown eyes.

'Stop it!' she inwardly told herself. 'He's here to help you!'

Ben and George suggested taking a few days to think about whether she was happy for them to represent her. But she felt so comfortable with the pair of them, it seemed ideal, so she confirmed she didn't need to think about it, and if there was anything to sign, just to let her know.

By the time they had finished talking, it was almost half past one. They had organised a light lunch, but she could hardly eat a thing. Ana went off to make a phone call, and Ben went over to Helen, just as she was grabbing a sandwich.

"It's a lot to take in, isn't it?"

"What do *you* think?" she replied, laughing.

She suddenly felt incredibly stupid and awkward.

"I bet most of the big winners you deal with are a lot more vocal and aware of what they are going to do with their winnings, aren't they?"

"Don't you believe it," Ben replied. "Some people think they can manage everything on their own and don't want or need our advice. Those are usually the ones who end up in a worse situation than before they won the lottery. Better to be cautious. Give it a few more days to sink in, and we can have another chat, if you'd like to? It would be good to catch up and see how you are doing."

He reached out and put a comforting hand on top of hers and smiled. The way he said it, and the touch of his hand, seemed more than professional guidance, but she was hopeless at reading men. He then casually walked off to talk to George.

Ana came back into the room.

"I can't believe all this is happening, and Ben seems fab! Do you like him? I think he likes you!" she giggled.

"For goodness' sake, Ana, he is an advisor from the lottery. He's just doing his job."

"I know," Ana said. "But do you like him?"

Blushing, that said it all.

When they reconvened, George and Ben asked if there were any other questions.

Fortunately, Ana was as organised as usual, sitting there with her notebook, and writing everything down so it could all be discussed later. She could tell Helen was struggling to take it all in and that there would be so much to go through in the next few days.

Helen wasn't sure if it was a good idea to mention her initial thoughts to George and Ben, but it was her money, and they were there to offer advice.

Nervously, she began.

"I have had some ideas, but you'll probably think I am crazy…"

Giving them the notepad that contained her list, she explained that the most urgent item on there was to help Alice and Dick at the B & B.

They both looked at it thoughtfully. Along with the notes, which were scrawled all over the pages (and were far from neat), were several doodles.

After a while, George looked up. "Well, I don't think we've ever had a request to help a B & B in Clacton before," he said, roaring with laughter.

She knew George wasn't mocking her, he just seemed highly amused by the idea.

"But could it be done?" she asked earnestly.

Both George and Ben looked at her, and before either could say anything to dissuade her, she continued.

"At first, I was overwhelmed by all this money, and to be honest, I still am. However, now, I am pleased I have won so much. As far as I am concerned, I would like to buy myself a house, a new car, and treat myself and Ana to a few nice holidays, but other than that, I really don't need anything. I could just live off the interest, as you mentioned earlier, George."

"However, as well as benefitting myself and Ana, I want to use it to help my brother and my friends, but, if possible, anonymously. My concerns though are how I can do this. I would also like you to advise me how best to invest the money to make even more, so I can help other people as well?"

George looked at her, contemplating what she had said. He was obviously processing everything very thoroughly before he replied.

"It would take some very careful thought and planning, but yes, I suppose it can be done."

He sat back in his chair.

"I have no doubt that it is going to be an interesting journey working with you, Miss Pond."

Once again, George laughed.

She knew then she was in safe hands, as George seemed to 'get' her.

Looking at Ben, she noticed he was smiling. He also seemed to approve of what she was trying to do, although he probably thought she was mad. She could feel herself blushing again.

Ben and George said they would spend some time thinking about how the plans could work and then come back to her.

"Well, that was fun!" Ana said, as they got into the taxi that had been ordered to take them home.

"Yes, I must admit, I quite enjoyed it," Helen replied, laughing at how absurd and surreal the whole situation still seemed.

She was both happy and proud that it could potentially be possible to do something good for the people she cared about.

The taxi dropped Ana off first and then took Helen home. Life was great. After a light tea and an episode of *Coronation Street*, she decided to pamper herself. In the bathroom cabinet, she found the expensive candle Ana had bought for her last birthday and put on a face mask. Looking after herself felt long overdue. The smell of the candle wafted around the whole flat. After taking off the face mask, she decided on an early night, suddenly realising how exhausted she was.

Surprisingly, that night, she slept soundly for the first time in ages. Now there was the beginning of a plan, she felt more comfortable about having the money.

Ben rang first thing in the morning.

"Hi, Ben here. I hope you are OK? I would like to thank you for one of the most interesting meetings George and I have had in a long time. I really enjoyed getting to know you, and Ana too. George and I carried on chatting for quite a while after you left, as you gave us plenty to think about. I wondered if you would like to grab a bite to eat, to go through our thoughts with you. It would help me better understand you and how you think all this will affect your life. Are you and Ana free later today, maybe for lunch?"

Ana had an appointment, but Helen said she would love to go but would be on her own. She knew Ana would be excited and expect a full report when she returned. Her heart skipped a beat, thinking about seeing Ben again, and of course, George.

6

Ben had suggested meeting at a little wine bar just outside Knebworth. Although Helen was aware of it, she had never been before as it was expensive. *It may be a future dining location, now I can easily afford it,* she thought.

As soon as she had put the phone down, there was panic. It was important to find a dress to impress!

Scouring the wardrobe, there didn't seem much choice; everything seemed too casual, only suitable for the dance floor, or far too formal. In the end, she settled for a navy and white patterned dress which was pretty but not too over-the-top.

Thinking about Ben, she felt the butterflies returning. It would also be lovely to see George again, too. He was really sweet, like a protective father, and she knew he would give her great advice, which would be so important moving forward.

For one of the first times in her life, she was early. Sitting in her car, she was wondering whether to go in or wait until half past twelve, which was the time they had arranged to meet. She hated going into a place first, but as Ben said he had booked a table, she knew she could always sit there and wait. Venturing out of the car, she went in and was surprised to find it wasn't very busy.

Just as she walked through the door, she saw Ben. He looked at her and smiled. How she loved that smile! She could feel herself blushing and tried desperately to look calm, composed, and hopefully, sophisticated.

He came over, and the waiter directed them to a table.

"George is late," she said, puzzled. "He struck me as someone who was always on time."

Ben blushed.

"Oh, I am sorry if I gave you the impression George was coming. I hope you are not disappointed that it's just you and me."

He looked straight at her. She gulped; the intensity of his gaze caught her off-guard.

"Oh, er, no, no that's fine."

She felt very nervous being on her own with him, but then reminded herself this was a business meeting, and Ben was her life coach, nothing more, and this was probably a normal situation for him.

After ordering their drinks, Helen felt shy and awkward, not knowing what to say. Ben, on the other hand, seemed much more relaxed, expanding on his work with the lottery, and then asking her about family, work, and, of course, Ana.

She told him about Ana's illness, and how, since the win, she didn't seem to want to talk about it anymore.

"I said I wanted to try and source a cure for her. She told me there was no point, but I still want to discuss it with you or George. I am unsure how I can find potential treatments. I can't lose her, I just can't."

She started to cry, forgetting where she was, and not caring about her mascara, which was probably running down her face.

Ben reached out his hand and put it on top of hers to comfort her.

Then the waiter turned up.

"Sorry to interrupt you two lovebirds. Are you ready to order?" he asked, assuming they were a couple.

He then looked at Helen and noticed her tears.

"Er, I'll come back in a little while" he said, swiftly departing, leaving them to it. At least it lightened the mood.

"The poor waiter must have thought we'd had a big argument!" Helen laughed, trying to diffuse the intensity of her emotions.

"Are you OK?" He seemed really concerned.

"I will be. Sorry, Ana has been my friend for so many years, we have shared everything together," she said, wiping away the tears.

"Well, who knows what is possible. Where is she today?" he asked.

Explaining Ana was at an appointment, she told him how increasingly tired her friend was becoming, probably because of the treatments and medication. Ben asked how they had met and about their friendship. She had never discussed her relationship with Ana to anyone else before, but with Ben, she felt she could talk about anything. He made her laugh, seemed genuinely interested when she told him about certain things that had happened in her life, and was really paying attention to everything she said. It was interesting though – she noticed Ben didn't give anything away about his own life. It made sense, she supposed, as it was probably a life coach's job to listen, observe, then offer advice.

The meal was lovely, but she declined a dessert. It just felt too extravagant.

Glancing over, she noticed Ben had just picked at his meal. He looked at his watch.

"Good grief, is that the time? I can't believe we've been here for so long. I am afraid I'm going to have to dash, as I have some work to prepare for a meeting. We didn't really get to talk about the things George and I had discussed, did we? That's remiss of me, but not to worry, as this was in my own time and not the company's. I hope you will forgive me on this occasion. Let's arrange another date, er, I mean, another appointment?" he said, looking embarrassed by his choice of words.

They arranged another meeting, and after he insisted on paying the bill, he walked her to her car.

"You can ring me any time, day or night. I have only worked with one other big winner in the past, so this is very exciting. You are my top priority," he said, with a smile.

Being a very tactile person, she didn't know whether to give him a hug or just a handshake as they said goodbye. As a result, they ended up in a very awkward half-hug, and blushing, she jumped into her car.

Watching him walk away, she wondered if there was something more than a business relationship between them. It felt like it. Either way, would that exist, if she hadn't just won over £18 million? He had seemed really interested in her life and learning more about Ana, but how could she tell? She was never good at reading men. She wasn't sure what was happening, but maybe this was how a life coach behaved, to put clients at ease. She had no idea.

As soon as she got home, she rang Ana to tell her about meeting up with Ben.

"Well, it sounds more like a date to me!" Ana giggled.

"No, it was strictly business," Helen replied, unsure, herself, what to believe.

"Hmm. I've known you long enough to know that you like *him!*"

"Yes. No. Oh, I don't know." Helen was flustered by her friend's questioning. "There are bound to be all sorts of rules about dating your life coach, so I am sure it can only ever be platonic. And anyway, what's to say he wouldn't just be after me for my money?"

"Oh, Helen!" Ana scolded. "What's wrong with you? You are pretty and clever. Anyway, even if you had a bit of fun with this Ben, when was the last time you went out with a man? If I remember rightly, it was that creepy Simon with the tattoos, which must have been at least eight months ago. I am so pleased he's no longer on the scene."

Laughing, Helen also shuddered, as she remembered him. "He was awful, wasn't he? By the way, the next meeting with George and Ben is on Thursday at two o'clock. What time shall I pick you up?"

There was a moment's silence, and then Ana said she would have to pass.

"But I need you there!"

"No, you don't. Anyway, I am seeing someone on Thursday."

"Who?"

"Why do you always need to know my business?" Ana snapped.

"Sorry I asked. I'll speak to you after the next meeting."

Abruptly hanging up, Helen was more than a little hurt by Ana's reaction. It seemed as though Ana's attitude was changing towards her, and she worried it might be because of the money. Was there a feeling that Helen didn't need her now she was rich? Or did the money make her feel awkward and uncomfortable?

On Thursday, Helen took a long shower before picking out what to wear for the meeting. She had treated herself to a couple of pretty dresses and some expensive perfume, which made her feel more confident.

Apprehensively, when she was ready to leave, she rang Ana. They had not spoken since Helen had mentioned the meeting. However, she needn't have worried. As soon as Ana picked up the phone, she seemed to be the same as always and didn't mention how the previous call had ended. She wanted to know what Helen was going to wear.

George and Ben had suggested meeting at Helen's, but with the flat being so small, she wasn't keen to show them the place she called 'home'. The sooner she started looking for something else the better. The meeting was arranged to be held in the reception area of a hotel not far from her flat. George said they had used it for meetings before during the day, and it was never busy. If it was or he felt it wasn't private enough, they could always ask to use a small conference room. He assured her confidentiality was his priority, and the details of her win would not be compromised.

George was already waiting in a quiet corner of the reception when she arrived, and Ben walked in just a few minutes later.

It was a good choice of venue. George had been right. There was no one sitting in the huge reception area, so they sat down in a corner, away from the entrance. After ordering some drinks, George and Ben started going through the discussions they'd had following the initial meeting.

"Ben and I talked about your plan to help your friends at the B & B," George said.

"I know you want anonymity, so we need to tread very carefully. Our thought was that they could be informed they have been bequeathed an amount of money by an anonymous donor, with the specific instruction it must be used to refurbish the B & B. I can get a solicitor I know to handle things for you, so everything is arranged through them. That way, your anonymity is maintained. Do you know what figure you were thinking of?"

When Alice had talked about the B & B, Helen had the foresight to ask how much she thought it would cost to bring the place up to scratch. Alice had given her a ballpark figure, and Helen suggested George add a further £10,000, just to cover any unforeseen costs. He raised his eyebrows.

"Are you sure you want to spend that much?" he asked.

"Yes, I really do. If I can make a difference to two people who helped make my childhood memories so special, then it's worth the money."

George was still concerned.

"I'd really like you to think it over for a few days first. I know you say you are sure, but it is a considerable amount of money and there is no immediate rush. Then if you still want to go ahead, I'll put you in touch with the solicitors. You can then meet with them, and they can discuss everything in more detail with you. You'll also need to talk with the bank about arranging for that sort of payment to go ahead."

The meeting didn't take long, as George and Ben had another appointment to go to. Helen had been hoping for an opportunity to speak with Ben about their last meeting, but she was unsure what she would have said to him anyway. Perhaps she had read too much into things…

A few days later, Helen confirmed to George that she was still determined to go ahead with arrangements for Alice and Dick, so he put her in touch with the solicitor he recommended and suggested she also let the bank know that she was spending some of her money.

Timothy at the bank was excited to speak with her again, suggesting she come in to talk further about investments. But on this occasion, her main goal was to ensure there was no problem with accessing the money sitting in the account.

Soon, the solicitors drew up the paperwork and everything seemed to be sorted relatively easily.

Crazily, life then seemed to go back to 'normal' for a while. Top priority was to start looking for a house. It was difficult, because Helen wanted Ana's advice about the type of house and the area she should look at. She was unsure about contacting Ana, as she had told Helen she no longer wanted or needed her to attend medical appointments. This hurt, as it felt like she didn't need her support, and she missed her friend terribly. Ana also started to mention a girl called Carmen. In all the years they had known each other, she had never heard of her before. Was Ana replacing Helen with *her*? It felt as though the friendship was severely fractured, especially as they seemed to be seeing each other less and less. She was unsure what to do to put it right.

When Helen saw her for the first time a few days later, she could tell Ana had lost weight, but seeing her again was wonderful, and there was no awkwardness, they just picked up where they had left off. It had been made very clear Ana wouldn't discuss her illness, so there was no point in raising it. Instead, Helen brought Ana up to speed on the meeting with George and Ben, and the plan on how she was going to help Alice and Dick. Ana was impressed George had managed to put things in motion so quickly.

Helen hadn't spoken to Ben since the meeting, and she felt he was ignoring her too; but then, he was her life coach, not a proper friend or boyfriend.

Just over two weeks later, she received a call from George with an update on how things had gone with Alice and Dick.

"The solicitors rang them to give them the news, and they were thrilled and very surprised about the money.

As you can imagine, they have been trying desperately to guess who their benefactor is. You'll be pleased to know your name wasn't in the mix. They have agreed with the request for the money to be used to renovate the B & B, but they want to change the purpose of the accommodation."

She was dumbfounded and a little saddened to think they wouldn't be using the money in the way she had hoped.

"Oh! I wanted them to use the money so they could continue to run it as a B & B. I thought that was what they wanted."

Hearing the note of disappointment in her voice, George continued.

"I don't think you will be upset with their plans. They don't want to improve the place for the kind of people who would be able to afford to stay somewhere more upmarket. As someone had done them a good turn, they would like to pass that on and will be using some of the rooms specifically for families who wouldn't normally be able to afford a holiday, charging them a greatly reduced rate so they can go away."

She was taken aback. "I wouldn't have thought about suggesting something like that."

"It was a lovely gesture, and as you can see, now it is not only Alice and Dick's lives who will benefit from what you have done."

There was a pause before he continued.

"By the way, how's Ana?"

He sounded really concerned, especially considering he didn't know her very well. Explaining things were difficult between them, she mentioned that the cancer was really taking hold now. She could feel herself getting emotional as she told him.

"Just make sure you are there for her but also respect her wishes if she wants you to step back a little. It must be a lot for her to cope with, and I should imagine she probably wants to protect you from what she's going through. If there's anything I can do, let me know."

"Have you heard anything from Ben lately?" she enquired, trying to sound casual.

"Ah, I wondered if you might ask after him," George replied, laughing. "He asked me the same question about you! He is a lovely man, but he has been hurt in the past. He needs to let his walls down."

It seemed an odd thing to say. Was he indicating Ben liked her but was being cautious? She didn't like to look stupid by asking any further questions, so she didn't pursue it.

Helen was also keen to discuss how to help Julian, and George explained he would need more information, so she would have to undertake further investigative work to find out more details. When she had that, he suggested she give him another call.

"I don't think life is going to be dull working with you."

She could almost hear the smile in George's voice, as if he was quite enjoying the anticipation and 'challenges' of her wacky ideas.

"Anything else?" asked George.

She paused for a moment, as the next request was much harder.

"I really want to help my brother, Sam."

He desperately needed a new car as his was old and cost a fortune each time to repair. Helen also knew he had a few debts and could benefit from some cash to pay those off to put him in a better financial position.

It was particularly tricky, as she didn't want Sam to know about the money. There were two reasons for this. The first was his lack of ability to keep anything quiet, and to be fair, this would be such a huge secret to expect him to keep. In addition, she didn't want her relationship with her brother to change. It sounded a horrible thing to say but, if he knew she had money, who knows how their relationship might be affected.

George sighed. "It is a difficult one, worse in some ways, as it is family. You could play it in a similar way to Alice and Dick, perhaps giving him money from a benefactor? Maybe some distant relative you weren't aware of? Of course, if you did that, then you would both supposedly have to receive a sum of money, otherwise it may look odd. The solicitors could say the benefactor wanted the payment to be anonymous. However, Sam may want to do some further digging, and then it might start to get awkward?"

She confirmed she would think about it and contact George again when she had decided what to do.

"Don't forget you have Ben, too, if you need any advice. He is, after all, your life coach," he said, with a little too much humour in his tone.

George was right when he said it was more difficult when it was family. She had never lied to Sam and didn't want to start now, but equally, she really wanted to help him without blowing her cover. Losing both their parents, when Helen was twenty-four and Sam only twenty-one, was the worst time in their lives, and they had supported each other as best they could. As the older sister, she had tried to protect him and shoulder all the arrangements and responsibilities herself. Sam wasn't mature for his age, and she knew how much he had struggled with their parents' death. Also, she had been fortunate to have Ana to help her through the bad times, but Sam had no one other than his sister. Although he tried to put on a manly front, she knew he hadn't coped with it well.

Looking back, there were plenty of regrets. Helen wished she had helped him more as, after their loss, he seemed to go off the rails for a few months. It was understandable. He was trying to make sense of his life while coping with the death of his parents. His way of dealing with it was with drink and going out regularly with the lads. He did bounce back, but there was no way of knowing what the full impact of their deaths had really had on him as he didn't talk about it. However, from that point on, he generally seemed to keep people at arm's length, which is probably why he had never had a serious relationship. Looking back, she wondered if she had done the same. *Winning this money is really making me reflect on my life*, she mused.

A payment (in principle to them both) from a benefactor who wished to remain anonymous did seem the best route. Helen turned to the solicitors who had dealt with Alice and Dick's money. It was decided the letter should be as brief as possible, to avoid too many questions. They would both receive a letter, and the payments would be the same – £40,000 each, which was a significant sum and would really make a difference to Sam's life. She knew he wouldn't be too bothered who the benefactor was, he would just be grateful for the money.

Within a week, the letter had been drafted, and after casting a very quick eye over it, Helen mentioned to the solicitors there was a small caveat she wanted to include…

The solicitors informed her when the letters had been sent and she held her breath, waiting for the inevitable phone call from Sam.

7

At *The Bedfordshire Post* newspaper, it was business as usual.

"Do I have to cover yet another feel-good story?" reporter Alan Fletcher asked Phil, his editor.

"Well, there is nothing else for you at present. I can always give it to someone else if you think it's beneath you," Phil replied curtly.

He was getting fed up with Alan's continual negative attitude. However, knowing what a good journalist he was when he put his mind to it, he was happy to indulge him a little.

Reluctantly, Alan took the details of the piece that needed covering. Yes, he did feel it was beneath him. He'd been with *The Bedfordshire Post* for eleven years, since leaving university. His initial thoughts were to stay at the paper for a couple of years before getting the really big scoop that would catapult him to the attention of one of the nationals. He had always felt he was better than this local 'rag'. His contempt was evident to his colleagues and, even worse, often the people whose stories he was covering. He wrote well (if he liked the subject), but it was becoming increasingly rare these days. Consequently, to be handed a story about a local kids' dance group trying to raise funds for a trip was not what he had hoped for on that Wednesday morning.

He took John, the photographer, with him. Alan didn't particularly like him. He talked too much for a start, but equally, he was an amazing photographer. Although he would never admit it to anyone, especially John, the photographs he took to accompany Alan's articles always enhanced the piece. He felt the main problem with John was that he had no ambition, which annoyed Alan intensely. Everyone liked John and there wasn't a ruthless bone in his body, which is why Alan felt he was still plodding along at the same local paper. Why waste so much talent? Together at a national newspaper, they could be a phenomenal team.

From John's perspective, he had always known he wanted to be a photographer but hadn't been sure what he would do with his passion, or even considered if it could become a career. As a result, he had left school and started work as a trainee carpenter. However, his photographs quickly came to the attention of *The Bedfordshire Post* when he had entered one of their photographic competitions. They had contacted him soon after to ask if he would like to work for them as a junior photographer and he had eagerly accepted. He had married young, and children followed soon after. *The Bedfordshire Post* gave him a reasonable income and was generally sociable hours, which was good enough for him.

He did have an amazing eye for a great shot, resulting in him winning several awards for his photographs, both in an official work capacity and through entering other national competitions. Now in his fifties, he was happy with his life and didn't begrudge the decisions he had made. He loved working with journalists to enrich a story through his photographs, and it always gave him a buzz to see them in print, knowing hundreds of people would also see them.

Sitting in Alan's car on their way to the job, John was obviously in a good mood, whistling along to the song on the radio.

"You could, at the very least, whistle in tune, John. In fact, it would be better if you just didn't bother," Alan suggested rudely.

John was used to his colleague's attitude. He turned to look at him.

"Did we get out of the wrong side of bed this morning? Or was it the wrong bed?"

He smirked at his own joke.

Alan went red. There was nothing he normally liked more than to brag about his conquests with women, but whether they were all true or not, John wasn't sure.

Alan was a good-looking young man and could really lay on the charm with women he liked until (in his own words) they became 'too clingy'. Then he would immediately drop them like a stone without any consideration for their feelings. John knew he was currently seeing at least two women and was pretty sure they didn't know about each other. He had met one of them recently, a lovely girl called Diane. She was probably mid-twenties, appeared bright, very engaging, and funny, and John had liked her. He had accidentally met her when he and Alan had gone to a cafe after a story, and she was getting a takeaway for her boss. She was keen to talk with John while Alan ordered coffees. She wanted to know more about what her boyfriend did and why he often had to work so late in the evenings, meaning she only saw him a couple of times a week, and often at short notice. John knew Alan rarely worked late, so it was obvious he was seeing someone else. When he quickly ushered John out of the cafe, his suspicions were confirmed.

Alan was also happy to trample over anyone he didn't regard as 'useful', and this was particularly evident in the office. He had made most of the girls cry at some point, as he felt they were beneath him, both in intellect and ability. There were only two females in the office who could really hold their own with him; Polly, who was in her early sixties, and Jane who was a couple of years younger than Alan. Neither took any nonsense from him. Jane was hungry for the best local stories but normally lost out to him as he was more forceful and would take them for himself. She wasn't willing to stamp on people to get what she wanted, and as a result, unlike Alan, everyone in the office liked and respected her. John suspected Alan fancied her and saw her as a challenge, but despite his bravado, he doubted he would ever try his luck for fear of her rejecting him and the office finding out. He would never be able to live that down.

The journey to the assignment continued in silence. It wasn't far to the local community centre, much to John's relief. He didn't want to be in the car with Alan any longer than he had to if he was in a mood.

As they walked in, they could hear music, which directed them towards the room where the dance troupe were. There, children of varying ages were dancing what looked like quite a complex routine. John was really impressed – they all seemed to be in perfect sync with each other. He could see his ten-year-old granddaughter enjoying something like this. He'd have to tell her about it when he got home.

When the song came to an end, one of the women in the room noticed John and Alan and approached them, eyeing them suspiciously.

"Can I help you? This is a private dance class."

John held out his hand.

"Hi there. We are from *The Bedfordshire Post* and are here to do an article about funding a trip abroad."

He could see the woman soften, understanding why they were there.

"You need to speak to Nicky. Come with me, and I'll introduce you."

Nicky was the woman who had been watching the children intently, giving out advice to the girls during the dance. John guessed she was in her mid-thirties. A pretty woman, but she looked extremely stressed. When she saw John approach, she suggested to the girls they went and grabbed a drink. After introductions, she sat down with them and started to explain about the group.

"I run the Daffodil Dance Group. Any help or publicity you can give us would be really appreciated as I don't know what else to do. We've exhausted all other avenues."

"We'll do our best," John replied, trying to sound reassuring as he started to take out his photographic equipment.

One of the other ladies came over. She looked directly at John.

"Would either of you like a tea or coffee?"

Alan grimaced. He hated the way John always had such an easy rapport with people. It was a skill he personally had never mastered, unless it was with a woman he was trying to charm. This group should be more grateful to him for being there as he was the one helping them and would make the biggest impact on their story. Feeling disgruntled, his initial thought was that he didn't want to invest any real time and effort into this article. Looking at Nicky, however, he had second thoughts. She looked reasonably fit, and he'd noticed straight away she wasn't wearing a wedding ring. She was slightly older than he would normally go for, but she could be interesting if he had a free night…

With the girls enjoying their fruit juice, John and Alan were able to learn more about the group.

"So, Nicky, tell us why you're looking to raise the money? I understand it is to do with some little competition in France?"

Alan's tone sounded flippant and dismissive, and John could see by the look on Nicky's face that she had also noted his attitude. However, she was desperate for the publicity, so she bit her tongue. Remaining composed, she explained.

"The Daffodil Dance Group has been running for five years."

She pointed to a dark-haired girl who looked to be about thirteen years old.

"That is my daughter, Abi. All she has ever wanted to do, since she was five or six, is dance. She used to dance all the time in her bedroom in front of the mirror, in the garden, at school, everywhere. She begged me to let her go to the local dance company in town, but I just couldn't afford it. They are a professional group, and you must pass an audition to even get in. On top of the weekly fees, there is the cost of costumes for shows and then additional lessons just before competitions. I'm a single mum, so money is tight. It is the only thing Abi ever asked for, and it broke my heart not being able to afford it.

"When I was young, I dreamt of becoming a professional dancer and was lucky enough to be accepted on a scholarship with a professional dance academy. When I left, I managed to get work as a backing dancer in a few West End shows, as well as working on a cruise ship for a while, until I got married. I understood Abi's passion, and I could tell she had real talent."

Nicky seemed to be reminiscing about her own dreams and how she had managed to achieve them. You could tell that, as a mother, all she had ever wanted was the same for her daughter.

"Talking to other mums, I realised it wasn't just me who couldn't afford the dance fees, and there were probably quite a few children who would have liked the opportunity, but money was the issue. So, I came up with the crazy idea of setting up my own dance group, at a more reasonable price. Also, unlike the dance group in the town, there would be no audition to pass; it would be open to all, irrespective of ability, and soon I had a few children who seemed interested. I figured if we ever did the odd show which required costumes, we could do a little bit of fundraising. As it turned out, one of the mums could sew, so she volunteered to make costumes."

John looked at the woman in front of him. He was impressed by her tenacity and ability to bring other people together to share her dream.

"As well as my full-time role as an accountant, I took on extra jobs: weekends and some evenings behind the bar at a local pub, and another offering to help people with their tax returns. The extra jobs pay for the hire of the hall once a week (which we get at a reduced rate) and basic costumes or materials. We started off with just seven children, but before long, the group had grown to eighteen. I never expected the kids to reach the standard required for competitions, but they did. They were so full of enthusiasm and just seemed to come alive! We started entering competitions, and initially it was only small, local ones, but we were doing so well, we started entering nationals. We cover tap, hip-hop, jazz, and modern, as well as contemporary dance. We entered an international competition, not thinking we would get through each stage, but thinking it would be fun to have a go. Through hard work and determination, the kids won all of the UK rounds, ultimately winning the UK finals."

Nicky looked away for a moment, grabbing a tissue from her pocket and quickly dabbing her eyes before the tears could fall. She didn't want the children to see her upset.

"I never dreamt we would do so well, but there lies the problem. The championships for amateur groups like ourselves are held in France, and we can't afford the costs to get there. I really don't want to let the kids down. They've come so far."

Nicky explained how much they had already managed to raise, but they still required almost fifty per cent more, to cover all their expenses.

John stared at Alan, who seemed bored, as he was constantly looking at his watch. He wasn't taking many notes, just writing down the odd word or two.

John felt annoyed and upset – with a well-written article, *The Bedfordshire Post* could give this group the publicity needed to help them obtain the funding required. Fortunately, John had a great memory, and he could fill in any gaps Alan had when they returned to the office.

Seeing how upset Nicky was, John decided he would try to lighten the mood.

"Nicky, what an amazing achievement. Well done! Why don't we have a group photograph of all the kids, while Alan is reviewing his notes? Can you get them all together?"

John was such a natural with the youngsters and soon had them eating out of his hands, making them laugh by pulling funny faces, and getting them to say other words rather than the traditional 'cheese' when he was taking the photographs.

Up to that point, Nicky had stayed out of the photos, but now the children were a little calmer, John suggested this was as much *her* story as the dancers, and as a result, she should be included in the photographs. He soon had her in a central position and took three or four shots before Alan declared, "I think you've got enough photos now, John."

Alan then turned his attention to Nicky, holding out his hand to shake hers, and when she did, he covered it with his other hand.

"It's been a real pleasure to meet you, Nicky. The article will appear on Friday, both online and in print. Here's my card. If you fancy going through more details over a drink one evening, feel free to give me a ring."

John grimaced. It was obvious Alan hadn't shown any interest in the story and now he was trying to hit on the dance leader. Unbelievable! Nicky withdrew her hand, looking suitably embarrassed, but took the card before thanking him. As they turned to walk away, John silently mouthed 'Sorry' to Nicky, making her smile.

She sighed. She really hoped the article would make a difference. They needed all the help they could get.

8

"I've just received a letter from some fancy solicitor. Did you get one too? What is it all about? Do you think it is a joke? Can I come over this evening to talk to you about it?"

Sam was almost breathless on the phone, trying to get everything he wanted to say out in two seconds flat.

Helen confirmed she had received the same letter, and by seven o'clock that evening, he was knocking on the door.

"Got any lagers, Sis?" was his first request as he flopped on the sofa. As his sister didn't move, he went into the kitchen. Not finding any beers in the fridge, he had to make do with a coffee instead.

"Do you have any clues about who this mysterious 'benefactor' is? The letter is vague to say the least. Could it be a prank?"

He seemed to be both confused and excited in equal measure.

She pretended to think for a minute, having practised her responses to the questions he was likely to ask for a few days now.

"No, I don't think it is a prank. Why make up something like that? It could be a distant relative who we weren't aware of. We don't really know much about Mum and Dad's families, especially Dad's side, as he was estranged from them. You haven't rung the solicitors, have you, Sam?"

He confirmed he hadn't, which was what she had suspected.

"I rang their office today, and someone is coming back to me tomorrow with further information. Why don't you let your big sis deal with all the boring details, and I'll let you know what I have found out and when we are likely to receive the money?"

Sam nodded. Being the older sister meant she had often dealt with things for Sam, so it didn't seem unusual for her to do the same in this instance.

She knew she had to tread carefully with the next question she wanted to ask.

"So, what do you think you will do with your money?"

No hesitation from Sam at all with his reply.

"Well, I'll probably treat the lads to a weekend away in Barcelona to watch the football."

She sat there, incredulous. He had all this money, yet by the sound of it, he was going to blow a large chunk of it on his friends!

"No, Sam, you know that's not a good idea," she said firmly. "Use some of it to pay off your debts, buy yourself a better car, and save some. Don't just squander it."

He looked hurt and angry.

"It's *my* money, I can do what I like with it. You decide what you want to do with *your* money, that's your right, but don't tell me how to spend mine."

She could see him bristling.

Remembering her own initial response to the lottery win, she had also talked about blowing money on holidays, nice cars, etc., so how could she blame her brother for wanting to do the same? It was true. She had given him the money and, as a result, shouldn't try to put conditions on it. He was right, and she told him so.

He sighed.

"No, you are right as usual," he said apologetically, then smiled. "I could do with getting a new car and maybe paying off the credit card. It would make life a little easier each month, wouldn't it?"

She nodded, trying to think of a compromise before answering.

"But you could still go away with the lads. Just don't pay for them! Maybe have one night, where you put more in the kitty to buy a few rounds of drinks," she suggested.

"Yes, I suppose."

He seemed distracted, and she could see he was looking at the letter again.

He frowned.

"By the way, what do you think the bit at the bottom means?"

Not sure what he was referring to, she studied the letter more closely, then smiled. On the bottom of the letter, it read:

This money is given without any restrictions on how you decide to spend it. However, it is hoped that should a situation arise in the future where you can help someone else, be it in a financial or practical way without any gain for yourself, you will do this willingly, as a 'repayment' for this sum.

Initially she had thought the solicitors hadn't taken her seriously when she had suggested it, so she was happy they had taken her thoughts and worded it so perfectly.

She pretended to take time to think about it.

"I think what they are trying to say is that, since someone is giving us an unexpected gift, we should try and help someone else if we can. Sounds as though it doesn't have to be money, just some kind of gesture."

She hoped the explanation would be enough.

"This benefactor sounds like some mad bloody anthropologist," her brother said, rubbing his head.

"You mean *philanthropist*, you idiot!" she replied, laughing.

They talked more about what Sam might spend his money on. Some of his ideas were a little wild and wacky, but she could tell he was joking. The money was a considerable sum, especially for someone like Sam, and not an amount he would ever have dreamt of having.

He then asked what she was planning to spend *her* money on.

She tried to look as though she was giving it some thought before replying. She said she would probably spend a little on decorating the flat, maybe a weekend away with Ana, and save the rest for a rainy day. He seemed happy with her answer, as he knew she was always careful with money. She did feel guilty for lying. How she wished she could tell him everything.

When he left, she thought about how happy the money

had made Sam. Should she have given him more? What if he *did* spend it on the lads or on something frivolous? Well, it was his money now, *he* had to make that judgement call, the same as she had to do with the lottery win.

After confirming to the solicitors the account to pay the money into, Sam received the payment a couple of days later.

The following Sunday, Ana was round at Helen's enjoying a lazy afternoon watching one of their favourite old films. Suddenly, they heard a very loud car horn.

"What the hell?"

Helen got up off the settee and went over to the window to see who was making so much noise.

Across the road, she noticed a fancy red sports car. Sam was sitting in the driving seat, and next to him was a man she didn't recognise.

Sam saw her looking. Grinning and waving, he beckoned her outside.

"No, no, no, no," she murmured and immediately headed towards the front door.

Ana was literally a couple of steps behind, eager to find out what was going on. They stood there in astonishment, looking at the gleaming red car.

"Well, at least you can see and hear him coming," Ana piped up.

"Not funny, Ana," she replied, curtly.

"What do you think, Sis?"

Sam was grinning like the Cheshire cat.

"What's going on?" she asked, trying to remain calm but fearing the worst.

"I thought I'd blow the lot on a nice set of wheels. Well, let's face it, this opportunity won't come again in my lifetime, will it?" he said, getting out of the car. The man next to him gave the girls a smarmy grin. He *had* to be the salesman.

"Er, can you give us a few minutes?" Helen asked the salesman, and she grabbed Sam by the scruff of his neck, virtually dragging him into the flat.

Sam tried to pull away.

"Get off me! What's got into you? You could get one too. We could have the same car in different colours. I bet they'd give us a discount or an upgrade for two—"

"What do you think you are playing at? Are you *mad*? The money could do so much and make life easier for you," Helen spluttered.

"Yes, but how boring would that be," reasoned Sam.

"Take it back," she said firmly, crossing her arms.

"No, I won't," Sam replied stubbornly. From his tone and the look on his face, she knew it was important to tread carefully, otherwise he would just do the complete opposite to spite her.

He continued.

"Anyway, I haven't bought it. Yet. I am looking at all options, and Mark over there" – he waved at the guy in the car, who smiled again and waved back – "has said he can get me a great deal."

"I bet he did. I don't care what Mark says. Honestly, you need to grow up, Sam. Take it back."

Sam looked at her sternly.

"You may be my older sister, but you can't tell me what to do. Get off my back for once. Let me have some fun."

Before she had a chance to say anything else, he was out the door, had jumped in the car, and with a roar of the expensive engine, gone.

As they went back inside, Helen looked at Ana.

"Don't say a word," Helen said.

She was fuming. She wandered into the kitchen then straight back into the living room, not knowing quite what to do.

"What the hell is he thinking?"

Ana came and sat beside her.

"He's not. He's a lovely lad whose head has been turned by the money. You can't blame him. You've got to let him make his own decisions. He is right. It's up to him to decide what he spends his money on, whether you approve or not."

She knew Ana was right, but it still made her angry.

"Yes, I know," she replied sadly, "but he is still my little brother, and I just want to do the best for him."

Had she done the right thing giving Sam so much money?

"I should have got the solicitors to put in the letter the money must be used for paying off debts or to buy a sensible car. That fancy thing was just… ridiculous."

"He *is* looking to buy a car, which is one of the things you hoped he would do with the money," Ana pointed out wisely.

"Stop being such a smart arse."

Helen knew she was right and smiled. "Did you see how ridiculous he looked? He is far too big for it. His knees were under his chin, and as for that creep of a salesman…" she said.

They both rolled about, crying with laughter.

After she had calmed down, Helen decided to ring Sam. She cut in before he had a chance to speak.

"Before you say anything, I am not ringing for an argument. I am sorry for being too sensible. I just hoped you would be too."

Sam took a deep breath before replying.

"I appreciate what you are saying, and you are right. I just got caught up in the moment. You will be relieved to know I am *not* buying the car, much to Mark's disappointment. I could see the thought of all the commission lighting up his eyes!"

His reassuring words eased the mood.

"However, I've decided I am going to spend a little, but promise I'll be more careful. I've had my bit of fun. Do you know, I have never even sat in a Mazda MX-5 before, let alone driven one. Amazing! Well, I'll speak to you later. I am going to start looking for a boring, cheap, second-hand car, and then pay off my debts, just like you suggested. You see, I *am* becoming a sensible old fart."

"Well, what a relief," Helen commented to Ana, as she put down the phone from her brother, filling her in about what had been discussed.

As they sat there, she decided now was the time to reveal her most recent ideas to Ana.

"I think I know what I want to do with a large part of the money."

Ana rolled her eyes, wondering what was coming next. "What daft scheme have you thought of now?"

If anyone else had said that to her, she would have

been offended, but Ana knew her so well and would give her an honest opinion, which was important.

"Hear me out 'til the end. Large charities are always supported by so many different people and big corporations, although I know they can always benefit from additional funds. But what about small organisations? I've decided I would like to find local people or small community groups, who are struggling for one reason or another, and help them out. People like Alice, Dick, and Julian. These are the kind of people who would normally be overlooked."

Ana offered no reaction, as she began to try to comprehend what was being proposed. Helen continued.

"I also want to manage it anonymously if I can. I am beginning to realise not everyone I help will spend the money the way I would like them to, and I need to find a way to come to terms with that. In addition, I would like one 'loose' string attached; basically, when the time is right, if a situation arises where whoever is receiving the money can help someone else, they should do it. Just like in Sam's letter. It doesn't have to be financial. Even if one or two people or groups do that and make a difference to another person or group as a direct reaction to what I have done for them, it will have a small ripple effect across our community. What are your thoughts?"

"Who do you think you are, a modern-day Mother Theresa?" Ana laughed.

Noticing the expression on her best friend's face, she realised she was serious.

"Oh, OK, so you *aren't* joking. How do you think you are going to pull this off? The chances of blowing your cover by doing something like this are enormous. There's no way you would be able to protect your anonymity, you do realise that don't you? It's alright just doing a one-off, but this would be virtually impossible. It would take incredible planning, organisation, and—"

"And your point is? I am sure there is a way we can do this. Imagine seeing people's faces or hearing about the difference the money would make. Potentially, I have an opportunity to change people's lives. The money could do so much good," Helen interjected.

She was very excited. This was what she wanted to do, and she hoped Ana would support her and, more importantly, want to be part of it.

She looked at her, and it was her turn to think carefully about her response.

"Look, I know you think you are doing this for what you feel are the right reasons, but not everyone wants their life changing. Even if they say they do, you could make it so much worse, just like you've seen from newspapers about individuals who win the lottery. People may become more selfish, plus, as you said, they may not do what you had hoped they would with the money. I can see this going horribly wrong, and you being *very* disappointed."

Helen was very upset that her friend wasn't being more supportive.

She tried to justify her thoughts.

"Well, I know I will need to take some advice. I can ask George to set up a meeting, and he can tell me what he thinks. And maybe Ben could come too, to talk about the emotional aspects and the impacts it may have on people…"

Ana looked at her and smiled.

"And there it is! Is this just an excuse to see Ben again?"

Helen was angry. She had thought Ana would immediately back her suggestion. But no, her best friend felt it was about wanting to get together with Ben!

She became angry, expressing her 'thoughts' that Ana was mocking her, knocking back all her ideas and plans and what she was trying to achieve. She also pointed out that Ana could never understand as she wasn't in her position, which, in hindsight, was a cruel blow. Another argument between the two best friends. It was horrible. Ana stormed out and went home.

Lying in her bed that night, Helen cried. She really wished she had never won the lottery. Her worst fears were coming true; the money was causing pain and destruction in her life. She was also really cross with Ana. Her only wish was to try and help people. Thinking about the possibilities, her mind started to drift, and before she knew it, she was asleep. What followed were nightmares of losing Ana, Sam finding out about the win, and people hounding her for money.

Despite the nightmares, she was up early the next morning. After showering, she wrote out some questions to discuss with George:

1. How much of the money should be devoted to the project?
   She had always been careful with her wages but had no comprehension of managing this amount of money.

2.   Where will I find people to help?

3.   Is there an easy way to ensure people don't know the
     money has come from me?
     She couldn't stick a wad of cash in an envelope
     and post it through someone's door.

4.   How will it be administered?

5.   What if I don't approve of what people do with the
     money?
     She could hardly *force* them to spend it as
     she hoped if they changed their minds. She
     also wanted to include the caveat put into
     Sam's letter, saying if upon receiving the sum,
     people should try to help someone else, if an
     opportunity arose. Again, this couldn't be
     enforced.

6.   Regarding question five (above), how do I come to
     terms with people deciding to do something different
     with the money?
     She couldn't ask for it back. Was it best not to
     get any feedback?

Finally (and most importantly):

7.   Can it work?
     Would it be possible to retain her anonymity?
     Or was Ana right? Was she being stupid and
     naïve to believe that any of this was a good idea

and, more to the point, achievable? Despite everything, it still felt possible, but it was so easy to get caught up with your own ideas and think they are amazing.

Having left George a message on his mobile, she waited for him to call back. He didn't ring until the following day. When they spoke, she told him what had happened with Sam and the sleazy salesman, and the sound of George's familiar laughter was heart-warming and comforting. It was good to talk with him again. She didn't mention her argument with Ana.

She told George she was going to the cafe later to try to speak with Julian's dad, Jasper, as Julian would be at university. They agreed to talk again after she had spoken with Jasper.

Just after the lunch time rush, Helen entered Jasper's. She felt sad, as her last two trips there had been without Ana. Pushing the thought out of her head, she continued. She was on a mission.

Jasper greeted her with his familiar "Buongiorno!" and wrapped her up in a big hug. In his late fifties, Jasper was still a good-looking Italian guy. He flattered all the ladies (which is why they always came back for cake and a chat), and with his wonderful accent, he could charm anyone. The cafe was very busy, so Jasper suggested she find a seat, and he would bring a cup of tea over when things calmed down and take her order. Realising she hadn't eaten all morning and was now ravenous, she looked at the menu. Initially ordering the home-made lasagne with chips instead of her normal salad, she even managed a portion of the tiramisu afterwards.

By the time she had finished, the place was virtually empty. Taking the plates up to the counter and sitting on a bar stool there would give her the opportunity to have a proper chat with Jasper. It wasn't something unusual, as the girls often did that if there weren't many people around.

Jasper was excited to tell her about the new range of cakes he was selling. Once he had finished, she began to ask how Julian's university course was progressing.

"I know Julian worries about me finding the money to help him with his studies. But as a father, that's what you do, isn't it? He will be a great doctor, and I hope one day, a great heart specialist. It will be an amazing achievement for our family. I am so proud of my little bambino," he said with tears in his eyes.

He looked at her and laughed.

"You naughty woman, you make an old man cry."

"You are an amazing father, Jasper. Which explains why Julian is such a brilliant young man."

"You lovely, beautiful lady, saying these things. But I know your plan," he said with his wonderful Italian accent.

He wagged his finger at her, as if telling her off.

"You say that, so I give you a free meal!" he laughed.

Despite Jasper's protests, she paid the bill and left. She was more certain than ever that she wanted to help Julian and make it easier for them both.

Ringing George when she got back, she was disappointed to hear he was in a meeting. He rang later in the evening and was keen to discover how her 'secret mission' had gone.

"I had a lovely home-made lasagne and spoke with Jasper. I really do want to help Julian and pay for his studies to take the pressure off his dad, but I know he is a proud man. I would love it if we could get together to discuss it, now I have more details, and to talk about some other ideas I have for the money. I have written quite a few notes. Basically George, I have decided I want to help people," she explained.

There was a pause before she heard George laugh. "Say again?" he asked.

"I want to do good."

This time, there was an even longer pause.

With a lack of any response, she continued. This was not the reaction she had hoped for.

"I sound ridiculous, don't I?" she said, feeling a little deflated.

"No, not at all," George replied slowly. "I am sorry, it was very rude of me to laugh at you. Now, let's hear your thoughts. I am intrigued."

After going through her plan, she waited with anticipation for George's reply.

"So, why do you want to do this?"

The question caught her off-guard.

"Well, I guess I'd like to help make people's lives better," she said, feeling proud of herself.

"And what makes you think giving them money will make their lives better? I am sure Ben has told you, lots of lottery winners don't end up happy, and wouldn't consider their lives better for their win; in fact, often the reverse is true. Giving money to people isn't always the best answer."

George's reply sounded very similar to what Ana had said to her.

She was instantly irritated and tried to explain.

"Yes, you are right. But I don't want to just *give* them money, I want to use the money to help people who need it, just to touch their lives and make a little bit of difference."

"But what do *you* hope to get out of it? What's your motive?"

George was pushing her. Startled by the question, he was making her feel uncomfortable. To lighten what felt like an intense question, she nervously replied: "I thought you were on my side, George."

Quietly and slowly, he continued.

"Whatever we do in our lives, be it good or bad, we do for a reason. Also, helping others financially isn't necessarily the best course of action and can make their situation worse. I am trying to understand your reasons. I hope you aren't attempting to be some sort of super-hero who wants to save the world."

She felt crushed and upset. Earlier in the day, she had been so excited about her ideas.

"That sounds awfully harsh, George. Why shouldn't I use my money to help people? Put a smile on someone's face because they haven't got to worry about university fees for example? I am not looking to save the world; I am not that naïve. I am not trying to be a super-hero. I have so much money, more than I could ever wish for, or even need. But do you know what the worst part of it all is?

Despite all this money, my best friend is dying, and I can't do anything about it."

Overwhelmed with her feelings, she began to cry.

George sighed.

"I am sorry for upsetting you, it really is the last thing I want to do. However, if I am to be your financial advisor and give you the best advice, I need to know what kind of person you are, what makes you tick, and why you want to do the things you do. I know you are a kind and thoughtful person, but there are some things you just can't fix, however much you try and compensate for it. I am on your side, Helen, honestly. Let's talk about it again in a few days. I'll check my diary, and we'll speak soon."

After the call, she sat on the settee, reflecting. Life seemed so unfair. She would give the money back in a heartbeat if it meant she could change things for Ana.

While she was feeling sorry for herself, the phone rang. It was Ben.

"Listen, are you busy this evening? There is someone I would like you to meet. She is a previous client of mine. I offered her advice when she won the lottery. She didn't win quite as much as you, but still a very substantial amount. She also wanted to remain anonymous, so it took a lot of persuading to get her to agree to see you. But I think it would be good for you to understand how she has retained her anonymity and how the win has affected her life. Can you come to mine at half past six? I am working until then. Here's the address…"

She eagerly agreed, excited at the prospect of seeing Ben again. However, she then began to wonder if it was a good idea. Did she want to meet another winner? It could be a positive or negative experience. But equally, it would be good to know the ins and outs of how it had made her life 'different', and maybe she could learn from any mistakes this winner had made. In the end, feeling she had nothing to lose, Helen began to get ready. It would also be interesting to see where Ben lived. She debated about ringing Ana but then thought it best to speak later when they had both calmed down and there was more information to give her.

9

The car wouldn't start. Great. Panic began to sweep over Helen, as she wondered how much it would cost to fix and how she would pay for repairs. Then she giggled, suddenly remembering her win.

"Don't be stupid. Just go and buy another car!" she said to herself.

She was still struggling to get her head around winning. In the meantime, though, she didn't have a car to get to Ben's, so phoning Sam, she asked if she could borrow his car for the evening. She hadn't thought what she would say if he queried why she wanted it, but he didn't, fortunately. She said she would return it later in the evening, and soon, she was on her way.

Ben's house was in a nice, leafy suburb just outside Hemel Hempstead. She had guessed with his job at the lottery, he would be earning a reasonable wage. Walking up the steps, she noticed the wisteria growing around the door. She pressed the doorbell and waited for him to let her in. The door opened. He stood there in just a towel from the waist down. Nothing else. She could see how well toned he was.

Wow! She hadn't been expecting that! She started to blush and felt embarrassed. Looking at her face, his state of undress suddenly dawned on him.

"Er, come on in. Sorry, I've literally just got back from work. It was a press shoot on a farm, and unfortunately, I slipped in something not too pleasant."

Well, with that scenario now in her head, it completely ruined any romantic thoughts she might have had.

"Make yourself at home while I get dressed," he said, gesturing to a room on the right.

Wandering into what turned out to be the living room, she was surprised. The room was very 'homely,' like it had a woman's touch. And then it hit her. She had never even asked him if he had a girlfriend, a wife, or a family.

You silly woman, she thought to herself. *Of course he would be married or in a long-term relationship. Stands to reason, with someone so good-looking, successful, and kind.*

She felt a twinge of disappointment and started to look around the room for evidence. There was just one photograph, and when she saw it, her heart sank. It was of Ben with his arms wrapped round a cute little girl, who looked to be about four or five years old, and they were both smiling happily for the camera. There was a definite likeness. So, he had a daughter at the very least. It wasn't what she had been hoping for.

Ben walked into the room a few moments later, this time dressed but his hair still slightly damp, and she could smell his aftershave. He looked amazing. Her heart skipped a beat.

"Sorry to have kept you. Do you want a quick drink before we leave?"

She declined, so they left and walked to her brother's car.

She *really* hadn't thought it through.

Although *her* car was old, it was tidy and clean. Sam's car, on the other hand, was not only old but *very* messy.

Immediately feeling ashamed, she realised it probably wasn't what Ben was used to and felt the need to explain that she had borrowed her brother's car and the reason why. Staring into the car and seeing the large number of cartons, receipts, and other items strewn everywhere, Ben tactfully suggested they should go in *his* car, to save her brother's fuel.

Walking round the corner, they came to a gated area full of expensive cars. Ben clicked his key fob, and the lights flashed on a navy Jaguar XE.

The cream leather seats were beautiful, and of course, the car was spotless.

"This is so lovely," she sighed, jumping in and admiring the car. Suddenly he pressed a button and raised her seat slightly. It took her by surprise, making her squeal and laugh.

She turned to him and realised he was staring at her.

"You look so beautiful when you smile," Ben commented.

Realising what he had said, he started fiddling with the sat nav, looking a little embarrassed.

Now this was confusing. *Did* Ben like her? Was there a wife or partner as well as a daughter? Was he just finding her 'interesting' because of the win? She had so many questions. One of Helen's rules had always been that she would never date a married man or someone in a serious relationship, but sitting this close to Ben, she knew she was becoming more and more attracted to him, which made situations like this very difficult.

Perhaps he was naturally flirty. They drove along in silence, so she sat back, watching the countryside go by.

Before long they came to a small housing development comprising of what looked like very large four and five-bedroomed houses, all with double garages. Lovely, yes, but they weren't huge mansions with vast acres of land. What was Ben doing bringing her here?

They pulled up outside a house with a neat front garden and a standard modern car, which was two years old, parked in the drive. A woman, probably in her late fifties, came to the front door. She was dressed in jeans and a T-shirt, and Helen immediately recognised the distinct Primark trainers she was wearing, as she also had a pair. It then dawned on her that this woman must be the housekeeper or cleaner. She was puzzled, though, as to why someone who had won a large amount of money would live somewhere like *this*, rather than in a much larger house?

The lady smiled as they got out of the car.

"Hi Ben, how are you doing?"

She then looked at Helen and held out her hand.

"Hi, I'm Jan. Come inside, it's not too warm out here, is it?"

Stepping through the doorway, she took them through to a large living room. It was lovingly decorated, tasteful, but not extravagant.

"What would you like to drink: tea, coffee, or something stronger?" she asked.

Having agreed to coffee, they sat down and soon Jan was back with three mugs and a tray of cakes.

"I couldn't believe it. When I checked, I had run out of cake, so I had to pop down to Lidl about an hour ago. It was so busy I was worried I wouldn't get back here before you arrived."

This *can't* be the lady Ben had wanted her to meet. She was shopping in Lidl and Primark, for heaven's sake!

As she was trying to take it all in, Ben interrupted her thoughts.

"Jan won the lottery four years ago. Like you, she wanted to remain anonymous. As I mentioned, it can be difficult for this to happen without some serious thought and planning. If you buy a huge mansion, top-of-the-range car, expensive clothes, and go on extravagant holidays, it soon becomes obvious to everyone something major has happened," Ben explained.

Jan continued.

"When I won, my husband Tom and I talked with Ben and the lottery team about what lifestyle we wanted to have and how we could go about it. The team asked a lot of questions to make sure they understood exactly what we wanted to achieve. Yes, we wanted a larger house but, because the kids had left home, we didn't want something too big and miles away from anywhere; just something slightly bigger than we had and in a nicer area."

Passing the cakes around, she continued.

"We still wanted to be fairly close to friends and family. So, we sold our three-bedroomed house and bought a five-bedroomed one here. We'd always been careful with money, and although Tom wasn't quite at retirement age, with the win, he was able to take early retirement. Most of our close friends didn't question it. Anyone who did, we simply said, with Tom's pension and the savings we had built up over the years, we could afford to buy this place. It wasn't really a lie, as it was 'savings' of a sort!

"It would have been so easy to 'splash the cash', and believe me, we had all these grand ideas at first. But we wanted to keep under the radar, and when you think seriously about what you *really* want in life, which Ben suggested we do, it became easier. In our case, our car was only five years old, so we waited a year before we bought a newer car, which was six months old; so again, it was easy to justify as we weren't buying a Ferrari or something flashy and expensive. I must admit, at first, I bought clothes from some really exclusive boutiques, but having scrimped and saved all my life, it seemed a waste, spending vast amounts on a dress or a top. Now, I have reverted to shopping in all the stores I went to before, plus a few more upmarket ones, but I still get a buzz if I can pick up a bargain! I am not pretentious and don't feel I have changed."

Helen realised how similar they were, both in their upbringing and outlook on life.

"The people on this development have never questioned how we have made our money any more than we would quiz them. If anyone does start to ask deeper questions, we are able to bat them away. The lottery team gave us suggestions of simple things to say that don't reveal our win and aren't lies or cover stories, which can be hard to keep up."

"You make it sound so easy," Helen remarked wistfully.

"I must admit, at first, we found it very difficult, as it did feel like we were lying to friends and family, but what was the alternative?"

Jan stopped for a minute to enjoy a sip of her coffee and a piece of chocolate cake, not seeming to worry too much about the crumbs she dropped on the beautiful, grey, deep pile carpet.

"Our friends are still those we have had for years, but would our relationship with them change if they knew we had won a lot of money? Would they feel resentful or expect us to support them if they hit hard times? The intervention may not be appreciated and could result in people feeling beholden to us, which could feel awkward too. Being a little 'economical with the truth', for us, is the best option. We do go on more expensive holidays than before and stay in grander hotels, and sometimes we decide to fly business or first class, but generally, we have remained grounded and have everything we want."

She was amazed at how easy Jan made it sound.

Jan swung her legs onto the sofa to make herself more comfortable before continuing.

"Money has been invested for the children's futures, and we have treated or helped them out now and again, but we want them to make their own way in life and understand the value of money, and they don't know about our win. We've also left something for other family members in our wills, but other than what you see, our life isn't vastly different from how it was before. The exception is, as I mentioned, my husband has now retired, which he probably wouldn't have been able to do for quite a few more years, and it gives him the opportunity to relax and play golf more regularly at a much nicer golf club!"

She smiled.

"Mind you, my win was a little more modest than yours from what I understand, although Ben hasn't given me any details. Professional to the last, eh, Ben?"

He looked a little embarrassed.

Jan seemed to have found the right balance for her circumstances, and it was impressive how she had made her transition into money seem so easy. But perhaps if her win was a lot less than Helen's, decisions weren't so difficult for her.

She really warmed to Jan. She was extremely easy to talk to and she found herself recounting how she had helped Alice and Dick. Jan couldn't stop laughing when the story of Sam's 'test drive' was revealed.

Leaving shortly afterwards, Jan gave Helen her number in case she wanted to ask her any other questions later. It was good to have someone else who really understood what a big win was like, and it was obvious that confidentiality was as important to her as it was to Helen.

On the way home, Ben was happy to chat about anything and everything. It had been a good suggestion to go and see Jan. Helen felt lighter and more comfortable, feeling that maybe there was a way to manage her winnings while still having the anonymity she craved.

There was one question that had been on her mind for a while, and this seemed to be the perfect time to raise it.

"Ben, why do you do the job you do? Doesn't it upset you, dealing with all these people who have come into money, that you aren't in the same position? Do you ever feel resentful or a little jealous?"

He turned to her, and she could tell from his expression her words hadn't come out the way she had hoped.

"What do you mean? Do you honestly believe I am *jealous* of people who win the lottery? Why would I envy them when I am forced to watch so many not taking the good advice they have been given, resulting in them making bad investments, poor choices, going through bitter divorces or much worse? Money does not necessarily bring you happiness. I know how money can rip people and families apart."

She sat there, stunned, surprised to see a side of Ben she hadn't witnessed before. There was so much pain and anger in his voice. Where was all this coming from? She had obviously struck a nerve.

The next moment he swung off the road into a layby and turned off the engine. His action jolted her, catching her off-guard.

He sat there for a moment in silence, obviously thinking very carefully about what he was going to say next, trying to find the right words. His reaction had been so strong, she felt nervous, and wondered what he was going to reveal. She just hoped it wasn't going to be too difficult to hear.

"My family had money when I was young. A great deal of money, actually. My dad had a very successful business. I went to one of the best boarding schools in the country, but I was sent there mainly because he didn't have time for me and sending a child to boarding school showed off his wealth to others. His sole aim was to earn as much as he could and enjoy a grand lifestyle. We had a ten-bedroomed mansion in the countryside, with a swimming pool and tennis court, a wine cellar filled with the best wine, and Dad bought lots of expensive artwork. Mum and Dad also hosted lavish parties to show off to Dad's so-called 'friends'. All his tailored suits came from Saville Row or Italy. Unfortunately, Dad began to think he was better than those around him, becoming arrogant, insensitive and trampling on people. Making bad decisions, his business relationships began to suffer.

"He took more and more risks, thinking all would be fine.

"Well, it wasn't. Within a couple of years, he was ignoring advice given with good intent and alienating the few people who had stood by him. He ended up bankrupt.

"Our house had to be sold, I had to give up my last year at boarding school as we no longer had the money to pay the fees, and my mum had to go out to work for the first time in her life. Not that she complained. She was never driven by the money. My dad wallowed in his own self-pity, blaming everyone but himself for his downfall. The few hangers-on dropped us as soon as the money was gone. We weren't 'good contacts' or useful, so we no longer added anything to their lives. My dad began drinking heavily every night, and it ended up killing him."

Ben paused for a moment. She could tell he was really struggling to recount his life.

"When I had to leave boarding school, I had not completed my A levels, but study was no longer the driver for me. It was more important to keep a roof over our heads. I took on a variety of jobs, sometimes a day and an evening job, as my mum went to pieces at first, and my sister was only young. When we were a little more financially stable, I started studying at night school, initially to pass my A levels, but then to gain accountancy qualifications to get a better job. Once I had them, I found a junior role in an international financial organisation, worked tremendously hard, and quickly rose up the ladder.

"I began to make a great deal of money but didn't want to go down the same path as my dad, so I slowed down a little. I saw a job advertised for a night volunteer at a charity, helping people with their debts. I then completed some life coaching courses and started teaching people how to handle their money and be happy with less. Then, ironically, a few years ago, a friend told me about the job with the company who run the lottery, so I left the financial sector, and I've been here ever since, although I still help out a couple of nights a month at the charity. I love my job, but I hate the damage money can potentially cause. That's why I work so hard to try and encourage people to think carefully about how they manage their newly acquired wealth. It can be so tough when George and I see where some people end up, despite our advice."

Ben's head was in his hands. She could see how hard his life had been, and despite what she had initially thought, he knew exactly what it was like to have it all and then suffer the tragic consequences of his dad's bad decisions. Now all he was trying to do was use his own experiences to help and protect people. And she knew his only concern now was to do the same for her. She put her arm around him to offer some comfort. He looked up at her with those beautiful big brown eyes and… kissed her.

She knew from that one kiss how important Ben could be in her life. It was so passionate, yet soft and gentle. Suddenly, he pulled away, saying, "I shouldn't be doing this. I am your life coach."

The mood immediately changed. He put on his 'professional front' again and started up the car.

The rest of the journey home was in silence. He dropped her off at his house to pick up her brother's car, and she left, feeling quite deflated.

It had been a packed day, and she was drained. After dropping off Sam's car, she returned to the flat, realising there had been no call from Ana, either on her mobile or the answerphone.

Tossing and turning for most of the night, her lack of sleep was becoming a regular occurrence. There was so much to worry about: her argument with Ana, wondering where she now stood with Ben and seeing how hurt he had been, as well as thinking about the money. Things just kept spiralling down and down. She had taken a couple of good steps forward helping Alice and Dick and her brother, but now she felt she had taken many more steps back.

After just a few hours' sleep, she was once again up very early the following morning. Being awake had made her review all that had happened, and the first thing she needed to do was to make things right with Ana. Friendships were important and, as she knew only too well, life was short.

After making a cup of tea, she picked up the phone and dialled Ana's number. The answerphone cut in.

"Ana, it's me. I know I've been a real idiot. I am so sorry."

She waited a few seconds, expecting Ana to pick up the phone, but there was no response. She obviously didn't want to talk, but based on their years of friendship, she was sure Ana would want to put an end to the silly argument, so maybe she had gone out.

But hang on, it was still early. *Really* early. Looking at her watch, she realised it was barely seven o'clock. Where would she be at this time in the morning? Just to cover all options, she rang Ana's mobile. Still no response. In case she had been in another room, she left another message on Ana's house phone, saying how guilty she felt about the way things had been left. Something wasn't quite right, but it was impossible to put her finger on it...

Then there was Ben. She hadn't a clue what to do about what had happened. She had been hoping he would go with her to buy a new car, as she had casually mentioned it on the way to Jan's, but it seemed inappropriate to ask him now. A line had been well and truly crossed, and it would probably be difficult to return to a professional footing after the kiss.

Trying to think positively and wondering what to do with her current free time, she decided a new car really should be her priority. It wasn't practical to keep borrowing Sam's, and there was absolutely no point in getting the old one fixed. So, with no Ana to give general advice, she turned to the only person who had some knowledge (but not a lot) about cars. Sam.

As it was a Sunday, despite being woken up so early, Sam was more than happy to go with her, to spend money.

It was important to remember she had also 'supposedly' been given £40,000, and Jan's words kept ringing in her head – 'keep under the radar'.

Sam arrived at Helen's for ten o'clock, and they were soon heading off to a local car dealership. There was such an array of cars, it was difficult to decide. However, she soon spotted a second-hand, cherry-red, Ford Focus with just over four and a half miles on the clock. At nearly £16,000, it was more than she had hoped to pay, but it would be reliable, and in the grand scheme of things, financially for her, it was a drop in the ocean. After a test drive, with Sam telling her it was 'a good, solid car', she signed the paperwork and said she would pick it up in a few days' time when the logbook and insurance had been sorted.

Just as they got back to her flat, her phone rang. It was Ana's mobile number.

"Oh Ana, I am so, so sorry. I was stupid and thoughtless. Let's not throw our friendship away for something so silly?"

However, the voice at the other end was not Ana's.

"Is that Helen Pond? I'm ringing from St Luke's Hospital. We have just admitted Ana Moreno, and she has your name down as her emergency contact. Can you come as soon as possible?"

Not hesitating for a second, she asked Sam to drive her to the hospital.

10

am dropped her at the main entrance of the hospital. He said he would wait, but it was impossible to know what she might be facing or how long she would be, so she said she would phone when she had more details.

Having discovered which ward Ana was in, she found her in a side room, her long, dark hair and pale skin making her look like some beautiful woman in a horror film having the life sucked from her by a vampire.

She smiled when Helen entered, but it was clear to see she was in a great deal of pain and was trying to mask it. She looked so tired, and in a flimsy hospital gown, you could see how much weight she had lost. Her lovely little gold bracelet seemed far too big for her tiny wrist. The cancer was obviously progressing at a much faster rate than Helen had realised.

Ana had apparently blacked out at home, and when she came to, although slightly disoriented, she had still managed to phone for an ambulance. She had told them where she lived and that her neighbour had a spare key.

"How's my favourite diva? Any big tantrums lately?" was the greeting Helen received. The nurse who was fiddling with a tube in Ana's arm looked up, surprised at the way she had greeted her friend.

She gave her a hug and there was a sense of relief that all had been forgiven, but there wasn't the opportunity to chat properly until the nurse left them alone a few minutes later.

"I am so, so sorry. You are right to call me a diva. I've just been caught up with everything and been an absolute idiot," Helen said, squeezing her friend's hand.

"Don't worry. It's been a crazy time, hasn't it?"

Ana was really struggling to breathe, but she still had a million questions.

"First things first. How is it going with the gorgeous Ben? Any developments?"

Helen told her about the meeting with George, Ben taking her to see Jan, visiting Ben's beautiful house, the photograph of the little girl, and the revelation about his life. Then she told her about the kiss.

"Wow, you have been busy!" she exclaimed.

"I just don't know what to do now."

"Let the dust settle, I am sure he'll be in touch," Ana replied wisely. "Mind you, not very professional is it, kissing your client!"

Changing the subject, Ana asked, "So, what else have you been up to?"

It was exciting to be able to tell her about the trip out with Sam to buy a car.

She asked the same question that many of their female friends would have asked. Not what *make* of car it was, but its colour!

Conversation was quite light until Ana said, "I've been thinking about your idea of how to spend some of the money. Hopefully, I should be let out for good behaviour the day after tomorrow, so let's make plans when I'm home. Will you have picked up your new car by then?"

Before there was a chance to answer, the nurse came back in.

"I think you need some rest now, Ana," she said firmly, as she started plumping up her pillows. She checked the monitor and then left.

"Why do nurses always have to do that?" Ana exclaimed crossly, getting Helen to re-arrange the pillows the way they were before the interruption.

"Anything else you need?"

"Ooh, a copy of *Hello!* magazine would be good, if you can get one. I might as well see what interesting things are going on in someone else's life!" She laughed.

Then she turned her head away.

"I am having a number of tests tomorrow, nothing to worry about, but it probably isn't worth coming to visit me, as I'm likely to be tired," she said, in what she hoped was a reassuring manner. Helen wasn't convinced but knew better than to question her.

The rest of the visit passed quickly. Neither of them seemed to want to address how serious Ana's situation was becoming. Like ostriches, they both continued to bury their heads in the sand, at least for the time being. Seeing how tired Ana appeared, Helen thought she ought to leave.

"I'll let you get some rest. Let me know when you are being discharged. If my new car isn't ready by then, we'll get a taxi. See you soon," she said, giving her a quick cuddle.

She pasted a smile on her face before heading out of the room. She was really worried about her friend, she had never seen her look so ill, and she only just managed to get outside before the tears came. She knew the best thing she could do for Ana was just to be there and offer as much support as she could. However, it broke her heart seeing her in a hospital bed. The realisation suddenly hit her that things were only going to get worse. She pushed those thoughts to the back of her mind, as they weren't helpful.

The following day was very quiet. Helen picked up a novel to read, but she couldn't get into it. She was worrying about Ana, and her mind kept spilling over with ideas about how she could help people.

Up until now, any ideas had been written on various scraps of paper, but if her plans were to come to fruition, it would be important to write everything down in a systematic way and look as though she was serious. She decided to go into town to buy a book to write up all her notes and plans for future spending.

In the big department store in town, she found a thick, brown, leather-bound book with lined, cream pages. She also treated herself to an expensive Parker pen. Ever since her school days, she had always wanted a good quality pen, and this one was beautiful; light blue and inlaid with mother of pearl.

There was hardly any food in the fridge, so her next stop was the supermarket. Feeling the need to splurge, she bought items she wouldn't normally buy and was shocked when the cashier revealed the bill to be nearly £200. There was a feeling of guilt, as her normal weekly shop was usually around £90. However, she had also bought Ana the magazine she wanted, a nice box of chocolates, and a big bouquet of flowers.

Ana called in the evening to say the hospital had confirmed she would be discharged the following day after the doctor had undertaken her rounds and she had collected her medication. She would give Helen a ring when she had an idea of a time. It was a relief that she was coming home.

Ana rang just before lunch, so Helen grabbed the notes she had carefully written in her new book, along with the new pen and some milk, bread, and eggs from her fridge, as she wasn't sure what Ana would have in, plus the flowers, chocolates, and magazine. The new car wasn't ready for collection, so with Sam at work, Helen booked a taxi. She was quite overloaded when she walked into the hospital.

By the time she arrived, Ana was dressed and had already picked up her medication, so she was quite keen to leave. They waited for a taxi and went straight back to Ana's.

She settled onto the settee, and Helen told her she had been putting her ideas together. Ana smiled. Going into her bedroom, she came back with an A4 lined pad, the pages full of her neat writing.

"I had also been making a few notes before I ended up in hospital," she said.

After a light lunch of egg and beans on toast, they spent a great afternoon working through their thoughts and comparing notes. As usual, despite Ana's initial misgivings, their ideas were very similar. They got out the laptop so they could get rid of all their notes and begin to put everything in some sort of semblance.

"Right, let's get cracking!" said Ana, full of enthusiasm.

Combining their ideas, they broke them down into categories.

Before long, it felt like they had a solid, workable plan to present to George and Ben.

It read as follows:

THE BIG WIN
(Not very original, but the best title
they could initially come up with)

1. *Everyday money*
   Draw a monthly 'salary' from the interest to cover day-to-day living expenses and 'luxuries' (holidays, etc).
   This would be Helen's 'fun' account. George could advise her of a suitable monthly figure, which could always be reviewed, to make sure she could enjoy herself. No point in having all that money if she couldn't do what she wanted! Also, at some stage in the future, she would need to access a much larger amount, to enable her to buy a house and furniture. Having a budget would also help rein in any rash spending.

2. *Help friends and family*
   Only Sam and Ana. Advice on what provisions could or should be made for them.

This was a difficult one. What did either of them need? Helen's only relative was Sam, and she had already given him £40,000, of which £12,000 had been spent on a car. It was reassuring to know he was starting to think about what to do with the rest of the money too. Later down the line, it would be important to put some money into a trust fund for Sam, for his future and that of his family, if he had one.

Ana had made it very clear she didn't want or need anything and to cross her off the list. However, Helen knew she wouldn't begrudge her paying for them to go away somewhere nice when she was feeling a little better. Also, if it was possible to pay for treatments or anything to make her more comfortable, she was going to do it, whatever the cost. But she kept her thoughts to herself. She wished there was more she could do for Ana, but for now, it wasn't a possibility. However, with a little more time, some new treatment could arise, and she vowed not to stop looking.

3. *How to find people to help?*
Scour local newspaper stories online and keep an ear to the ground, which may give leads.
George and Ben's input would be crucial. Helen didn't know if they had any experience of what she was proposing, so it would probably be a learning curve for them all.

4. *Expenditure on projects*

What was a suitable monthly allowance for projects? And how much should be spent on a single project? Should I only look at small, local organisations or was it worth considering small national ones too?

Again, she hoped that George and Ben could advise her. There must be other people who supported small charities, albeit without any secrecy. She may be able to use them as a model.

5. *Ripple effect*

*All payments should have a stipulation that states 'The benefactor requests that **if it is possible in the future** (and with no time limit set), the individual or organisation benefitting from the donation should try to help somebody else (not necessarily in a financial way), therefore producing a 'ripple effect'.*

Was this practical, or was she being delusional? Perhaps it was a ridiculous thing to suggest, and it could be interpreted in so many ways by the person or organisation receiving the money or, equally, could be ignored completely. But if only one other person was helped by this action, it would be worth it. George was good with words and suggestions, and she knew he would be totally honest with his opinions.

6. *Updates on projects*

Was it a good idea to check on how things were going with a project, perhaps three or six months after the money had been received, to see what had happened? It would enable me to check if the initial goal(s) had been achieved or if the person or organisation needed any further financial support.

The downside to giving the money away was that things may not go to plan, or even worse, the money may just be squandered. How would she cope with that? Would there be feelings of frustration and anger? There was also the possibility it may put her off giving to others in the future. Ben would need to give her advice on how to handle any disappointment she may face, as it would be naïve to believe all projects would go to plan.

Ana chipped in. "It just proves the point," she said. "When you give someone the money, you have to do what they say in *Frozen*."

She looked at her friend for a moment, before they both burst out the chorus to 'Let It Go'.

She knew it would be difficult. That was what had happened with the donation made to Alice and Dick. They hadn't done exactly what she thought they would do with the money, but in fact, they had gone one better. However, she was all too aware it *could* work the other way, like Sam's initial idea of buying a new fancy car. And if she did 'stipulate' what the money was to be for, there probably wasn't a way of *making* someone use the money for the desired purpose and, to be honest, should she have that much control anyway? If she did, whoever was receiving the money, would probably resent the fact they were being 'told' what to do with it. This wasn't going to be as easy as she had initially thought. She was relieved to have George and Ben's input.

7. *How easy would it be to ensure that people couldn't link the money back to me?*

Was it possible to make a completely anonymous donation? Could it be traced, if someone really wanted to?

This was what terrified her most about the whole idea. Could it work? Was she trying to be too ambitious? If there was any possibility her anonymity could be compromised, she wouldn't do it. But she felt so passionate about her plans, and she really didn't want them crushed at this initial stage.

And lastly:

8. *How would everything be administered?*

The lottery support is on-going, but is this kind of project covered?

She knew the probable answer. It was unlikely this kind of work would fall under the lottery's remit, so she would need to look at other options for support. And how easy was that likely to be? George and Ben would hopefully have some answers.

The girls hadn't realised four hours had passed since they started going through their notes, and by this stage, they were both hungry. "Let's go wild and order a takeaway," Helen suggested.

Ana's response, in her typical ironic style was, "Wow, you *really* know how to live dangerously!"

Ana didn't eat much, but Helen made up for it. They had ordered Chinese. Trying not to get sauce all over the notes, they carefully reviewed their work, most of which were now typed up onto the laptop anyway. They were sure George would be impressed with the ideas and what had been covered, especially as they had been systematic and considered potential pitfalls. Hopefully, he might just agree their crazy ideas had wings.

The following morning, not feeling able to bring herself to ring Ben, she tried George again. The answerphone cut in, and she left another message. He rang back in the afternoon. Explaining about the previous day's productive session, she asked when he thought they could have another meeting to discuss things further.

He pencilled in a day early the following week, ensuring it worked around Ana's appointments. It was disappointing that the get-together seemed so far away. Helen was anxious to get things moving now they had the bare bones of a plan. George made no mention of whether he had recently spoken with Ben, and she didn't like to ask.

The next day, the car was ready for collection. Helen was so excited. As Sam was working, she took a taxi down to the car dealership.

The car was just as beautiful as she remembered and a dream to drive. It was perfect for her: nippy around town, economical, and she loved the colour. The boot was bigger than she recalled (*great for future shopping expeditions*, she thought), and the car had that wonderful 'new' smell. All the cars she had ever owned had been at least ten years old, so the luxury of an almost brand-new one was not wasted on her. Sam was quick to make sure Ana knew it was on *his* advice she had chosen that specific car. It had felt amazing to say to the salesman there wouldn't be the need for a finance deal; the car would be paid for in full. Always the 'bargain hunter', she had asked what extras could be thrown in. The salesman had agreed to a spare wheel, car mats, and a full tank of petrol, which was great. The car also had cruise control and sat nav (no more bad 'attempts' at map reading and getting lost on the M25). Those little extras may be what people automatically expected from a car these days, but it was all so exciting and new for her.

The car's first proper outing was a trip with Ana and Sam into the countryside, followed by lunch in a pub. Helen proudly picked up Ana and then Sam. It was great to be able to treat them both to a meal and not worry whether there was enough in the bank to cover it. Ana must have been shopping, because over lunch, she produced a nodding dog – perfect (*she* said) for the back shelf of the car! Seeing its wagging head made them all laugh.

From that point on, life seemed to almost go back to normal. You wouldn't have known there had been a lottery win or that the stormy clouds of Ana's illness were gathering in the background. The pair of them decided to just enjoy how things were while it lasted.

The following week, the girls set off for their meeting with George and Ben. They were both so excited, and Helen was keen to show off her new car, hoping George and Ben would like it too.

In the days before the meeting, to keep herself busy, Helen had gone into town and photocopied four sets of their typed-up notes so everyone had a copy at the meeting. Each page had a wide margin to ensure there was room to write any notes or action points.

It was important to her that George knew how serious she was about her proposals.

She was desperate to see Ben again, but she was also scared, not knowing how awkward it might be. She was pleased their first encounter since the kiss would be in a group setting.

The meeting was back at the National Lottery offices. It seemed so long since the first time the girls had been there, full of nerves and excitement. They were told their 'colleagues' were already waiting for them, and they were taken upstairs. As they walked in, they saw George, but looking round the room, there was no sign of Ben, but there was someone else.

It was a woman. George and the woman both got up as they entered. Who was she and what was she doing there? George was about to give them the answer.

"Girls, this is Kathy Hodgson. She will be taking over from Ben as your life coach. She has years of experience working for the National Lottery, in fact, longer than Ben has, and I am sure you will find she'll be a great asset to you. I have brought her fully up to speed on your win and what you are planning to do," he explained.

Looking at each other, the girls wondered what was going on. Where was Ben? What had happened? Helen tried to put on a smile but found it difficult to hide her surprise. It obviously wasn't possible to quiz George about the change of life coach in the meeting, but she would definitely ring him later to find out what had happened. But would she want to know? She felt quite deflated, but now wasn't the time to think about it.

"Lovely to meet you," Kathy said as she came over to shake their hands.

Kathy seemed nice and obviously had a great deal of experience, but she wasn't Ben.

As they sat down, Helen handed out copies of the typed notes. George looked surprised.

"My, my, ladies, you have been busy!" It was obvious from his reaction he was impressed with their hard work. "Equally, I shouldn't have expected anything less," he continued.

Going through each point in detail, George was brilliant, and to be fair, Kathy chipped in from time to time with some very useful suggestions.

Although George thought their ideas were rather unusual and had a number of concerns, he also commented that they were well thought through.

With regard to a personal expenditure, George suggested a monthly amount that was the equivalent to more than six months of temping! He explained it was better to overestimate so it was there if it was needed, but it didn't necessarily mean it had to be spent each month.

As she had suspected, George confirmed what was being proposed would be out of the lottery's normal remit. To retain her anonymity and to reduce the stress and pressure of what she was proposing, he suggested setting up a small company to handle the donations, with an agreed amount paid into the account every quarter. A board of directors and trustees could be set up, and George said he knew someone who could organise and find the right candidates. They would be discreet and run the business on her behalf, which seemed a really good solution.

Having directors and trustees meant they could also source suitable individuals and groups to help and then send the details to her for consideration and approval. Quarterly meetings could be held to discuss the pros and cons of all the suggestions, and she would have the final say on which ones to support.

George said he was happy to initially be involved and oversee what was being considered. He advised against looking at any further donations until the company was set up. However, if anything arose that she wanted to support before arrangements were formally in place, he suggested using the solicitors to handle those donations but warned her confidentiality may be harder to maintain. He reiterated his involvement in the venture could only be a temporary measure.

He was keen to explain the advantages of having a formal company. Not only would it mean there would be transparency from a legal perspective, but if anyone was curious about the benefactor or wanted to talk to someone about the donation, they could liaise with one of the trustees, meaning there was less of a trail back to her. Also, George pointed out that as a legitimate company making donations, it could be set up as a charity, meaning it was possible to claim some of the tax back. Nice to know, but it was hardly an issue! However, it would mean there was more money to help others. An advantage of the quarterly meetings was she would still maintain overall control over the donations made if that was what she wanted, or she could take a step back, knowing the business was in safe hands.

Again, George reiterated there were no guarantees people would use the money in the way she hoped, and he was concerned about how she would cope if that occurred.

Kathy interjected.

"As much as you could stipulate what the purpose of the money was for, at the end of the day, if it wasn't used in the way you had hoped, you would just have to accept it was no longer your money. You need to view it as a gift, and once received, it would then be up to the individual or organisation to use it in the best way they saw fit. If you felt you couldn't do that, you need to think whether this is the best way of using your money."

It made perfect sense.

Kathy continued.

"If you like, I can spend some time with you, working on some techniques to help you deal with donations that don't go to plan, so you can let it go."

Helen and Ana immediately looked at each other, smiling, remembering their recent rendition of 'Let it Go'. It was unlikely Kathy would break into song. She didn't seem the type.

Kathy said she would arrange a time to discuss it further.

"You also need to make sure you don't get too attached

to any cause," Kathy commented. "Attachments complicate things."

Helen didn't know how to respond to that statement. She wondered if she was talking about the donations or her attachment to Ben. How much did Kathy know, she wondered?

George asked if she had any thoughts on a name for the company. She replied she hadn't but would discuss it further with Ana over the next few days. George expressed the urgency in doing so, as the company could not be set up without it, so it was added to her list of action points.

She was feeling quite light-headed at the end of the meeting but pleased because, despite all the hard work that would be involved, everything was starting to come together. George seemed to really understand what she was hoping to achieve. With him onboard, she was sure it would all come together but, as he had mentioned, his involvement would be brief. She realised how much she would miss him, despite only knowing him for such a short while.

"I must admit, you two have really thought this through. I am very impressed and beginning to think this could possibly work. Still a lot more to be organised, but well done," George said.

Kathy smiled and nodded in agreement.

The girls beamed at each other.

"You are a very interesting and determined lady. I can see why people are attracted to you. I am sure we shall have some very interesting discussions in the next few weeks! Well, I've got to go off to another meeting, so I must dash but, once again, well done. I'll be in touch."

George winked at Ana, shook Helen's hand, and left.

She wondered what he meant when he said, 'I can see why people are attracted to you.'

She had been hoping to speak with him privately to ask about Ben, but obviously that wasn't going to happen now.

Kathy still sat across from them.

"Any further questions?" she asked.

Neither of them knew what to say.

"No, um, I think we've covered everything."

"I look forward to seeing you again," Kathy said.

She gave out her business card, and after shaking their hands, Kathy left, leaving the two girls alone.

They sat there for a minute or two, not quite believing everything was finally coming together.

"I think we were pretty spectacular!" Ana shrieked, giving her friend a high five. "I didn't ask in the meeting, but can I be a trustee? Or is it a conflict of interest with our friendship? Oh, it's going to be so much fun!"

Just seeing her enthusiasm and excitement made it all worthwhile for Helen. This was obviously giving her something to focus on beyond her illness.

There was still the difficulty of deciding on the company name. They started to think about options.

"What about Lottie?" Helen suggested.

"What about it?" Ana replied blankly.

"Well, I won the lottery and that's where the idea came from."

Ana cringed.

"No, *definitely* not! It's a ridiculous name for a company."

"The thing is, I want the name to mean something."

Continuing to bounce around a few ideas, nothing seemed right.

Someone knocked on the door and asked if they had finished with the room.

They nodded, packed up their notes, and then made their way back down to reception. Turning to Ana, Helen asked, "Are you coming back to mine or shall we go to yours?"

"Sorry, I'm tired," Ana replied. "I need to get some sleep. I'm meeting Carmen tomorrow."

"Who is this 'Carmen'? You've never mentioned her until recently. And now it feels like she is replacing me as your best friend."

She tried to make it sound like a joke, but there was an element of seriousness, and she knew there was more than a hint of jealousy in her voice.

"Don't be silly," Ana replied quietly. "I've known her for a while. But don't worry, she won't be around for much longer."

What an odd thing to say, Helen thought. And Ana had looked at her strangely when she said it. Why wasn't her best friend opening up to her and explaining what was going on? They had never had secrets in the past.

Not wanting to cause another argument, they walked to the car in silence.

On the way back, however, Ana was so animated, her mind buzzing with ideas about the company. Not really listening to what she was saying, Helen tried to sound as though she was paying attention with the odd 'yes' and 'no' here and there and hoped it made sense, but her mind was elsewhere.

She was more interested in knowing why Ben was no longer her life coach, and whether she would ever see him again?

11

When Helen got home, she noticed there was a missed call on her phone, but the person hadn't left a message. When she rang 1471 to check the number, it was Ben's.

She panicked, not knowing what to do. Should she ring him back? Or did he ring and then change his mind, thinking it would be a mistake to call? She was unsure what to do, as she didn't want to potentially face another rejection. Mind you, theirs had never been a 'relationship', just one kiss. Why then, was she so bothered?

She knew the answer. From the moment they had met, she could tell he was different from anyone she had known before and that, potentially, there could be something special between them. Maybe he felt it too.

No, she reasoned, she had probably read the signals wrong. But then again, he had kissed her! And he had tried to ring. She was totally confused as to what her next move should be.

While she sat there pondering, the phone rang. Hesitantly, thinking it might be Ben calling back, she picked up. However, it was Ana.

"I've potentially found our first project!" she exclaimed excitedly. "I was looking at *The Bedfordshire Post* online. There's a dance group for local kids. They've been entering dance competitions. The woman who runs it set it up because her daughter and some of her friends wanted to dance but the fees for other local dance groups were too expensive. This year, they have got through to the European Dance Championships in France. The event is sponsored so costs are reduced, and they have already raised £8,500 from various fundraising activities. However, they still need to find another £8,500 towards travel, accommodation, and costumes. The balance has to be paid within the next couple of months, otherwise they are not going to be able to go. It would be great to give them the money, wouldn't it?"

Ana then proceeded to remind her of their dance club days, which made her smile. Being so graceful, Ana had very different memories of discos than Helen did, with her two left feet and complete lack of co-ordination! With that awful thought in her head, she realised Ana was still talking.

"I could come over after I have been to my appointment tomorrow, and we can look at it in more detail, if you like?"

Helen immediately agreed.

Putting the phone down, she was becoming more excited about the future. In addition to helping Julian, there was now another potential project, by the sound of it.

But, she also felt it was time to think of herself.

She decided to look at houses, to get an idea of the kind of place she would like to buy.

Flipping open the laptop, she went on to the Parkinsons Country Properties website, an estate agency that managed more prestigious homes.

Wow! There was the perfect property! About forty-five miles away and set in its own grounds, it had eight bedrooms, an indoor swimming pool, jacuzzi, sauna, gym, games room (Sam would like that), and there was even a separate self-contained bungalow. At the bottom of the garden was a tennis court. Cost? £3.2 million! That sounded like such a lot of money. But then again, a house is usually the most expensive thing you purchase in your life and a small amount of her win, in the grand scheme of things. Crashing back to reality, she realised it was too far from Sam and Ana. She could also hear Jan's comments ringing in her ears about keeping under the radar. How would it be possible to justify being able to afford something so expensive when she was temping?

She decided to look on a local estate agents' website instead. She found a few lovely properties in some of the surrounding villages. There were some that looked interesting, and having written the details down, she decided to discuss them with Ana.

She would need to come up with a really good cover story to explain to Sam how it was possible for her to afford something bigger. Although she had supposedly been given £40,000, she had spent £16,000 of it on a car. And even buying a modest cottage would be too much on a temping budget.

And then it hit her! When the company was set up,

her cover story could be she had managed to secure a permanent live-in job as a senior personal assistant with an excellent salary. Obviously in reality, it would be her own home and company. This would also solve the problem if people enquired what she did for a living, or if Sam asked how she was able to afford a house, when the time came. That wouldn't be a complete lie, it would just need to be thought through very carefully. Adopting this story would make it easier if she let slip about one of the projects she was working on in her day-to-day 'job'.

Being realistic, however, it wouldn't be a good idea to buy a big house, as it would require upkeep. And it wasn't as though she needed that much space; as long as it was big enough for Ana and Sam to come and stay. Perhaps she could get Kathy's advice when she saw her next.

By nine o'clock the following morning, Ana was at Helen's, keen to show her the newspaper article. Looking it up online, there was a large photo of the dance group looking so happy and excited. However, the woman in the middle looked tired and her smile forced, as if she had to oblige for the camera.

"What an amazing opportunity for the kids," Helen sighed.

They agreed it was definitely one for the list.

The appeal had a GoFundMe page, so they decided to look at it in more detail. This was the kind of project Helen was keen to support, as the group had managed to raise a considerable amount of funds on their own, which was impressive.

They started to look at other GoFundMe pages to see what other causes there were.

Big mistake. There were *so* many, all worthy of money.

"This is crazy. I can't believe how many people and groups need help. How do we choose?"

"You can't help everyone," Ana reasoned wisely.

She was right, of course. It was then the enormity of what she was looking to undertake hit her. Hopefully when the company was set up, the trustees would give guidance and much-needed advice, she reassured herself.

When Ana left, Helen began thinking more about her, and how things seemed to have changed between them in the past few weeks. She had noticed Ana was often 'unavailable', and the excuses were often quite feeble. She couldn't help wondering if the money was making her friend nervous. Perhaps she was worried that, if she said the wrong thing, their relationship could be affected. She wasn't sure how to voice her concerns without causing another argument.

It was impossible not to notice how weak Ana was becoming as time went on. That was another reason why she felt it was better not to say anything if she couldn't see her. It was important she didn't get stressed or worn out.

But when the two of them were together, they had as much fun as they always did. Her input, support, and advice were invaluable. Plus, she was the only person who would always give an honest opinion.

However, nothing could have prepared Helen for what was about to come…

When she first heard the phone, she thought it was a dream, but no, it kept on ringing. Looking at the clock, it was only 2.15am. Who would be ringing at that time? It couldn't be good news. Her first thought was it must be

Sam. Maybe he had been involved in an accident. Sitting bolt upright, she picked up the phone.

"Miss Pond? This is St Luke's Hospital. We have re-admitted Ana Moreno."

Helen's throat was dry, and her heart was beating fast.

"Please can you get here as soon as possible. She is asking for you."

Without hesitation, she quickly grabbed her coat, putting it on over her pyjamas, and changed her slippers for a pair of trainers before picking up the car keys and rushing out the door. What the hell had happened? Had she blacked out again?

Trembling as she jumped into the car, she took a minute before starting it. She knew she needed to keep level-headed and calm as it was a twenty-minute drive to the hospital.

She parked as quickly as she could, which was relatively easy, because at that time in the morning, the car park was almost empty.

Dashing into the reception area, she explained she needed to find her friend as soon as possible. The receptionist was looking at her strangely and she suddenly realised why. Her coat was wide open, and the receptionist's attention had been drawn to her bright pink pyjamas with little white bunnies on them. In addition, she realised, with her untameable hair, she probably looked like a banshee. But at that moment, she didn't care. All that mattered now was Ana.

The receptionist checked the computer and directed her to the second floor.

When she arrived on the ward, a nurse immediately came up to her, obviously sensing her distress.

"I am here to see Ana. My name is Helen, I'm her friend and I've had a phone call. Is she alright?"

The nurse pointed to a chair in the corridor of the ward, indicating for her to sit down. Helen was getting agitated. All she wanted to do was see Ana. Why couldn't she just go in and see her?

The nurse sat next to her, speaking softly.

"I need to prepare you. Ana is very sick. She was admitted about seven hours ago, and at first, we thought she would pull through, but the doctor has indicated she is rapidly deteriorating. She asked for you, and we have you down as her next of kin."

Trying to process what was being said, it couldn't be right. Ana wasn't that sick. Yes, she was dying, but she had months, possibly longer. She had said so.

And then it hit her. It *was* a few months since they'd had the initial discussion. Helen could feel herself getting both angry and upset. Ana couldn't leave her now, not when they were so close to setting up the business and enjoying the mad situation they had found themselves in. No, she couldn't die, that was selfish of her. She was needed; it was important she was there to help her with all the plans they were making. She couldn't leave her now! Tears began to prick her eyes.

Suddenly, she was aware the nurse was talking again.

"Give me a minute. I'll see if it's OK for you to go in. Carmen, her private nurse, is with her."

With that, she left, making her way into what Helen thought must be Ana's room.

Now it all made sense. She had talked about 'her friend Carmen' but had avoided saying she was her cancer nurse. No wonder she had never heard of Carmen before and why Ana hadn't wanted to talk about her.

Had she been so caught up in her own world that she had failed to be there when her friend needed her the most?

The next minute the door opened and a woman in a slightly different uniform came out. This must be Carmen, Helen reasoned. She was about the same age as Ana and looked terribly sad.

"She's not dead, is she? She can't be," Helen heard herself asking and immediately regretted it.

She came and sat by her side.

"Hi, you must be Helen. I've heard so much about you and wish I could have met you under different circumstances. No, Ana's having difficulty breathing, but she's hanging in there. She wanted to see you while she was still conscious. Spend as long as you want with her, she has been asking me every two minutes if you are here, driving me nuts, if I am honest," she said with a rueful smile.

"But what do I say, what do I do?" she asked, trembling. "I don't know what to say, I…" She faltered.

"You'll find the right things to say. She is your friend. Just being there will be enough."

Following Carmen into the room, it was difficult to know what to expect.

The room was dark, but there was a small, dim light at the side of the bed, and then Helen saw Ana. Her darling, best friend, Ana. It looked like her, but equally, it didn't. There were lots of tubes, she was attached to a drip, and everything was connected to a machine, which was bleeping every few seconds. She looked so frail. However, she managed a weary smile as Helen entered the room.

"What are you doing calling me out at this time of the morning, no time even to brush my hair and still in my rabbit pyjamas!" was all Helen could think to say.

Ana started to laugh, her friend's words obviously lightening the mood.

"It's alright for you, I've had to listen to the constant bleeping of that bloody machine for the past few hours," was Ana's weak reply, pointing to the metal contraption at the side of the bed.

Sitting next to her in the chair, Helen could feel the tears rolling down her cheeks, despite her best efforts to hold them back. She really wanted to be brave for her friend but was failing miserably.

"I'm so sorry. I didn't realise you were so ill. I haven't been paying enough attention. I've not been there for you, I should have done more. I could have waited a while before trying to sort out our plans for the money. I shouldn't have pushed you so hard, it's all been too much for you."

The words just tumbled out as she buried her head against Ana's leg.

"Don't be silly! What do you think has kept me going over the past few months? This has been so exciting."

She touched Helen's head with her hand.

"I've loved every mad moment of it. Oh, and I am sorry I lied about how sick I am," she said just as Carmen came back into the room with another nurse.

"God, I feel so selfish. It's all been me, me, me recently."

Ana completely ignored her friend's self-pity.

"So, have you heard from Ben?" Ana asked.

"No," Helen replied. "I think that ship has sailed."

"Well tell him your best friend is in the final throes of her life. Play the 'dying sympathy card'," she suggested, smiling.

"Ana!" Helen was shocked. She knew her friend was trying to make light of the situation, but it didn't make her feel any better.

"Seriously, you need to get your own house in order before you start trying to sort out everyone else. This situation has made me realise that Ben would be great for you. Also, the pair of you would have adorable kids. Oh, and if you do have any, one of them has got to be named after me. But only if you have a girl, of course!"

Her breathing was becoming more and more laboured and shallow. The nurse looked at the monitor and went to change a setting.

"I am going to change the dose a little, which should make it a little easier for you," the nurse said to Ana.

"No, don't give me a stronger dose, I want to be lucid. Please?" Ana pleaded.

The nurse nodded and smiled respectfully before adding, "If you need me, press the button. I can always give you some more pain relief if you want it."

Carmen and the nurse left. Once again, the girls were alone.

Ana grabbed her best friend's hand and held it tightly.

"Promise me you won't just let your life drift. You have been given an amazing opportunity, so grab it with both hands. Don't mope around when I am gone. I shall watch over you, and if you don't do as you're told, I'll see if there is a way I can come back and haunt you!"

They both laughed through their tears. Ana was really struggling to breathe, yet her grip remained so tight.

"I don't want to go, but my time has come. I want you to know how proud I am of you. You've been the best friend anyone could have asked for, and I am so pleased you chose me to be your friend. I love you, and I always will."

Suddenly, the machine started bleeping madly, and Helen recognised that all-too-familiar flat line, which she had witnessed on so many TV programmes.

"Nurse, Carmen, anyone. Come quickly! Save my friend, please save my friend!" Helen screamed, running into the corridor.

It was too late.

12

The next couple of days passed in a blur. Not wanting to speak to anyone, Helen took the house phone off the hook and put her mobile on silent. Pulling the bedcovers over her head, she just wanted to shut out the world. When she couldn't sleep, she drank, hoping it would block out the pain, but as soon as the alcohol wore off, the unbelievable aching in her heart was still there, so she gave up drinking.

On the third day, there was a knock at the door. She thought if she ignored it, the person would go away. But they didn't. They just kept hammering on the door. Eventually, the knocks did stop, and she settled back down under the duvet.

Suddenly, she could hear someone moving around the flat, then the bedroom door opened, and the duvet was roughly pulled from her. It was Sam.

"How are you? God, you look awful! And this room needs some fresh air."

He pulled back the curtains and opened the window. Light flooded the room, much to his sister's annoyance.

"How the hell did you get in?" she asked grumpily, trying to pull the covers back over her.

"I knew you had given Sally at 2B a spare key when you went away before, so I thought she might still have it. Now, come on, get up, I am putting the kettle on," he ordered, as he disappeared from the room.

Reluctantly getting out of bed, she dragged herself into the living room.

Soon, Sam was back with two mugs of tea and some biscuits.

"When was the last time you ate anything?" he asked.

Helen ignored the question.

"Look, I am *really* worried about you," he continued, the frustration and concern showing on his face.

"I am truly sorry about Ana. But lying in bed isn't going to help. Now, drink your tea, then jump in the shower."

Obediently, she drank the tea, enjoying the warmth it briefly offered, before reluctantly going to have a shower. When she came out and went into her bedroom, she could see that Sam had laid out a clean set of clothes on the bed. She smiled, as the items didn't really match, but she appreciated her brother's good intention. Pulling on the top and grabbing some jogging bottoms from the drawer, she went back into the living room. Sam was just emerging again from the kitchen, this time with toast.

"You've not much in the fridge, but I found some bread. A little dry, but as it is toasted, you won't notice the difference."

She wasn't used to her little brother taking charge. Perhaps he was growing up. Or maybe he had grown up a long time ago and she had never given him the chance to show it.

Taking a bite of the hot buttered toast, she realised how hungry she was. After eating it, she immediately felt guilty for enjoying it so much when her best friend was no longer there.

Tears began to fall down her cheeks, and it was impossible to stop them flowing. Sam picked up a tissue from the box on the side table and came over, giving her a huge hug.

"Oh Sis, I am so, so sorry."

She didn't know how long she cried, with Sam just holding her.

When there were no tears left, she sat up, exhausted.

"Thank you for being here, Sam."

She noticed he had also been crying.

"I miss her too. She was like a sister to me."

He got up, embarrassed she had seen him so upset. It hadn't occurred to her how important Ana must have been for him, but as she had watched him grow up and helped support him, he probably missed her as much as she did. She had been the only other constant in his life.

He took the tray back to the kitchen and, noticing the phone was still on its side, put it back on the docking station, turning up the ringer. Immediately, the phone rang.

Sam answered it.

"Sorry to trouble you at this difficult time. Is Helen there?"

Sam mouthed silently to her it was 'George' and looked at her quizzically. He was obviously wondering who 'George' was.

Taking the call, she was grateful to hear George's voice as he offered his condolences.

But then he said something she was clearly not expecting. Ana had made a will just a few weeks before she died. Helen was surprised to find out she'd apparently had a private meeting with George on one of the days she couldn't see her. He'd agreed, as a favour, to help sort things out in advance of her death. They had discussed her funeral and arranged for the will to be drawn up, with Helen as the beneficiary of all her assets.

Having known George for such a short period of time, it was amazing the impact he had made on their lives, and it made her realise how much of a real friend he had become, rather than just a formal financial advisor. Ana had given Carmen his details, to enable her to notify him after her death.

George said he would like to come round to discuss everything with her as soon as she felt OK to do so. As Ana had named Helen as her next of kin in the absence of any family, she would need to sort out the funeral arrangements, despite knowing how difficult it would be. George said he would help her through it all, every step of the way, so she didn't have to do it on her own. When would be a good time?

As she wanted to get things moving, she arranged for him to visit the following morning.

When she came off the phone, she could tell Sam was wondering who George was. To keep it simple, she said he was a colleague from one of the jobs where she had temped, and he'd become a good friend, which is why they had stayed in touch. He seemed to be happy with the explanation.

Helen knew she needed to pull herself together, for Ana's sake. Asking Sam if he could get some food from the supermarket while she tidied up, she hastily drew up a list and gave it to him with some cash. He duly trotted off to the shops, a little worried about leaving her. She smiled, wondering what he would come back with, not really knowing his shopping skills.

When Sam returned, he filled up the fridge and freezer with everything she had asked for. He could see she had tidied up and to help, he offered to do the hoovering. She couldn't believe it, and even joked she wasn't aware he even knew how to use a hoover!

After another cup of tea, they sat and talked about Ana, Helen telling him about some of the funny things that had happened during their friendship. It was also lovely to hear Sam relay his own stories and special memories of her.

He recounted an occasion when he had first joined their high school. Although Helen had never realised, being short, he had been bullied and had confided in Ana. The following day, she had found one of the two lads who were bullying him, pinned him against the wall, and 'advised' him to leave Sam alone, if he knew what was good for him.

Not the correct way to deal with the situation, but that was the end of that.

"I didn't know!" Helen was shocked.

"I didn't want to bother you with it, or let you think I couldn't handle things," Sam replied. "But Ana could tell something was wrong, and we had a chat about it. She has given me some good advice over the years."

Sam stayed at Helen's all afternoon, and by teatime, she ordered a takeaway for them both. Sadly, she realised how little quality time she had spent with her brother over the past few years and immediately regretted it, vowing to change that in the future.

"Do you want me to stay the night?" Sam asked.

She knew she didn't want to be alone, but equally, she needed to start moving forward with her life again and find some sort of normality.

Trying to sound convincing, she said: "No, you're fine. I'll manage. You've got work tomorrow, and George is coming round to see me in the morning."

"So, prospective boyfriend material, is he?" Sam asked warily.

"Good grief, no!" she replied, surprised at Sam's assumption. "George is old enough to be my dad, and he's married. He's just become an amazing friend to both me and Ana."

"Why you *and* Ana, if he was a work colleague?"

She could tell Sam was curious, challenging the original explanation of who George was.

It would be so easy to get herself in a tangle if she tried to come up with another lie, so she just answered defensively, "Don't be so nosey, Sam. I am allowed a life."

It sounded harsh, and Sam looked offended.

She immediately apologised.

"Look, I'm sorry for being snappy. As you can imagine, I'm finding everything very difficult at the moment."

Hoping he would accept the explanation, she hugged him.

"Wow, you must really be feeling off if you are giving *me* a hug!" Sam joked.

She was embarrassed, as it suddenly dawned on her she couldn't remember the last time she had hugged him.

She used to hug Ana all the time, so why not her own brother?

Sam said there was a pizza in the fridge if she wanted something quick and easy the following day, before leaving her to it.

When he had gone, the flat felt so empty and quiet. Tears started to form again as she thought about Ana, and she immediately tried to pull herself together. She needed to be clear-headed and organised for the discussion with George in the morning.

Surprisingly, she slept relatively well that night, but she was still up early. After showering and getting dressed, she put on a little make-up, as she was conscious of how pale she looked. George was arriving at ten o'clock, and he was, as expected, on time.

Opening the door, she let him in.

"So, how are you bearing up?" he asked, the concern etched on his face.

Taking one look at him, the tears started to flow again. George guided her to the settee and sat down next to her.

He didn't really know what to do, and she buried herself into his chest. He put his arm around her to offer some comfort, letting her cry. When she was more composed, he tried to lighten the mood.

"Well, I'll definitely have to change this shirt before my next appointment!"

She didn't understand what he meant, until she looked down and noticed his once nice, clean, white shirt was now covered in black mascara.

"Oh no, George, I am so sorry! What will your wife say?" She was horrified at what she had done.

George laughed. "Don't worry. She knows all about you and what has happened, so she will believe me. She also knows I am too old to be chasing pretty young ladies these days! Now, how about a cup of tea?"

George ambled off in the direction where he thought the kitchen might be. With it being such a small flat, there weren't many options.

She could hear him opening cupboards and rummaging, looking for mugs.

He briefly popped his head back round the door and asked, "Right, where's the teapot?"

"I haven't used a teapot in years, George, although I do think there is one somewhere in the kitchen."

She couldn't tell whether or not he found it, or just shoved a teabag in each mug, but soon he came back through with two mugs of tea.

They sat there for a while enjoying it, until eventually, George broke the silence.

"Would you like to hear what Ana discussed with me? I wrote down what she said verbatim."

Nodding, she was unsure if she was ready to hear what he had to say.

George took out a folded piece of A4 paper from his pocket and started to read.

"Listen, fuzzy head," George looked at her, instantly appearing rather embarrassed. "Just for the record, I want to establish these are *her* words, not mine!" He laughed.

She smiled, remembering how Ana had come up with the nickname. It was on their first school trip away from home. They had shared a room, and waking up late,

Helen's hair was a big fuzzy ball, as it always was first thing in the morning. Ever since, 'fuzzy head' had stuck.

George continued.

"I don't want a big fancy funeral, just something simple with all my closest and dearest friends. There is a list of names, addresses, and telephone numbers in my bedroom cabinet, top drawer. Not many people, but enough.

"Also, I don't want everyone wearing black. I like the idea of all my friends, including the men, wearing pink, which as you well know, is my favourite colour. I don't care if it is a tie or socks, but whatever pink item it is, it does have to be visible. There, that will get the men cursing me! I don't want any hymns, but to appease my mum when I see her again, and to ensure I get into heaven, I better have a semi-religious Church of England funeral."

George took a sip of his tea before continuing.

"A simple coffin is enough. Don't waste money on anything fancy; it will only be burnt, as I want to be cremated. I would like my ashes to be put in with my mum in her little plot at St Mary's. Entering the crematorium, I want them to play 'Let Me Entertain You', and, as I go, 'I Want to Break Free'. Might as well make people smile a little during such a grim time. There are a couple of more sensible songs I want during the ceremony and a poem, which I have made George aware of.

"During the service it would be nice if a couple of people would get up and say a few words about my life. That includes you, Helen, but don't say anything incriminating. I may be dead, but I don't want *too* many secrets of mine being shared!

"Also, would you put together some lovely photographs or videos of my life to be shown during the funeral and after? Just make sure you don't use anything embarrassing, especially not the video where I was unintentionally flashing my knickers at your brother's party and you didn't tell me!

"I would prefer it if people gave a donation to a cancer charity. It will have a much bigger impact than flowers, which will only end up in a bin. Anything to try and stop others going through this awful disease or to provide people with additional support while they do. However, I would like it if you would place some peonies in the crematorium chapel or on my coffin. As you know, they are my favourite."

Sitting there, incredulous, Helen couldn't believe in all the madness of the past few months, between Ana's medical appointments, her illness, and helping Helen with her lottery win, Ana had still found time to make sure that when she died, everything would be in place, so there was nothing to think about.

George turned to her, checking she was OK.

"I know this is probably a lot to take in, so I am more than happy to help you with everything," George said.

Gratefully, she told him she would accept any assistance he could give.

George folded up the paper he'd just read and passed it to her. He then delved into his briefcase and handed her an envelope.

"While I remember, this is also for you. Ana asked me to give it to you after she passed. She said for you to read it whenever you feel able."

Putting the envelope on the table, she recognised the all-too-familiar writing. It would be a long time after the funeral before she would be able to open it and read whatever the contents held.

The tremendous loss she felt was unbearable. It was as though she had lost half of herself.

How would she function without her best friend? And organise her funeral? Being pragmatic, perhaps the way she could prove how much she had loved her, was to make it the best funeral she could possibly have.

George apologised but said he would need to get going, bearing in mind he would have to change his shirt before his next appointment. She thanked him for his time and all the help he had given Ana. He really was a remarkable man.

Late afternoon, she decided to go round to Ana's. George had said he would accompany her if she wanted him to, but she knew this was something she had to do on her own.

Opening the door and looking around the lovely little cottage, this place had been like a second home to Helen. Everything was as it normally was, but it was so quiet. For a moment, it felt that at any minute, Ana would come bounding out of the bedroom, like she always did. But her heart sank, as she knew it wasn't going to happen. Laying down on her bed, listening to the unusual silence, once again, she could feel the tears starting to form. She went to the wardrobe and grabbed Ana's favourite pink jumper, breathing in her scent, still evident on the soft cashmere. How Ana had loved her cashmere jumpers! She decided to take it home with her. Then, when she was feeling low and missing her, she could close her eyes and wrap it around her, so she could pretend Ana was still there.

The list of names and addresses was exactly where Ana had said it would be.

Over the next few weeks, George was a tower of strength, helping plan the funeral and contacting everyone. George lived up to his promise of supporting her with every aspect. She didn't know what she would have done without him.

During that time, she also got to know Pat, George's wife. She had suggested George invite Helen round for a coffee, and then, one evening for a meal. Helen thought Pat felt she needed a motherly figure, and it wasn't long before she felt comfortable popping round to see Pat when George wasn't there. She gently encouraged her to eat when she didn't feel like it, even if it was just a bowl of soup, to keep her strength up and her mind clear. She was always there for a hug, to talk, or when the tears came, which was so welcome. She really appreciated the huge amount of love and support from both Pat and George during such a difficult time.

With their lives so intertwined, Helen knew most of the people Ana wanted to invite to her funeral. Because Ana had been so popular, everyone loved her, Helen was confident they would make every effort to come. Whenever she contacted someone, it was a painful reminder her best friend was gone, and she found it incredibly difficult to hold back the tears.

However, as well as tears during that initial period, she found herself becoming very angry and resenting the money she had won. What good was it if she couldn't share it with one of the most important people in her life? She would have given it all back in a heartbeat if it meant Ana was back by her side. Life was *so* cruel.

Slowly, as the days passed, the pain eased, but Helen knew it would never completely disappear.

13

Waking up to sunshine on the day of the funeral, Helen *thought* she was ready for it, but it soon became clear she wasn't. It was obviously going to be a very difficult and emotional day. As per Ana's wishes, she wore a pink dress with a matching cardigan and pink shoes. Sam had arrived early to hers, as they were travelling to the funeral together. He was wearing a pink waistcoat and matching tie. He looked so lost and vulnerable. It was the same look he'd had at the funeral of their parents, and she realised the day would affect him just as much as her. She knew what a difficult day it would be, and it was important she remained strong and in control for his sake as much as her own.

Soon the hearse was outside. Taking a deep breath, Helen got into the car with her brother.

She was stunned at what she could see as they arrived. As per Ana's wishes, *everyone* was wearing something pink, including George, who had gone the whole hog by wearing a pink suit! She had no idea where he had found it, as she knew it was not the kind of outfit he would have in his wardrobe.

Looking around, she was amazed at the number of people there. Even Alice and Dick had come up from Clacton.

As they reached George, who was standing at the entrance, Helen introduced him to Sam.

Beautiful pink and white peonies adorned Ana's coffin. In addition, she had also requested the crematorium be covered in peonies, and the scent permeated every corner of the room as everyone went in.

Helen sat in the middle of George and Sam, and next to George, was Carmen. It felt only right that she should sit at the front, having played such an important, albeit brief, part in Ana's life.

The eulogy was the part Helen didn't think she would be able to get through. George had kindly asked if she wanted him to stand with her while she read it, and she gratefully took up his offer in case she broke down. Just having him at her side was so comforting, and as a result, she managed to get through the tribute to her best friend without crying. From her perspective, it was important everyone knew the impact Ana had on her life and what an amazing person she was. But everyone there knew that already. In addition, George, Sam, Alice, and Carmen spoke about her too. Considering George and Carmen had only known Ana for a short while, it was so lovely they wanted to share their feelings.

Emotions were contained until the coffin was gently lowered, but then Helen's tears didn't stop. She stayed inside the crematorium on her own for as long as she could before making her way outside.

George was great, chatting to everyone, and Helen noticed he was even glancing over regularly to check on Sam, making sure he was OK.

Most people had made donations as Ana had requested, but in addition, there were many heartfelt messages on the few wreaths and sprays outside. It was obvious Ana would be missed by so many people.

Helen spotted someone out of the corner of her eye, standing away from most of the crowd, and realised it was Ben. She hadn't seen him during the ceremony, but he must have been there. He came over, looking slightly awkward.

"How are you holding up?" he asked.

"As well as can be expected," she responded rather coldly.

"Look, I am so sorry for your loss. Ana was one in a million. Did you know she contacted me when she was in hospital, a few hours before she died? She said if I had any feelings for you at all, to get in touch and stop being such an arse. But the timing seemed to suck."

She was taken aback. She hadn't realised Ana had spoken with Ben, but on reflection, it was the kind of selfless thing she would do, trying to tie-up loose ends. Ben chatted politely, but it felt quite awkward, and it was difficult to know what to say. Realising this was not the time for an in-depth conversation, Ben gave her a hug, said "I'll be in touch", and headed off towards the car park.

He didn't come to the wake to celebrate Ana's life, and in a way, Helen was pleased. She didn't need that complication on the day of Ana's funeral. She wasn't looking forward to this part, having to be sociable and talk about Ana, but surprisingly, it was very uplifting. Sam and Helen had gone through Ana's playlists (although there were plenty of jokes between them about some of her choices), and they chose many of her favourite songs. It was easy for Helen to find herself remembering the significance of most of the songs that made her smile, including dancing around their bedrooms with hairbrushes and drooling over a particular singer or boy, dreaming of the day they would meet them, fall in love, and get married. Immediately, she felt a sense of sadness, realising Ana would never meet her special someone or have kids, something she had always hoped for in the future.

People also came over to tell their own stories about Ana, and the love she had brought into their lives. It was wonderful to hear their tales about the madcap antics they had got involved in because of her, which was just typical of Ana.

Alice came over, giving Helen a great big hug. She had tears in her eyes, which nearly caused Helen to well up again, but she managed to hold it together. Alice handed over a bag containing a delicious banana cake. Apparently, she had hidden it from Dick, wanting to make sure Helen had something nice to eat if she didn't feel like preparing anything later that day.

Helen also took the opportunity to have a long chat with Carmen. Although she hadn't known her, Helen instantly warmed to her and was so pleased she had been with her friend during those last few months. Apparently, when Ana couldn't see her best friend and was being secretive about her plans, Carmen was always there by her side, seeing specialists and discussing what was best for her at every stage of her care.

It was understandable why Ana hadn't wanted Helen there. Carmen's calm approach, reassuring presence, and her ability to ask sensitive and practical questions would have been much more useful to Ana.

Despite not wanting to donate to large charities, it felt only right for Helen to make a personal donation to the company Carmen worked for, as a thank you for her involvement in Ana's life. She knew Ana would have approved of the gesture too, especially if the money was used to provide the same level of care for someone else.

By the time everyone had gone home, Helen was exhausted. She really didn't want to be alone that night and didn't think Sam should be either, so he agreed to stay the night.

She slept reasonably well, but upon waking, she felt incredibly lost, and the ache in her heart was unbearable. It all seemed so final now. She had no idea what to do in the short term, let alone further down the line, without her best friend.

However, she had known that after the funeral she would need to get away and have some form of distraction.

With that in mind, a few days earlier, she had rung Alice and Dick to ask if it would be OK to go and stay at the B & B. Despite still being in the middle of renovations, they were happy to put her up for as long as she wanted, provided she didn't mind the mess and was prepared to muck in.

She told Sam what she was proposing to do and asked if he would be OK without her there. He thought it was a good idea, saying he would be fine and had lots of things to keep him busy. So, later that morning, Helen packed a suitcase and headed off to Clacton.

By early afternoon, she had arrived at Alice and Dick's and was immediately confronted with builders, scaffolding, dust, and chaos. However, it was lovely to get caught up in the pair's excitement about the plans for the B & B. They soon found her a pair of overalls, and before long, she was painting skirting boards. It was good to get involved with something that took her mind away from the loss of Ana. Being exhausted from all the hard work, she also found it much easier to sleep.

One morning as they sat and ate breakfast, Alice and Dick began talking about their mystery benefactor, trying to guess who had helped them out. They were still talking about it while they were painting the walls in one of the bedrooms.

Alice said, "Dick thinks it was a little old lady called Sally who always used to come down and stay for a week or two at a time. She knew our policy about no pets, but she always sneaked her cat in. She used to bring it with her in a big bag, thinking we wouldn't notice, but when you see something moving around, you know it is not a book and a sandwich, don't you?"

They all laughed. If they wanted to believe it was Sally, that was great. It meant they had no idea who the donor was, and Helen was relieved she wasn't in the frame, but equally, there was no reason why they would think it was her, anyway.

George rang regularly to check how she was getting on. He knew she felt broken and lost and was pleased she was with friends during such a difficult time. She rang Sam every day, just to check he was OK too.

As each day passed, having the normality and familiarity of being with Alice and Dick and some structure, she started to relax and heal. They showed her the plans for the rooms, and it was lovely to hear about all their ideas.

Thinking of the donation, Helen suddenly remembered Ana's suggestion to help the dance group. The company hadn't been set up yet, and she wasn't sure how long it would take, but she knew they were desperate for money to be secured as soon as possible as their trip couldn't be far away. Deciding to look at the GoFundMe page again while it was still on her mind, she opened up the laptop and went onto the relevant page. Looking at the photograph again, she agreed with Ana's comment about how sad the group's leader looked. This was the only donation Ana had suggested, and wanting to honour that, she knew she would be so proud if a payment was made. It really seemed worthwhile, and a donation would have an immediate impact. With that in mind, she decided to sort this one out herself, making a one-off payment on their donation site. She clicked on the link and promptly paid £8,500 – the balance they needed. These days it was amazing how easy she found it, saying goodbye to such large amounts of money.

Damn! She suddenly remembered what George had said about protecting her identity. It was a stupid thing to have done, donating and not marking it as anonymous. If the company had already been set up, this slip-up would definitely not have occurred.

With her heart pounding, Helen knew she needed to rectify her mistake. Googling the Daffodil Dance Group, she found a contact number for Nicky Brightman, the leader of the group. Trembling, she dialled the number, not thinking through what she was going to say. Nicky answered quite quickly.

"Um, sorry to trouble you. I saw your GoFundMe page and have just paid some money into your GoFundMe account."

Nicky was obviously quite surprised someone had rung and thanked her for the donation.

"I don't think you understand," Helen continued. "I have paid the remaining balance, so you don't have to raise any more funds."

"Is this some sort of wind-up?" came the wary reply.

"No, please, I need to explain. I have paid the money you needed. The thing is, I meant to make it a private donation, but I didn't click the right button to make it anonymous. I am happy to have made the payment, but if anyone asks, can you just say it was an anonymous donor? I need to protect my identity. It's very important."

It was obvious from the tone of Nicky's reply that she still didn't believe the balance had been paid, but she confirmed if asked, she would not reveal Helen's details. Putting the phone down, she was relieved to have resolved her error. Perhaps managing the money and remaining anonymous wasn't going to be as difficult as she had first thought. Phew!

14

After the phone call, Nicky Brightman was curious to see if what this woman had said was true. Logging on to the GoFundMe page, she was astonished to find the outstanding money required for the trip had indeed been paid. Why would a stranger do that? Who was this 'H. Pond?' It was an incredibly large sum of money. Well, whatever the reason, it didn't matter. The group could now concentrate solely on the finals.

Nicky decided to let *The Bedfordshire Post* know they had secured the funding as it was probably due to the article.

Alan smirked as soon as he heard her voice, immediately assuming she wanted to take him up on his offer of a drink. He answered her call and put on what he regarded as his 'sexy, suave voice'.

"I knew you wouldn't be able to resist the offer of a night out with me. I am just surprised it took you so long."

Nicky was taken aback by his arrogance.

"I am ringing about the article you wrote for us about the group needing some financial assistance. I just thought I would let you know, someone has stepped in and paid the remaining amount, so thanks for writing the piece."

He sat bolt upright. Who would donate £8,500 to an amateur kids dance group? There could be more to this story, he thought.

"Well, do you want to tell me who was so generous? Was it a company?" he enquired.

Nicky knew she needed to be careful what she said, bearing in mind Helen's request.

"Er, um, I did say I wouldn't reveal their identity. The person wishes to remain anonymous."

Alan was *really* intrigued now. He tried another angle.

"Perhaps we should do a follow-up; to let everyone know you now have the funding. People love a happy ending, and this was for such a worthwhile cause. Those poor kids now being able to go on the trip of a lifetime. I know you say the donor wants to remain anonymous, but I am sure they will get a great deal of satisfaction seeing how much their money is appreciated. Our readers would also love to know about your great news," he schmoozed.

There was a short silence before Nicky reluctantly agreed to allow him to interview her again the following day at the pub where she was working part-time.

They arranged to meet half an hour before Nicky's shift was due to start. They sat at a table, and he knew he would have to use all his charm to get Nicky to reveal details of this mystery benefactor.

He leant back in his chair, trying to appear relaxed.

"It's great you have all the money you need to enable the kids to go on the trip to Holland. What a happy ending. I am so pleased to have played an important part in making it happen."

Nicky looked at him. She knew he wasn't interested in the kids; it was all about what was in it for him. She had met men like him before.

"France," she said simply.

"What?"

"It is France, not Holland, where the finals are being held," she replied firmly.

"Oh, it doesn't really matter where it is, does it? You got your happy ending," he replied flippantly.

He took a sip of the beer she had bought him before continuing.

"Well, what a turn-up for the books, someone just handing over £8,500 like that. What do they want from you?"

"Nothing," she replied.

Alan snorted. "No, that can't be right. You don't get something for nothing in this world. Who would just donate so much money to an unknown little dance group?"

Nicky looked at him incredulously. Why couldn't he believe someone just wanted to help without expecting something in return?

He realised he had overstepped the mark when he saw the disapproving look on her face.

He knew if he didn't say something quickly, Nicky would clam up and he would never find out who the donor was.

Speaking softly and thinking carefully about his words, he tried to sound sympathetic and concerned.

"Nicky, I am only thinking of you, your reputation, and those lovely children. Perhaps I ought to check him out, make sure he is not someone with a hidden agenda. I have lots of contacts and—"

"Why do you automatically assume it is a man?" Nicky asked. However, she immediately regretted her words, realising she had probably given too much away.

"Ah, so it's a *woman*! Well, well, well!"

Alan was pleased with himself. He was making some headway now.

Nicky was shifting awkwardly in her seat.

"Perhaps this wasn't such a good idea. If you could just put something to the effect that we have received the balance needed to go on the trip and thank people for their donations. Maybe you could write a further article after we've been to the finals. I am sure if you are really interested in the children, it would make a great follow-up story."

Alan could see he wasn't going to get anything else about the donor from Nicky, so decided he was wasting his time. But perhaps all was not lost...

"Don't forget, if you fancy a night out with a handsome, funny guy, just let me know."

Nicky was well and truly fed up with his arrogance.

"Do you know someone like that?" she countered. "I'd better go, my shift is about to start. Enjoy your drink."

She didn't bother to shake his hand. Without waiting for an answer, she got up and made her way to the kitchen.

Alan didn't like women who undermined him, and her attitude towards him made him very angry. She wouldn't have obtained the £8,500 if it hadn't been for him. He would get to the bottom of this anonymous donor and, if it painted the dance group in a bad light or there was more to this donor, then so be it. It would make a great story either way. Phil would be impressed.

But how could he find out who the donor was if Nicky wasn't willing to spill the beans?

He went back to the office and smiled at his colleague, Polly, who was by the photocopier. Normally he wouldn't take any notice of her. She was responsible for 'The Written Word', a weekly column that Alan felt was a total waste of time. It wasn't journalism. Anyone could choose a few poems from the ones that came into the office each week or write a review about a new book. However, today, he needed to be nice to her. He wanted something.

"Hi, Polly, how's your day? Anyone sent in an amazing poem this week?"

She eyed him suspiciously.

"What do you want, Alan?"

She knew he was after something if he was being pleasant as he hardly ever spoke to her.

"I was just wondering how easy it is to track down someone who has donated on a GoFundMe page?"

Polly's journalistic career had started in London. During her time there, from what he had gathered, she had covered several high-profile stories. She didn't brag about her achievements but often regaled the office with stories of famous people she had met or how she had managed to charm her way into restricted areas. This one-day-a-week job at *The Bedfordshire Post* was just keeping her going until she felt ready to fully retire. She didn't like Alan at all. She thought he was like many power-hungry journalists she had encountered over the years who didn't care what impact their stories may have on the people involved.

She thought for a moment.

"Well, if you know the GoFundMe page, you can see who has donated. There will be those who have publicly listed themselves as donating and their name will appear next to their payment. Mind you, most people these days make anonymous contributions, which makes it harder."

Damn, thought Alan. Whoever it was probably made an anonymous payment. Nobody making that kind of donation would be so stupid, would they?

He logged on to the computer and looked up the GoFundMe page for the Daffodil Dance Group. He scrolled down the list of donations. £5 here, £20 there, and… No! He couldn't believe it. H Pond –£8,500! Why would you make your donation public if you wanted to remain anonymous?

It didn't matter, as this was definitely to his advantage. Perhaps this was going to be far easier than he had thought!

He had a name. Now it was a case of trying to track the person down. He opened his little desk notebook and scribbled a spidergram with 'H Pond', in the middle and two branches from it – 'The Daffodil Dance Group' and '£8,500'.

It was most likely someone local, he reasoned, as they had probably seen the article in the newspaper or on the paper's online edition. Working on that assumption, and with the dance group based in Luton, hopefully, it would be somebody living in the area.

Looking on LinkedIn, he found two people by the name of 'H Pond' working in or around Luton.

He immediately dismissed the first one; an eighteen-year-old trainee in a garage. The other was a distinct possibility – a man, Harold Pond, who looked, from his profile picture, to be in his sixties. He worked as an import director for a London fruit and vegetable company. He would probably have the funds, although it seemed a very grand gesture. Maybe his granddaughter was a member of the dance troupe and he didn't want her to know? This would be worth exploring. But Nicky had intimated it was a woman.

To widen his net, Alan also searched Facebook. Everybody liked to be on Facebook and share all their details, didn't they?

He quickly discovered it wasn't the case, as looking for Harold, *he* didn't even appear to be on Facebook. However, he did find someone called Helen Pond. In her late twenties, no work status mentioned, and single. There was nothing on her profile that made her stand out. He concluded it was unlikely she was the donor.

Despite Harold Pond being a male, Alan decided he would concentrate on him first. Perhaps Nicky had been cleverer than he thought and was trying to throw him off the scent by suggesting it was a female, although she didn't seem bright enough to do that.

On LinkedIn, it mentioned Harold's company. Going on to the organisation's website, he looked for some kind of angle he could use to try to set up a meeting with Harold, and he quickly found it.

One of the areas the company was proud to advertise was its 'green and ethical credentials'.

Alan hatched a plan. He rang Harold, explaining he was writing a piece about the importance of ethical transportation of fruit and vegetables and how organisations chose companies abroad that they could work with in a fair and ethical way. Alan continued by saying he was sure people would love to hear what a local man was doing to promote this partnership, as well as finding out how Harold had achieved such a prestigious position in the company.

Harold loved having his ego stroked and was happy to meet him for lunch a couple of days later, if he was paying.

Alan then booked the day off for the meeting. At this stage, he wasn't prepared to tell Phil what he was up to. Best wait until he had a juicy, front-cover exclusive.

On the day of the meeting, Alan was sure he could convince Harold to spill the beans about the donation.

Just before twelve, he headed to The Bridleway, a smart restaurant set in its own grounds just outside Woburn. Not the cheapest of places, but it would hopefully be fitting for an import director, especially as their food was, wherever possible, locally sourced.

Harold was exactly what he had expected. He had the gift of the gab, a true salesman. He loved talking about his job and, more importantly for Alan, about himself. He was keen to make an impression and had even brought a box of fruit and vegetables, which his company sold, with him as a gift! Not that Alan was excited by a box of groceries. However, he feigned surprise and delight. He would give it to his mum as a present. She always said he never bought her anything.

Alan had his 'professional questions' prepared, so the interview would appear genuine. He started off with these, asking how the fruit and vegetables were imported and how they were ethically sourced. Harold was more than happy to explain how certain fruit and vegetables needed to go through plant health controls, which storage issues needed to be considered, how the company ensured the produce owners were paying fair wages to their employees, etc. In fact, it was over two hours before Harold seemed to pause for breath, other than while sipping at the glasses of whisky that were brought him. However, before long, this did loosen Harold's tongue, and Alan felt he could start asking questions relating to his real mission.

"You aren't making many notes," Harold observed, slurring his words.

Suddenly, he became defensive.

"You aren't going to put a spin on this, suggesting we don't do what we claim, as I can assure you—"

Alan put up his hand to stop Harold from continuing so he could explain himself.

"Of course not, Harry! May I call you Harry? I have an amazing memory, so I promise you, I am taking it all in. It is important people recognise how companies like yours work so hard to fulfil green and ethical expectations. And I can tell you are a man of integrity. Now, I've discovered all about the company, but what about you? What makes *you* tick and keeps you motivated?"

Harold beamed.

Noticing Harold's eyes were now glazed from all the alcohol, he felt the time was right to delve deeper.

"I bet you are the same in your private life, am I right? Do you do anything to support your local community? I mean, do you volunteer or donate money to charity?"

Alan stopped himself from saying anything further. He was a little worried he may have overstepped the mark for a moment with his last comment. If Harold was the donor and didn't want anyone to know, then he may get suspicious.

He leant over and spoke quietly to Alan.

"Look, I do my bit for the company. If I am honest, the fact it is an ethical company is irrelevant to me, it's the salary that keeps me there. Strictly between you and me, the wife wanted the big house, fancy car, expensive clothes, and luxury holidays. She was bleeding me dry. I had to work harder and harder to keep up with her demands. In the end, when I told her she would have to cut down her spending, she left me for a guy living in Primrose Hill. I had hoped to be retired by now, but the divorce has left me broke, so retirement isn't going to be an option any time soon," he replied bitterly.

Suddenly, Harold sat back, closed his eyes, and started to snore quite loudly, much to Alan's annoyance. This meeting had been a total waste of time.

From the conversation they'd had, it seemed highly unlikely Harold was his guy. If, as he claimed, he had gone through an expensive divorce, he would hardly be giving away £8,500.

He asked for the bill. He was shocked to find it was nearly £140! He couldn't believe it had cost so much for some extremely small portions of fancy food, wine, and a few whiskies. He didn't know how he would justify the cost on his expenses, especially as he hadn't cleared the idea for an interview with Phil first. *Never mind*, he thought. He could always charm the pretty redhead in accounts and persuade her to put it through.

This left only one immediate possibility: Helen Pond.

The following day, he re-visited her Facebook page. He studied it carefully. Most people never bothered with privacy settings, and fortunately, she hadn't either. Why were people OK with everyone knowing every aspect of their lives?

He noted she had a brother and a few friends, but nothing made her stand out. If it was her, why would she pay so much money to a small dance group?

From checking through her details, it appeared she had been to university and studied business and marketing, but there was no mention of her current job. Was she a high-flyer? Or was she wealthy and didn't need to work? He laughed to himself. Neither option seemed likely.

Phil walked past his desk and peered at his computer.

"What are you doing, Alan? Who's the woman on the screen? Another one of your conquests? I thought you were meant to be going out to investigate the potholes on Inkerman Road?"

Looking up from his computer, Alan responded indignantly.

"This could be my big scoop. It's much more important than a few potholes."

"Then please feel free to enlighten me about this supposedly big scoop," Phil continued sharply. "And while we are having this conversation, would you mind telling me why you have submitted a huge expense bill for lunch yesterday? You weren't even working."

Alan could tell Phil was cross.

"It's all connected to this potentially big story I'm working on. I am not prepared to discuss it now," he snapped at Phil.

Phil was fed up with Alan feeling he could do what he liked. He needed bringing into line.

"Well, I haven't given you any assignments that would warrant you spending such a significant amount of money on lunch, so I am not going to sign it off. Now, I need you to start working on the pothole story if you don't want to elaborate on this so-called interesting scoop?"

Alan shook his head in disbelief.

"Get going please, you have a three o'clock deadline."

With that, Phil walked off. He wasn't prepared to get into a debate, especially not in an open office.

Alan was fuming. He resented taking orders from anyone and didn't appreciate being shown up in front of everybody else, especially by Phil. They had both started at the paper at around the same time, and although Phil had three years more journalistic experience than him, he always felt cheated out of the promotion they had both applied for.

Potholes. Who wanted to read a dull article about potholes? People needed to get a life.

15

A few nights into her stay at the B & B, Helen rang George to tell him how things were going. It felt the right time to ask about Ben.

"By the way, George, have you seen anything of Ben lately?"

"Ah, I wondered when we would get round to him," he said. "He's fine. He works too hard, but you already know that. I saw him a few days ago, and he asked me about you."

"What did he say?" she enquired nervously.

"Had I seen or heard from you, and how were you coping without Ana."

"I miss him." She sighed and then gulped, realising she had said it out loud.

"Oh, Helen."

There was a pause before George continued.

"He likes you. A great deal. I have worked with him for a long time, and I have never seen him so caught up with one of his clients, as he has been with you, both professionally and personally. But that's the thing. You were his client, and the company rules are very clear. You never mix business with pleasure, especially in our line of work."

"But I am not his client anymore. Kathy has taken over. Do you think my money is putting him off? He told me about his upbringing."

George sounded surprised.

"I hadn't realised he had told you so much about himself. No, the money isn't the issue. I think he has just been hurt in the past, and now with Ana passing, he wasn't sure when would be the right time to talk to you or what to say to put things right."

Since George was being so honest, she knew there was a question she needed answering.

"The one thing that is bothering me slightly is his daughter. Is he married, separated, or divorced?"

George seemed confused.

"Ben doesn't have a daughter. Where did you get that idea from?"

She explained about the photo of the little girl in Ben's living room.

George started to laugh.

"She's not his daughter. But, it's true, she is a very special girl and extremely close to his heart. It's his sister's daughter."

Relief swept over Helen.

"So, he doesn't have a wife or partner?"

"No, definitely not, but if you don't get in there quick, someone like him won't stay around forever."

Of course, George was right. She decided it was time to think about heading home and start making some decisions.

She was unsure how much use she had been to Alice and Dick, but they said they were sorry to see her go. Much to Dick's annoyance, Alice packed her off with a big Victoria sponge, explaining her need was much greater than his.

Driving back, she felt much stronger and more prepared to face the world again.

She was pleased she had spoken to Sam daily during her time in Clacton, as she hadn't wanted him to grieve on his own.

When she reached home, she gave him a quick call and asked if he wanted to pop round that evening.

"Do you mind if I don't tonight, Sis? I am going out."

He seemed to be very cagey. Usually, he would say 'I am seeing Dave, Josh, or the lads'. There was obviously something going on. More questions needed to be asked.

"Who with?" Helen enquired.

"Um, er, well," he stammered.

She could tell he was struggling to think of a suitable excuse. He was hopeless at lying.

Then it dawned on her.

"It's a girl, isn't it?" she shrieked down the phone.

"Yes, it is, but don't get too excited, it's early days," he said, sounding a little annoyed he had been found out. She knew it must be embarrassing for him, talking to his sister about his love life.

"How long have you been seeing her? What is she like? How old is she?" It was important to get all the details.

"About five weeks now."

She was shocked.

"What? How come this is the first I have heard about it?"

She already knew the answer. Having been so wrapped up with Ana's illness, subsequent death and all the arrangements, then going off to stay with Alice and Dick, she hadn't really thought about what was going on in Sam's life, other than checking briefly that he was OK. He had been so mindful of her losing Ana; he must have thought he should keep it to himself until the time was right. In the past, he had often kept his girlfriends a secret, but there again, they never usually lasted longer than a week.

"Come on then, spill the beans!" she demanded, excitedly wanting to know everything about the girl who had managed to penetrate (and cope with) her brother's chaotic world.

Managing to establish her name was Sarah, she was a couple of years younger than him, and quite shy, she worked in a bank as a customer services advisor. He had met her when he went to the bank to talk about what to do with his 'inheritance'.

"So, she's good with money then? Thank goodness! One of you needs to be!" He knew his sister was having some fun at his expense and was enjoying it.

"Yes, you'd like her. She is sensible, funny, and she doesn't mind me going out with the lads now and again!" He laughed. She could tell he was smitten.

"Well, don't ruin it! When can I meet her?"

Sam wasn't keen to give a specific date, and she didn't want to push him. Wishing him good luck, she said she would ring the following day to find out how it had gone.

So, life was moving on. She was pleased, as it was what Ana would have wanted and expected. However, she would have been so intrigued about Sam's girlfriend. She could hear her now, quizzing Sam mercilessly until she had all the facts.

16

elen was still half asleep when she dragged herself towards the ringing phone the following morning. Her sleep had been interrupted by nightmares about the money and meeting Ben again, only for him to decide that they just weren't right for each other.

She clumsily grabbed for the offending phone but accidentally knocked it off the docking station and onto the floor instead.

"Hang on a minute, I've dropped you!" she yelled to whoever the poor individual was at the other end of the phone. She knew if it was a cold caller, they would probably hang up.

Retrieving it, she asked if anyone was still there.

"Yes, I'm still here," a male voice responded.

"So, who are you and what do you want?"

"Hi, my name is Alan Fletcher. Please don't hang up. This is not a sales call, just in case you are worried. I'm ringing from *The Bedfordshire Post*. We are conducting a survey, canvassing people in Luton on local trends. It will only take a few minutes, and you will be entered into a draw for a meal at a Beefeater."

She wasn't sure whether to hang up, but she had to admit, she was intrigued.

"Look, I'll be honest with you," he persisted. "I've rung forty-two people today, and hardly anyone will answer my questions. My boss is going to sack me if I don't get a good sample of replies, so if you could just spare a few minutes, you would be helping me keep my job."

Knowing how tough it was having a boss who gave you a hard time, and with this guy sounding so apologetic, she caved.

"Of course, I'll help you."

"Great, let's get started. First question. Can I ask what age category you are in: twenty to thirty, thirty-one to forty, forty-one to fifty, or fifty plus?"

Before long, she had confirmed the first few standard questions he asked: age, marital status, and that she had lived in Luton for most of her life.

"Working, out of work, homemaker, or retired?"

"Not working. I mean, I am in between jobs at present."

"What do you normally do?"

"Admin – nothing wildly exciting. I've had a run of bad luck recently."

"Oh, I'm sorry. What's happened?"

She froze for a moment, trying to think of a suitable reply. Best to keep it simple, she thought.

"Redundancy."

"Oh, OK. Next question. Do you donate to charity? If yes, do you make one-off or regular donations?"

She paused. This was a difficult one, and she was unsure how to respond.

"Er, occasionally, I, er, um, probably best to just put 'no.'"

It was an intriguing response. Surely you either did or didn't make donations? Was she hiding something? He needed to carefully keep digging.

"Are you sure? I mean, you sound like the kind of person who has a social conscience."

"Well, er, yes, I have given to charity on the odd occasion."

"What type of organisations do you normally support and what amount would you typically donate?"

Now she was beginning to panic.

"Um, I don't want to talk about donations. Best to put I give money from time to time, to whichever charity I fancy."

Phew! It felt as though she had delivered a careful, well thought through response, and she was certain Ben would have been proud of her too. It was a shame he wasn't currently in her life so she could tell him about it, she thought sadly.

"Thank you for answering my questions, you have probably saved my job," he laughed.

Alan was sure Helen was hiding something and needed to find a way to keep digging. A different approach was required. He decided to lay on all the charm.

"Look, I don't normally do this, but to say thank you, I would love to take you out for a drink. I realise you don't know me, but if you are worried, you can look me up on *The Bedfordshire Post* website, just to check I am not a mass murderer or something. What do you say?"

What Ana had said was true. Life *was* short. Ben was off the scene, and she could do with a distraction.

Totally out of character, she found herself agreeing and arranged to meet Alan a couple of evenings later.

When she'd had a shower, she decided to look at his details on the newspaper website, as he had suggested. It would be useful to know who she was meeting, after all! Studying his photo carefully, he was very good-looking, and to be honest, probably normally someone who was unlikely to talk to her if they had been at a club. Still, it was a night out, and she didn't have anything else to do.

As an experienced journalist, Alan was pleased with himself. Initially, he had thought he was wasting his time with Helen, but she had become unduly agitated when he had started to question her about donating. Why would it cause so much panic? *Could* she be the mystery donor? It seemed *very* unlikely. If you hadn't got a job, how could you afford to give away such a large sum? What would be in it for her?

Even if she wasn't the donor, he felt sure she was hiding something, and as a journalist, it was his job to find out what. It could lead to an interesting story, one way or another. It was a clever move on his part, to think about asking her out on a date. He could use all his charm to find out her secret. She wouldn't be able to resist.

Alan knew he would have to make a good impression when he met Helen. However, he didn't feel it would be too difficult to gain her trust. She sounded so flattered when he had asked her out and thought it highly unlikely she had men queuing round the block. She wasn't his type, not glamorous enough. However, if she had money or was keeping a secret, it might be worth hanging around for a while.

It may cost him some time to persuade her to open up, but it was possibly worth the investment.

In fact, time wasn't currently an issue for Alan. He had recently finished with the two women he'd had on the go. Diane had, as he feared, become too clingy and, as for his other girlfriend, he had called her by the wrong name. Twice. That hadn't gone down well.

Still, there were plenty more fish in the sea. In the meantime, Helen was work not pleasure, but it could be a nice little distraction, even if it was potentially only for one night.

17

The evening Helen was due to meet Alan, she found herself having second thoughts. What was she thinking? They probably wouldn't have anything in common, and she knew nothing about him other than he worked for a newspaper. Thank goodness they were meeting somewhere public.

He had requested to be a friend on Facebook, and she had accepted it. He wasn't her usual type; blond, highlighted hair, all smiles, and a great deal of confidence about him, judging by his approach on the phone and all the photos of pretty girls on his Facebook page! Meeting him felt disloyal to Ben, but she immediately put it out of her head. They weren't together after all.

The pub Alan had chosen was in Silsoe. She had been there once before, many years ago, but it had changed a lot; it was much more upmarket now. Most people in there seemed to be in their late twenties or early thirties, and it was extremely busy. Looking round to see if she could spot Alan, she felt someone touch her arm.

"Helen?"

She turned, unaware Alan had sidled up beside her. "How did you know it was me?"

"I looked for the prettiest girl in the room, and there you were," he replied.

Pretty corny, but she still found herself smiling. Thinking about it, he had seen her Facebook profile, so it wasn't rocket science.

There were no tables available inside and it was quite noisy, so after getting the drinks, he suggested sitting in the garden as it was a warm evening. Quite a few people said 'hello' as he walked past, so she guessed the pub must be one of his locals.

As they sat down, she studied him carefully for the first time. He was a little taller than her, probably early thirties, and she could tell he had expensive, but casual, taste. For some reason, she felt a little uncomfortable with him, but put it down to nerves. It was unusual to be asked out by someone she had never met before. She could understand why women would like him, but for her, there was no immediate spark like there had been with Ben, which was disappointing.

Ana certainly wouldn't have approved of him, as she would have regarded him as flash and too cocky.

It wasn't long before Alan was asking her lots of questions; it must be difficult, being in between jobs, how was she managing? Where did she live? Was her flat mortgaged or rented? What were her hobbies and interests? Did she like dancing? Was there a boyfriend or ex-husband? What family did she have?

It was all so intense, more like an interrogation, and it made her feel on edge.

"My goodness, this feels like an inquisition!" she said, laughing, trying to sound casual. Most men she'd been out with just wanted to talk about themselves, apart from Ben.

"I am sorry, I am just interested in getting to know you. The questioning is probably because of my job. I obviously don't know when to stop," he explained.

That made sense, she thought.

Just then, a couple came up to their table.

"Alan, fancy seeing you here. We've just been out for a meal and thought we'd pop in here for a quick drink."

The man then turned his attention to Helen.

"Hi, I'm Phil, Alan's boss, and this is my wife, Karen."

She could see that Alan was looking a little uncomfortable. Was there a problem between him and his boss, she wondered.

"Phil, I hope you don't mind, but we came out here for a quiet drink away from all the noise inside and to get to know each other."

His response seemed rather rude. His boss, however, didn't seem to mind.

"Oh, we'll leave you to it then. Nice to meet you." He indicated to Helen.

Her concerns were growing. There was something not quite right, but she couldn't put her finger on it. Also, the whole date was feeling more like a cross-examination.

A worrying thought then crossed her mind. Did Alan know about her win?

No! That was ridiculous! How could he?

However, it was important to be careful. He was a journalist after all. She would need to remain level-headed and on her guard, just as George and Ben had taught her.

After all, she didn't know Alan at all. Thank goodness she was only drinking orange and lemonade. Thinking about it, he had seemed very disappointed she wasn't drinking, even suggesting that if she did want to drink and relax, she could get a taxi home, or he would take her back. She shuddered, relieved she had the car. She didn't want him taking her home.

By half past ten, she was very tired. The questioning had continued the whole evening. Surely this wasn't how he acted on all his dates. Mind you, it would explain why he was still single.

She also noticed he didn't reveal much about himself and was also happy to eye-up several pretty women who came into the garden. She realised that going out with Alan had been a huge mistake. Her feelings for Ben were still so strong, and she didn't have the energy for something else at the minute, even if nothing ended up happening between her and Ben.

Finishing her drink, she told Alan it had been a lovely evening, but she really needed to go home as she had a meeting the next day.

It was odd. His reaction wasn't one of disappointment; the look on his face was more one of surprise. She imagined women didn't regularly reject him. But his next question was even stranger.

"So, what's the meeting about, anything interesting?" he enquired.

Why did he want to know that? Surely his first question would have been "Do you fancy going for another drink sometime?" Instead, he was more bothered about the meeting. Something *really* did feel wrong, and it made her even more on edge.

"It's an interview for a possible job."

"Oh. Good luck." He continued to sit at the table, not even offering to walk her to the car. *Ben would never have behaved in such a way*, she thought, sadly.

Alan finished his drink and went back to the bar. Being turned down by both Nicky and Helen in the space of a few days made him feel he was losing his touch. During his late teens and early twenties, women, both young and old, had never failed to succumb to his charms. He didn't even have to try.

Mulling it over in his head, he started to think about the evening and what Helen had said, and more importantly, what she *hadn't* said while answering his questions. There were things she seemed uncomfortable talking about, so he was certain she was hiding something. Although it did seem crazy, the more he thought about it, he felt there was a possibility she could be the donor. For example, how could she afford her flat? She had told him her friend had been ill, and in helping her, she hadn't really worked for a good six months. He had also noticed her car when she had parked. It was less than a year old. She had told him her parents had died several years ago, and her family had never been well-off. So how could she afford that with a limited income? What, he wondered, *was* her secret?

Just as he was trying to work it out, a woman who looked to be in her early forties came up to the bar and ordered a drink. She was attractive for her age and had obviously had a few drinks.

"A double gin and tonic please."

She smiled at him.

"On your own?" he asked. She looked him up and down and nodded.

"I can't believe a beautiful woman like you is not with someone."

He looked at the barman. "This one's on me," he said as he got his wallet out to pay for her drink. Then he added, "Why not join me?" He patted the bar stool next to him.

The woman didn't need asking twice and heaved herself on to the stool. Alan smiled. Generally, he liked younger women, but she looked like she could be fun for a night. Maybe the evening hadn't been a total waste of time after all.

18

Waking up the following morning, Helen immediately regretted the night before. Nothing had happened with Alan, not even a kiss, which she was relieved about. But just thinking about him and the number of questions he had asked, made her feel very uneasy. If he rang again, she would definitely fob him off. He hadn't bothered to ask about another date, so it was probably highly unlikely anyway. It did make her wonder what his motives were, but just as she was mulling it over in her head, the phone rang. It was Ben.

"Hi, how are you?" he asked gently. "Stupid question, I know, under the circumstances."

The call was unexpected, and it threw her, but equally, she was pleased to hear from him.

"As well as can be expected when your best friend dies, I suppose." She realised her response sounded a little harsh.

There was a pause.

"Look, I am *so* sorry. I just couldn't carry on being your life coach. It wouldn't have been professional with the way I felt about you. From the moment we met, I knew I felt something for you, but I thought I could control my feelings. The thing is, you really got into my head, and all I could think about was you and how much I wanted to see you. And then when I kissed you..."

He stopped short.

How was she meant to respond to him? It made her angry, and she didn't hold back.

"You didn't phone, there was no explanation, you just left me totally confused. And then I met Kathy at my meeting with George and wondered why she was there as my life coach and not you. You could have tried to speak to me and let me know what was going on. It was the least you owed me."

"I know," he replied, sighing. "I'll be honest with you. I have only had one long-term relationship before, and I have never been good at figuring out whether women like me or not. I didn't want to mess it up. But I guess I did that anyway. I should also have got in touch when both Ana and George told me to, bearing in mind I was no longer your life coach. But I just didn't want you to have to deal with me on top of everything else you were coping with. I also didn't want you to think I was only interested in you because of the money."

He sounded crestfallen.

Softening a little, she realised he had genuine feelings for her and now understood the reasons he had kept his distance. She felt more reassured there was the chance of a relationship going forward.

Ben had at least acted with integrity, removing himself from his role because of the conflict of interest there clearly was. She could also hear in his voice how difficult it was for him to say sorry.

"So, where do we go from here?" he asked, hesitantly. "Would you consider going on a proper date with me, Helen?"

Thoughts crept into her head. She was worried about getting hurt. What if it all went horribly wrong? Could she cope with that, especially at this time, when she had just lost Ana and was feeling vulnerable?

She could hear Ana's voice in her head, clear as anything.

"For goodness' sake, just take a leap of faith!"

Smiling to herself, she shyly replied.

"Yes, that would be lovely. I have to warn you though, I am still in a difficult place, after losing Ana."

"I understand. It's just a date, let's just see how it goes. I am not asking you to marry me!" He laughed.

The butterflies were in her stomach again, the feelings so different from her date with Alan. She just hoped she was doing the right thing. They agreed to meet up the following Saturday evening for a meal.

19

In the meantime, there was a meeting booked with George and Kathy, as Helen wanted to move forward and help Julian as soon as possible. She was eager to put a plan in place for dealing with her gifting longer term. It was important not to make another slip-up. As the donation to the dance group seemed to have resolved itself, she decided not to tell George about it.

The meeting was arranged for early morning, but the traffic was bad, and she was late.

George and Kathy were both sitting there waiting for her. It looked as though he had prepared a great deal of paperwork, as there were three binders spread out on the desk, one for each of them. He passed them around and said he would go through his thoughts, based on the last meeting, and would welcome any questions.

With teas and coffees poured, George began.

"Kathy and I have had a few discussions about your plans and, based on those, have produced the following report. Before we begin, though, I just wondered if you are aware of anyone else who has done what you are planning to do?"

She shook her head.

"Mind you, I don't know anyone else with that kind of money!" she answered, laughing.

Looking serious, Kathy continued.

She mentioned numerous high-profile people who had undertaken philanthropic activities in the past, such as Facebook founder, Mark Zuckerberg, and Bill Gates, of Microsoft fame. However, they were already in the public eye.

"Obviously, these are all billionaires contributing on a much grander scale. Although you aren't as wealthy as them, you still have an unbelievable amount of money, and I understand the wish to keep any donations secret, as it provides many advantages for you. For example, it will stop people coming to you requesting handouts and then being disappointed when you turn them down. Also, if people aren't aware of your win, you don't have to worry that they are befriending you because of your money. Believe me, it often happens, and you may not even be aware of it. In addition, although it may seem far-fetched, by keeping your wealth a secret, you avoid the possibility of a kidnap attempt."

"Gosh, I hadn't even thought of that!" Helen looked shocked as she tried to digest the gravity of what she had just been told.

Kathy could see she was visibly shaken.

"I am not trying to scare you, but you need to be aware of the facts."

Her voice softened.

"I know you said you have this feeling you want to 'give back'. Is there a particular reason why? Is it due to a religious or spiritual belief you have or a feeling of guilt about something?"

Helen thought carefully for a moment before replying.

"No, nothing like that. I just want to do some good with the money. Don't get me wrong, I *want* to spend some and have a comfortable life, but equally, I'd like other people to benefit from some of it. Life is too short."

She could feel herself getting upset as she immediately thought of Ana.

Kathy looked at George and then back to Helen.

"If you really want to do this, it needs to be managed very carefully, and it won't be easy. Remember it takes just one slip-up, whether it's an overheard phone conversation, confiding in someone, or an email message sent to the wrong person, and you've lost the anonymity you say you want to protect."

She understood what Kathy was saying and nodded.

"I know it will be difficult, and I am going to have to be very careful. But surely if I have good people around me to support what I am trying to do, it should be manageable? George, what's your view?"

She was hoping to get his reassurance.

George glanced back at Kathy before continuing the conversation. Helen could tell from the joint approach being taken, they had obviously discussed everything at length before meeting up with her.

"Setting up an organisation, as we discussed last time, would be the sensible option, but it is also not without its problems. Your identity could still be compromised, as

Kathy has pointed out. Organisations you are donating to have to protect themselves by knowing, at least in broad terms, where the money they are being given comes from. Whether these are grants, cash donations, or something else, companies must ensure they have undertaken due diligence to avoid any illegal payments being received. The other point you need to think about, as we have discussed, is potential unwanted publicity. When someone donates a sizeable amount, organisations are often so pleased to receive it, they want to advertise it. This is when journalists could come sniffing around, in case there is a story. What you could do is look at putting a stipulation attached to any payments, stating the sum is only assured if no publicity is made by the individual or organisation about the donation. Again, there is no guarantee this will work, but for small organisations, it would probably suffice."

Her thoughts immediately went to Alan, and she had the same uneasy feeling again. Could he have found out about her win? The only people who knew were George, Kathy, Ben, and Jan, and she trusted them all.

No, she reassured herself. It must have just been a coincidence. She was worrying about nothing and being paranoid.

The meeting continued in the same intense manner, and Helen realised if she was to undertake her plan, there would be much to take into consideration. How she wished Ana was by her side, taking notes, chipping in, and expressing her thoughts. She had an amazing brain and had always been better at this kind of thing than her.

"It all sounds so complicated." Helen was feeling disheartened.

Kathy could see she was struggling with the enormity of it all.

"Let's leave it for now," she suggested. "There's a lot to work through. Take the folder away and look at it in your own time."

George jumped in.

"I know it is important to maintain the secrecy, but you may want to discuss it with someone else too, to get a second opinion. Maybe someone you trust totally, who will give you good, independent advice?"

He winked at her, and she knew he meant Ben.

After the meeting, feeling completely overwhelmed, it seemed that she had taken one step forward and two steps back. How could trying to do something good be so hard and complicated?

It had been a difficult meeting, to say the least.

When she reached home, she decided to take the pressure off herself and, for now, forget about the meeting. Her immediate priority was to concentrate on Ben. Getting ready to meet him seemed weird, as she realised it would be their first proper date. She felt such a raft of emotions; nervous, scared, and excited, she wondered how the evening would progress.

Equally, she was happy to be seeing him again and just hoped neither of them would be disappointed when they got to know each other properly.

They had arranged to meet at a little restaurant in Offley, a small village about ten minutes from her home. It felt a good, neutral place to meet as she didn't know anyone in the village.

At quarter past seven, the taxi turned up, and Helen headed out the door. This time, she had booked a taxi, as she thought she might need a glass or two of wine for Dutch courage.

Although they were meeting at eight o'clock and she was early, Ben was already in the car park and got out of his car just as she was walking towards the restaurant. He had a huge bunch of red and white roses in his hand, and he thrust them at her.

"These are for you."

Laughing, she took them.

"My goodness, what a big bouquet!"

He looked very self-conscious.

"Well, I have a lot of making up to do. Are they OK?" he asked shyly.

Taking her by the hand, they walked into the restaurant. It was busy, but Ben had reserved a table, and it was in a separate area to the main bar. The waiter came over and took the drinks order.

When he came back with the wine, Ben watched as Helen took a very big sip from her glass.

"Good grief! You are either very thirsty or incredibly nervous!" Ben laughed.

"I *am* nervous," she replied. "But it is good to see you again."

They kept the conversation very light to begin with, and Ben asked how things were moving forward with her ideas. She told him about the recent meeting with George and Kathy.

"You won't go far wrong with those two," he confirmed. "What do you think of Kathy?"

She smiled.

"Well, she's very different from you, but she seems lovely. She doesn't have the same connection with George as you do. I could immediately tell you were comfortable working together, and the ideas you bounced off each other were very similar. However, I do think Kathy, as well as George, fully understand what I am trying to achieve."

Ben was quiet for a moment.

"Actually, it was George who first brought me onboard. I had previously worked with George in the finance sector. He was my mentor. He taught me so much, but two years after I joined the company, he got the job at the National Lottery. I missed him a lot, and when the vacancy arose for a life coach, with my background and experience of teaching people how to manage money, albeit for those who didn't have it, George immediately thought of me. It seemed an amazing opportunity, so I grabbed it. You are right, we do think alike, and I would trust George with my life."

Ben grabbed her hand across the table.

"Listen, I am so sorry. I tried to play it cool, but it just wasn't possible to continue working with you feeling the way I did, but equally, I couldn't stop because I wanted to keep seeing you. Even if you didn't feel the same way, I still wanted to be there to help you. Your dreams for the money seemed so selfless, and I have never had a winner want to do anything like you are planning. George and I love it, and we both admire what you are doing."

Helen was happy to think she had George's approval as much as Ben's. She told him George had suggested if there was someone she completely trusted, it might be useful to go through with them what had been discussed in the meeting. With Ana gone, she asked if Ben would be happy to look at the information George had provided and give her his thoughts, now he was no longer her life coach. He said he would be delighted to read it through, so she felt it was a good time to tell him about her latest idea.

"I have been thinking about what I could do in Ana's memory. About ten years ago, while we were holidaying in Clacton, Ana and I went walking round a little village in Essex. We came across a country estate that was open to the public and decided to explore. We enjoyed the day, wandering through the woods, and it was so peaceful.

"I remembered reading you could purchase trees there in memory of people who have died. Having checked, it isn't expensive, so I thought I would buy some trees and a bench in memory of Ana. She would love it, especially as it is preserving the woodland for the future. I think it is a positive way of life moving forward. Ana would have a real giggle, knowing that she had her own 'land'. Also, whenever I feel sad and want to feel close to Ana, it could be one of the places I visit. What do you think?"

"Sounds great," Ben replied. "But how would it work? Do you have to go down there and plant trees?"

"No. The woods they use are for dedication purposes and are already established. Most of the areas have mature trees in them and you aren't allowed to plant further trees there.

"Being a mature wood avoids the possibility of trees dying in the early years of planting. There are also spaces in the woods to provide meadows and grassy areas for both people and wildlife to enjoy, and for natural regeneration. Dedications are made available in woods of all ages, but most of them have trees aged ten years or more, which means people can enjoy them now."

Ben smiled.

"It is a wonderful idea. I didn't know Ana for long, but I am sure she would have really approved. If you like, we could go down there for the day to have a proper look? Or we could make a weekend of it, and you could introduce me properly to your friends, Alice and Dick."

"Well, *that's* rather forward when we are still on our first date!" Helen laughed.

Ben blushed, realising the possible intimation of his statement.

"You know I didn't mean it like that. We could have separate bedrooms, find somewhere nice, I wasn't necessarily suggesting…"

"I know, I am joking!" She was still laughing, trying to ease his embarrassment.

This was all going so much better than she had hoped. She really liked Ben and had never felt that way about anyone before.

The rest of the night passed quickly, and conversation with Ben seemed to flow naturally and easily. They were both sad when they realised last orders had been called. She hoped all their dates would be like this one.

As she hadn't ordered a taxi back, Ben offered to take her home.

He pulled up outside her flat, and they sat in the car, still talking as they had done all evening.

"Did you want to come in for coffee?" she asked, trying to sound casual, and not too sure what 'coming in for coffee' would actually mean.

"Yes, that would be lovely," he replied.

Maybe he felt as unsure as she was about how the night would end.

Unlocking the door, she turned off the alarm. Ben followed closely behind.

"Are you going to give me a tour?"

She laughed.

"I can do, but it won't take long, it's only a small flat."

Panic then engulfed her. What would happen when they got to the bedroom?

They started in the kitchen, and to calm her nerves, Helen put the kettle on and asked if he wanted tea or coffee.

She could feel how close he was standing behind her; there wasn't enough room to swing a cat in her 'bijou' kitchen, and with little to say about a kitchen, they waited awkwardly for the kettle to boil.

"How do you have your tea?"

"White, half a sugar."

She grabbed the biscuit tin as they headed into the living room.

"I'll show you the rest of the flat after we've had our tea," she suggested.

"Where's the bathroom?"

She pointed him in the right direction and settled herself on the settee.

Then she remembered the roses, so returned to the kitchen to get the only vase she had. As it was only small, it was a struggle to get them all in.

"These are beautiful, Ben," Helen said when he returned.

She was still arranging them as she placed the vase on the coffee table in front of them.

"Just like you," he said, as he leant over to kiss her.

Unprepared for his advance, she knocked the vase, which started to wobble. Trying to save it, she caught him with her elbow, smacking his jaw.

"Oh, my goodness, are you OK?"

Concerned, she moved closer to him, inspecting his face for any bruises.

"I'll live! Good to know you are as clumsy as me!"

Unfortunately, the incident had ruined the moment, so they sat in silence and drank their tea.

After a while, Ben cleared his throat.

"Listen Helen. I like you… A lot. I would never have given up being your life coach if I didn't. You are such a special person. I really want you to be a big part of my life. But I don't think we should rush and spoil things, so let's take it nice and slow. Is that alright with you?"

What a relief, she thought, nodding in agreement. It took the pressure off whatever 'this' was going to be.

"And just for the record, I am not after your money!" He laughed as he sat back, clearly relieved now he had said what was on his mind.

"Don't worry, if things get serious, I'll get you to sign a prenup!"

"There is one thing I have been meaning to ask you, though. Now you have all this money, what would you like to buy for *yourself*?" Ben enquired.

The question threw her. It was true, she hadn't really thought too much about herself, especially since losing

Ana. Yes, she had bought the car and thought about a house, but nothing else. Mulling it over, the only other thing she had ever wanted to do was travel, particularly around Spain as she had been having Spanish lessons. She told him that maybe she could go over there for a few weeks and immerse herself fully in learning the language.

He smiled at her.

"Do whatever makes you happy. Just remember, it's important for you to enjoy the advantages the money can bring too."

They talked about so many aspects of their lives that night. He asked about her family, and she explained there was only Sam left. He told her more about his sister and her daughter, Maddie. She revealed that seeing the photograph in his living room, she had initially assumed she was his daughter, until George had put her straight.

He laughed.

"I love her to bits. I had never been interested in having kids until she was born. I instantly fell in love with her. When she was four, she was seriously ill, and it broke my heart, seeing her in hospital, wondering if she was going to survive. I visited her every day. Fortunately, she recovered, and I now try to see her at least once a week, if I can."

You could tell how much Maddie meant to him, and she was happy he had such an attachment to his niece. She had always wanted children but didn't think she would ever find the right person to share those dreams with.

Ben yawned, and looking at the clock, Helen realised it was ten past two in the morning!

"Ben, do you know what the time is? *I* don't have to be up early, but I don't know what your plans are for the day?"

He was shocked at how late it was and got up quickly.

"I had better go. My first meeting isn't until eleven, but I have some prep work to do beforehand. I'll call you later on today if that's OK?"

He looked at her, and she melted.

"Of course."

He planted a quick kiss on her cheek, picked up his car keys, and was gone.

She sat there for a moment, unable to believe her luck. Ben was gorgeous, kind, funny, and clever, and she knew he didn't care about her money.

She went to bed tired, but for the first time in a long while, excited about the future.

20

Helen spent the next few days looking through George and Kathy's proposals and trying to get her head around them all. The amount of thought and effort they had put into their recommendations was impressive and there were some great ideas in the folder.

Setting up the company really made sense. It was true, it was less likely there would be a 'mistake' in revealing her identity with a company taking control, and it would take an awful lot of the pressure away from her. As Ana was no longer there to support her, it would be helpful to get other people's input as to where the money could go, and for them to implement it. It was important to be able to enjoy giving money away and not get caught up in the nitty-gritty or stress of it all.

George had spent a great deal of time with Helen, and it wasn't lost on her, as she knew he had many other clients who needed his advice. He had also mentioned, several times, setting up the company would be out of the lottery's remit, but he was still willing to help set everything up during the early stages. One thing he did suggest, however, was against looking at too many *local* organisations and not rushing them all through at the same time. His point was valid. As he explained, if a few groups or individuals were benefitting solely in and around Luton, it may spark an interest that there was possibly someone in the community 'giving' money away, and local press could start trying to put the dots together. True, the chances of them pointing the finger at her were slim, but it was still important to be careful.

Thinking about the potential slip she had made with the dance group payment, she shuddered. It was a relief to know it had gone through without any incident.

George was as good as his word. He contacted prospective trustees who could oversee the company, and he was keen for Helen to meet them to make sure she was happy with his choice and to start getting things up and running.

During the first year, he suggested she set aside around £200,000 for donations. Helen held her breath when that figure was mentioned. It seemed so huge! But George put it into perspective. Helping twelve people or organisations a year and limiting it to three per quarter, at a cost of up to £10,000 a time, the donations would soon add up. In addition, there would be the time and expenses of setting up the company and paying the trustees to administer everything. The balance of what was left would give a little 'wiggle room', in case there was the need to pay some groups or individuals slightly more. This was a logical and sensible approach, meaning there would need to be real focus to decide who really needed the help and would stop any rash decisions being made. When the company was set up, the amounts could be discussed in more detail with the trustees who would give advice based on their own expertise. It was great everything was starting to come together at last.

George continued. "Before you can set everything up, you still need the company name. Have you thought of one yet?"

She shook her head.

Trying to think of a suitable name was proving incredibly difficult. It needed to be something inspiring, but which wouldn't draw attention back to her. None of her ideas seemed right, and she promised to seriously think about it. She could tell George was becoming frustrated, as it was the only thing stopping them from moving forward.

She recognised it needed to be sorted quickly, as she was keen to make the first payment to Julian to help him with his continued studies. She had suggested to George an initial sum of £12,000 would probably be a suitable amount. George didn't seem phased by the amount. Although it wouldn't solve all of Julian's student debts, it would go a significant way towards his costs, and there could be further payments as required. George suggested that by putting money through the company, it may be classed as a grant. He also came up with the suggestion that when Julian's studies were completed, she might want to put an annual amount aside to help other students who couldn't afford university fees, to help them achieve their dreams. She thought it was a brilliant idea and exactly the kind of support she wanted to provide. She realised how much she would miss George's input.

Kathy was also in regular contact, to remind Helen she was there if she wanted to discuss the enormity of what was being proposed or anything else that may be of concern moving forward.

Once again, she reiterated that it was a huge undertaking to try to achieve what Helen was planning, and, as someone donating, there could be downsides to the money given. As they had discussed at previous meetings, realistically, disappointment could be one of them. Kathy really was proving to be professional and helpful, and although she wasn't Ben, it was still great, having her input and support.

Things were beginning to move along nicely.

Then, out of the blue, Alan rang.

He hadn't contacted her since their one and only date, so she had assumed he wasn't interested, which had been a relief. Therefore, it came as a surprise when he suggested meeting up again. There was no apology for not being in touch, just a sense that he expected her to jump at the opportunity of seeing him again.

"I am sorry Alan. I am seeing someone, and I want to see how things go with him."

His response left her dumbfounded.

"I don't mind if you want to see both of us. You might as well keep your options open."

What? She was shocked he would even suggest something like that. But in his world, maybe it was how he operated. It sounded a little desperate though.

"Thank you for the offer, but I'll leave it, thanks," she replied, quickly ending the call. She couldn't believe his cheek! She had regretted the date as soon as they had met up, and there was just no contest between him and Ben.

Ben was coming round the following night, so she mentioned how she was struggling with a name for the company. He suggested they discuss it over a bottle of wine. All she needed now was something nice to wear, so she decided to pop into town.

Haddenham's, the local department store, which had been in the town over 100 years, was closing. Before, she would never have ventured into the clothes section, as it was all designer labels and so expensive, but at the thought of a bargain, she decided to pop in. Picking out a beautiful sea-green camisole and matching trousers, the sales assistant commented on how the colour was perfect with Helen's hair and complexion. Admiring herself in the mirror, she felt really pretty in it, and being such a versatile outfit, she was sure there would be plenty of other occasions where she could wear it. She didn't even look at the price tags as she came out of the changing room and went straight over to the desk to pay.

However, taking it out of the bag when she got home, she realised it was completely over-the-top for an evening in, so in the end, she stuck with jeans and a pink silky top that were already in her wardrobe.

Stepping into the bath, the smell of the lovely bath oil Ana had bought her for Christmas wafted all around the bathroom and into the living room. Helen clearly remembered her buying it. They had been shopping together when she had seen the beautiful bottle and, opening the lid, commented on how lovely it smelt. It was funny watching Ana pick up the bottle and trying to hide it behind her back. She said she wanted to browse a little more and suggested Helen go upstairs to the cafe and get the teas in, before she discreetly went and paid for it. Saddened by the memory, she found herself trying to hold back the tears, knowing she would never have those lovely, funny experiences with her best friend again.

The sound of the phone interrupted her thoughts. Luckily, she'd had the sense to take the phone into the bathroom along with her glass of wine.

"Hi, Sis, how are you doing?"

Sam sounded quite excitable.

Before she had a chance to reply, he jumped in.

"What are you doing this evening? I was going to suggest we went to the pub tonight, so you could meet Sarah."

Oh no! Sam's call completely threw her. She was really looking forward to seeing Ben, but equally, she wanted to meet Sarah.

"I am sorry, I can't tonight, I'm busy. What about tomorrow?"

There was a pause down the other end of the phone, and then suddenly he yelled, "*You've* got a date, haven't you? Who is he? How long have you known him? What are his intentions?"

Sam was laughing at her, which made her slightly irritated.

"None of your business, and it's not a date. Well, it is, but let's just see how it goes. Concentrate on your own relationship and stop worrying about me."

Sam could tell she was annoyed. His tone softened.

"Sorry, Sis, I didn't mean to upset you. Seriously, I am pleased for you. We could always make it a foursome tonight, if you wanted?"

"No thanks, Sam. It's *very* early days. I'm sorry I was short with you. Why don't we arrange something for a couple of weeks' time? I could cook us all a meal if you like?"

"Do you think that's a good idea with your cooking skills? How about we get a takeaway?" Sam suggested, cheekily.

"Sounds great," she replied, ignoring her brother's disrespectful but accurate comment about her cooking abilities. "It will be my treat, and I'll get a nice bottle of wine if you like. Now, what does Sarah like to eat and drink?"

Putting the phone down, she felt mean. This was the first girl Sam seemed keen on and one of the few he had been happy for her to meet. In the past, it was usually obvious that none of his girlfriends were going to last, but there just seemed something different about the way he spoke about Sarah. She hoped they would both be lucky in love this time.

Needing to get ready for Ben's arrival, she jumped out the bath, hoovered, dusted, and tidied up, and by eight o'clock, she was pacing around, expectantly waiting for Ben.

Just seconds later, there he was. Sweeping her up in his arms always felt so special, giving her the fluttery feeling in her stomach. He smelt beautiful, but it was Ben who said, "You smell lovely," before kissing her.

"Would you like a glass of wine? Red or white?" she asked.

He sat down.

"Red please. Although I am driving, so I'll only have the one," he replied, and she disappeared into the kitchen.

When she came back into the living room, she told him about Sam and the suggestion of them all having a meal together.

"We could have met them tonight, if you had wanted," he said.

She explained she had declined, as she wanted to talk to him in more detail about the recent meeting she'd had with George and Kathy.

"I really would like your thoughts. I want you to be part of it all… whatever 'this' is," she said.

"Do you mean us or your win?" he asked with a smile. Giving him a playful nudge in the ribs, she went through everything that had been discussed with George and Kathy at the last meeting. It felt good to be able to talk it through with someone else, especially now Ana wasn't around.

"Well, from what you are saying, it seems you have things pretty much sorted. I agree with all their advice and suggestions. So, what do you need from me?"

She explained she was still struggling with a name for the company. She grabbed the notepad and a pen so they could jot down their thoughts.

Still, nothing seemed right. It was important not to make a rash decision, so Ben suggested she sleep on it for a few more days.

Ben was so lovely and easy-going. Even though they had made the decision to take things slowly, they were soon seeing each other almost every night, so it wasn't long before their relationship progressed and he would either spend nights at hers, or she would be at his. They seemed so in sync with each other, and she hated it when they were apart.

It felt like they had known each other for ages, so she had to keep reminding herself they had only been together a short time. Ana was still sorely missed and there were plenty of days where she would find herself thinking *I'll just ask Ana...*

If she was still in her life, everything would be perfect.

Formation of the company was progressing, much to Helen's relief. George had arranged for her to meet the three people he felt could be trustees and who would act as the face of the organisation. They were brilliant; all had great skills and expertise in running charitable organisations, and more importantly, she felt they could be trusted to be confidential. George had kept things as basic as he could with the trustees, explaining Helen had 'come into some money' and, not needing the money herself, wanted to use it in a philanthropic way but wanted to undertake this anonymously. The people George had picked were used to operating in this way and fortunately, they were all available to start straight away on a part-time basis and keen to embark on the new venture.

The only stumbling block now was the uncertainty of a name. It seemed impossible to find something suitable.

Burying her head in the sand for a few days, she arranged the meal with Sam and Sarah. She really hoped Sam would approve of Ben and that she would like Sarah. Ben even confessed he was a little nervous about meeting her brother, which surprised her, as he always seemed confident. She knew, however, that with his easy-going manner, they would get on well. Sam was right about her terrible cooking, and considering how cramped it would be for the four of them trying to eat a takeaway in her flat, they arranged to go out to a little restaurant Ben knew in Berkhamsted.

Ben picked them all up, and she could tell Sam was impressed with the car. Sarah was very quiet. Helen began to wonder if they would have anything in common.

However, after arriving at the restaurant and ordering some drinks, it wasn't long before Sarah began to open up and relax when she realised the 'older sister' wasn't judging her.

As they started to enjoy their meal, Sam turned to Ben and said, "So, how did you two meet?"

Helen and Ben looked at each other. Neither of them had discussed what to say, if someone asked that question.

"Oh, it's a bit boring really," she said, laughing nervously while trying to think of a plausible answer. Ben could sense the panic in her voice and took over, covering her hand with his for reassurance.

"Don't be so coy, darling," Ben said. "We were in a work meeting together, and I liked her views and input in the meeting. I discovered she was single and decided to ask her out. I wasn't sure if she would say yes, but she did. And here we are." He removed his hand and carried on eating his meal.

Wow! She was impressed at how easily he had dealt with the question. He must be used to it, because of his work. What he said wasn't a lie, in fact, it was very close to the truth – a neat bit of deflecting, she thought!

"Oh, another man you met at work then," Sam commented to his sister, while trying to twirl some pasta round his fork and failing miserably.

Ben looked at her quizzically, and she explained it was through work she had met her friend George. Ben then understood, and she noticed he had a wry smile on his face.

It was a wonderful evening and lovely to see that, despite being shy, Sarah was able to hold her own with Sam, even reining him in every now and again when he was getting out of hand. Helen approved, sensing how good she would be for her brother.

Ben paid for the meal, despite Sam's protestations, with Ben suggesting he could pay next time. It was lovely to see Sam relaxed, and she was happy he had now met Ben. Knowing Sam, he would ring her at the earliest opportunity, to give her his opinion, but she wasn't worried. After dropping Sam and Sarah off, they headed back to Ben's.

The following morning, Helen heard her mobile going off and decided to ignore it. With it being a Saturday, she didn't have to get up early and was looking forward to a lie in with Ben, but soon, it was ringing again. Squinting at her watch, she realised it was only twenty past eight! Ben stirred slightly but didn't appear to wake as she picked up the phone and walked out of the room.

"So, *that* was Ben!" her brother declared loudly.

It really was too early for the inquisition, but she was fully awake now.

"Yes. Do you like him?"

"Nice car, and he paid for the meal, what's not to like? You have obviously landed on your feet!" he joked.

"Helen, do you want a coffee?" Ben asked, as he walked past her and through to the kitchen.

"Ah, you aren't at yours, you are at Ben's! *That's* why I couldn't get you on the house phone. You stayed the night at his. This is moving very quickly for you, you floozy!" Sam laughed.

She felt embarrassed, like a naughty teenager caught out by their parent.

However, she knew Sam wasn't being judgemental.

"Good for you," he continued. "Ben seems a nice guy. Hope it all works out."

"The same to you, Sam. Sarah is lovely, and she can hold her own with you, which not many girls can do."

The line was quiet for a second, before her brother replied.

"I really like her. She's funny, kind, and thoughtful, and she's got one over on you – she can cook!"

"Well, next time it's a meal at yours then, with you and Sarah cooking!"

They agreed to arrange another night out. It was great to see Sam so happy and settled at last. Life did seem to be moving forward.

21

Another day, another dull job, Alan thought to himself. Why was he putting himself through it? Lately, it felt like Phil was constantly monitoring his work and assignments, so his investigations were having to be undertaken mainly in his own time or discreetly at work.

During his lunchbreak, he decided to revisit Helen's profile on Facebook. One of the first things he did when they had arranged the date, was to request to be a 'friend' on her page. Now, he could view all her entries as she hadn't made anything private. Nothing of interest on her home page. My God, what a load of drivel! Loads of motivational quotes. He shuddered. They left him cold.

Going through her friends, he checked to see if Nicky from the dance group was one of them, but no, she wasn't. He began to think this was a complete waste of time. Ooh, wait a minute! He spotted a beautiful girl. Slim, long dark hair, a real stunner. He would have to put a friend request through to her. He made a note of her name – Ana

Moreno. He had seen her in several photos with Helen. Even if she was married or dating someone, she may be able to provide him with further information that could be of help or at the very least, would be a very interesting distraction.

He looked at Helen's music page.

Who listens to Dolly Parton and ABBA? he wondered.

Well, she did, obviously. *No taste*, he thought.

He was about to give up when he clicked on her 'likes' page. He couldn't believe it! Listed under that category was none other than the Daffodil Dance Group!

Now this was just *too* much of a coincidence. She *had* to be the mystery donor. His hunch had been right.

Phil started to walk over to him, so he quickly returned his screen to the story about the missing dachshund he had been working on.

His thoughts kept returning to Helen. He was still mystified as to why she hadn't wanted to go out for another drink with him. He didn't fancy her, but he wondered why she would turn down someone like *him*. She wouldn't get anyone better than him, as she was very plain and ordinary.

But 'ordinary' she obviously wasn't if she was the donor for the stupid dance group. Why would you make such a large payment? There was no obvious connection. Nicky had said the donation was paid following the newspaper article, so apparently, this mystery donor hadn't been someone already known to her, and she had hinted it was a female. It was all too much of a coincidence, and he believed there were very rarely coincidences in life.

Just then, Susie, the girl who delivered the office post walked past, handing out the mail. He had been out with her on a few dates when she first joined the company. False nails, enhanced cleavage, and a very loud laugh. He had to admit, although she looked striking, there wasn't 'much between the ears', as his dad would have said. She was OK for a few dates though, as he had received many approving looks from other men when he had taken her out. She had been quite upset when there were no further dates. He decided to quiz her.

"Ah, Susie, my favourite postwoman. How are you?"

She looked at him curiously, unsure of what he was after.

"I haven't seen you in ages, have you been away? You are looking incredible! Have you done something with your hair?" he continued.

She beamed at him. He had overheard someone in the office saying she had recently been to the hairdressers for some hair extensions and a beautician for lip filler. When she explained, he confirmed he could really see the difference. He wasn't really interested but knew he now had her attention.

"While you are here, perhaps you can answer me a question?"

She seemed interested to hear what he had to say, and she perched on the corner of his desk.

"Let me give you a scenario. You aren't working, yet you've managed to buy a car less than a year old. In addition, you have donated £8,500 to a group you don't have any connections to. Why would you do that?"

She looked at him as if he were mad. "Well, I wouldn't. The car I can understand because you can get it on finance, but if it was me and I had that kind of money, I would go and have further enhancements."

She pushed up her already more than ample breasts to emphasise what she meant.

"You can get some great treatments for £8,500. I can't think of any reason why someone would give away so much money."

He knew she was the wrong person to ask, but he persisted.

"OK, but say that you *had* made a huge donation. What would be the reason for it, especially if you didn't have the money?"

She looked at him as if he was stupid.

"No one is going to do that if they *didn't* have the money. I mean, why would you?" She laughed, before adding, "Perhaps the person won the lottery or something."

She jumped off his desk, seemingly bored with the questioning and carried on delivering the post.

He sat there, thinking over what she had just said, and laughed to himself. Hmm, wouldn't it be something, winning the lottery! Of course, *that* hadn't happened.

But hang on a minute. Something was niggling at him. Hadn't someone in this area recently won the lottery jackpot? No, it couldn't be. Could it…?

He began to scan through newspaper articles the paper had printed over the past few months about the big lottery win. Yes, there in front of him was the article about the lottery win, indicating it had been won by someone in the Bedfordshire area. He also came across a story about a shopkeeper, James Elliot, who claimed he had actually sold the winning ticket at his corner shop in Lilley. Alan hadn't covered the story, but he remembered it clearly now.

Surely Helen Pond was not the winner of the National Lottery? That would be ridiculous. But the more he thought about it, the more he felt it could be a possibility. No one had come forward, and if it *was* her, it would make sense to be keeping a low profile. However unlikely, if it was her who had won the lottery, he would find out. He wasn't a good journalist for nothing. He just needed to work on a plan…

While he was deep in thought, Phil approached his desk.

"What are you doing Alan?" he enquired.

"Why?" Alan replied.

Phil looked surprised at his curt response.

"Well, if you are not too busy, I would like to see you in my office. I've had a complaint."

Phil walked towards his office, and stopped at the door, expecting Alan to follow him.

He did so, as he wasn't keen on the rest of the team hearing whatever Phil had to say. It must be about another member of staff and Phil needed some clarification about one of his colleagues, he thought.

Alan sat down. His first words were not a surprise to Phil.

"It can't be a complaint about me."

He waited for Phil to comment, but as he didn't, he thought for a moment. Was it possible someone had raised a complaint against him? If they had, he really couldn't figure out why.

"So, who's complained? Is it the blonde girl in sales? I took her out a couple of times, and I know it meant more to her than me. She must want to get back at me."

It came as no surprise to Phil to find him acting defensively. Whenever he made a mistake, his immediate reaction was to blame someone else.

"I have received a complaint following an article you wrote. She said you were making unwanted advances towards her."

Alan looked bemused.

"I can assure you, Phil, I know about women. I should imagine she was more annoyed because I *hadn't* made a play for her!" he smirked.

"Enough, Alan."

He realised Phil was not in the mood for jokes.

Phil continued.

"In addition to the complaint, you still put through the lunch expenses I told you not to unless you could prove to me it was work related.

"You have been late for work and assignments on several occasions in the past month with no explanation.

"I am *still* waiting for two articles I asked you to write last week, and the deadline has passed for one of them. To top it all, I find out you are writing articles I am not even aware of, and to my knowledge, haven't been authorised. Yesterday, I had some man ring me from a fruit and vegetable company, asking me why the article you said you would write hadn't appeared in *The Bedfordshire Post* yet. Do you want to explain? You didn't run it past me or discuss it at the team briefing. You know you are meant to bring me up to speed with any new stories before you take them on.

"You just don't seem focused at the moment. What the hell are you playing at?"

Alan said nothing, so Phil continued.

"I'm going to have to call a meeting with HR. Your attitude recently has been appalling, especially towards other staff in the building. It's totally unacceptable, Alan."

He sat there, stunned. How *dare* Phil speak to him like this.

Looking up, he was surprised to see everyone in the open office staring at him through the glass-panelled walls. He wondered why before realising the door to Phil's office wasn't shut properly, so they would all have heard Phil's rant.

Alan could feel himself getting hot under the collar. He'd had enough.

"I shouldn't have to justify myself to *you*," he sneered. "I've given this miserable company eleven years of my life. ELEVEN years!" He banged his fist on the desk. "And you give me ridiculous stories to cover; potholes, some old biddy's one hundredth birthday celebrations, or a little kid who managed to walk ten laps round a school field for charity! I should be covering 'proper' stories. They may have made you editor, but I've more talent in my little finger than you've got in your entire body. You wouldn't know a good story if it smacked you in the face. If only you knew what I was working on, I don't think you would be so quick to judge me and—"

Phil interjected.

"I would stop right there if I were you. You are digging yourself into a big hole."

"I don't care."

Alan was seething.

"Do you know what? I am too good for this stupid excuse of a newspaper. You can stick your job where the sun doesn't shine. When I have cracked this story, all the nationals will be clamouring to employ me, and you'll be sorry. *Very* sorry."

With that, he pushed back the chair and strolled out of the office. He expected everyone to be cheering him on as he came out. Instead, there was no reaction from any of them.

Phil sighed and remained seated. He was shocked by Alan's behaviour. Yes, he knew the discussion was unlikely to go well, but he hadn't expected his response to be so dramatic. In hindsight, he should have pulled him up long before it got to this point.

He shook his head. Alan's resignation would be a loss, but he was also becoming a liability, and his behaviour had become even more irrational recently.

Phil wondered what he meant about the story he was working on. Was it connected to this fruit and vegetable company? Now, he would never know. But his departure was probably for the best.

Alan was furious. He drove home, parked his car, and walked to the pub.

As far as he was concerned, *The Bedfordshire Post* was a backward-looking tabloid, and he knew he would never amount to anything there. His leaving was more of a loss to *them* than for him. Give it a day or two and Phil would be ringing, begging him to return. Well, it wouldn't happen without a decent pay rise and an apology in front of all the staff. *Then* he'd see who looked stupid.

Sitting in the pub, he realised losing his job was probably the kick up the backside he needed. He was sure a national newspaper would be delighted to have someone like him. Also, not working meant he could concentrate on Helen Pond and whatever secrets she was hiding. Even if she hadn't made the donation to the Daffodil Dance Group, there was still likely to be a great story there, too. Plus, he wanted to take some legal advice, to see if he had a case about how he had been treated at *The Bedfordshire Post*. Maybe life wasn't so bad after all.

22

Following Alan's resignation, work at *The Bedfordshire Post* continued as usual. Phil asked Polly to clear Alan's desk. He thought that, as a fellow journalist, she may find something in there that might provide some clues as to what Alan had been working on. As she wasn't too busy, she was happy to oblige. No one had seen him since his departure, and he hadn't been back to collect anything. Phil told her to put any personal belongings to one side, and he would arrange for them to be sent on.

Sitting down at the desk, Polly used the spare key Phil had given her and opened the top drawer. As expected, it was full of everyday stationery items: stapler, pens, paperclips, along with some old food wrappers. Something smelt like it had died in there, and she soon found two banana skins tucked right at the back. Gross! He had a bin next to his desk, why couldn't he have just thrown them in there? She put the stationery items into a box to be returned to office supplies, and the rubbish went in the bin, along with his business cards. He wouldn't be needing those anymore.

She had hoped to find his journalist's notebook, but it wasn't there. Although some of the younger journalists at *The Bedfordshire Post* used iPads or their phones these days to make their notes when they went out to cover a story, many were still 'old school', preferring notebooks.

However, there was a smaller notebook in the second drawer. Flicking through it, she found brief notes about some of his recent interviews. The way he worked was not her style. When she was younger and covering big stories in London, she did as much research as she could to put herself in the strongest position against the competition. There was a great deal of that in the City, as her colleagues had been ruthless if they were chasing a story. However, she could tell from Alan's articles that he covered only as much as he needed to and nothing more.

There was a short paragraph about the Daffodil Dance Group's interview, and he had written down the telephone number of Nicky, the leader of the group, at the side with a 'nine' written against her name. Honestly! There were also a few notes about Harold Pond from Freeland's Fruit & Vegetable Company, which she recognised as the interview Phil hadn't authorised. Polly knew that Harold Pond had rung Phil to find out why his interview had not been published, and Phil had said he would send another journalist to have a chat with him, explaining that Alan had left the company. It was probably a waste of valuable space in the paper and there didn't seem any angle to it, but equally Phil wanted to avoid potential bad publicity.

As she continued to look through the book, she was

intrigued. A few pages in, there was a spidergram with 'H Pond' in the middle and little lines and questions coming from the centre. The names Harold Pond, Helen Pond, and Nicky from the Daffodil Dance Group were mentioned. Under Harold's and Helen's names were questions: source of income? Donation of £8,500 to Daffodil Dance Group? Lottery?

Harold Pond's name had been crossed out, but Helen's name was still there with a question mark, along with her address, telephone number and a rating of 'four'. Why had he been investigating two people with the same surname? Were they related?

At that moment, Phil headed towards her.

"Thanks for going through Alan's desk, Polly. Anything interesting?"

She didn't give him the answer he was expecting.

"Phil, if no one has been assigned to the Harold Pond interview, can I take it on?"

Phil was surprised, as she had expressed no interest in undertaking stories up to this point, just her weekly 'The Written Word' articles, so why now?

She continued.

"I'm curious to find out what he was working on. You must also be intrigued, surely?"

Phil thought for a minute. It was true, they did need to sort out the article with Harold Pond, and if Polly was willing to chat to him and find out what had happened, that was fine. She probably had more time than any of his other journalists, so he agreed.

"By the way, Phil, do you know someone called Helen Pond?"

He thought for a moment, before shaking his head. "No, why?"

"It's just there is mention of a Helen Pond in Alan's little book. It seems strange don't you think – two 'Pond's'?"

He agreed it seemed odd but didn't appear particularly concerned about it. He returned to his office.

Deciding to focus on Helen, Polly went on to Facebook, as he had written that under Helen's name.

There were a few 'Helen Pond's' but only one who appeared to be local. She scrolled through her Facebook pages. She concluded that this must be her, as she had Alan down as one of her friends. Looking through her pictures, there were no photos of her with him, however. Poring over a few entries, there was nothing of great interest. She wondered if she was just one of his conquests, but she really didn't look like his normal type, and he had only given her a rating of 'four' in his book. Moving on to her 'likes', there wasn't much listed. Then she noticed the Daffodil Dance Group. That was another name mentioned in Alan's book. Why did that name ring a bell? She decided to pop in and have another word with Phil.

"Does the Daffodil Dance Group mean anything to you?"

Phil rolled his eyes.

"You are joking, aren't you? Have we had yet another complaint?"

Polly looked confused, so he continued.

"The group leader, Nicky, is the person Alan propositioned. He and John wrote an article about the group. They were after funding to go on a trip for some competition. I think he laid on his usual 'charm', and she took offence. Why do you ask?"

"I think she may be linked to whatever Alan was working on. Can I ring her, on behalf of the paper, to apologise for his behaviour? It may give me a lead?"

Phil agreed. Anything Polly was willing to do to cover the wrongdoings of his ex-employee was fine by him. He wondered for a moment if she was after Alan's job, but he immediately dismissed the thought, as he knew she was looking to retire in the next few years and seemed happy with the small number of hours 'The Written Word' took each week.

"Right, I'm off to lunch," he announced. He'd had enough stress for the morning.

First, Polly found the telephone number for Nicky at the Daffodil Dance Group and rang it.

"Hi there. I am ringing from *The Bedfordshire Post*."

Before she had the chance to say anything else, Nicky cut in.

"Ah, are you the photographer Alan was talking about? Can you do Thursday?"

Polly was confused.

"What photographer?"

"From *The Bedfordshire Post*? After the interview I had with Alan yesterday, he said he would arrange for a photographer to come out to take some photos."

Now Polly was really confused. As he was no longer working for *The Bedfordshire Post*, what interview was he undertaking? It sounded as though he had given Nicky the impression he was still working at the paper, which seemed odd.

"So, Alan came to see you yesterday?" Polly enquired cautiously.

"Yes. He was on his best behaviour, which was a relief. When can you come over? We are now meeting on Thursday evenings from seven at the Scout hut in Woodstock Road. I had hoped it would be the nice photographer who came last time, as the kids loved him. I think his name was John. But I am sure you will be just as great."

Polly thought for a moment.

"Er, yes, I am sure we can get John to come along. Actually, I am not a photographer. My name is Polly, and I am one of the other journalists here at *The Bedfordshire Post*. We just need some additional information to complete the article, so I'll accompany John, if that's OK? See you Thursday."

What the hell was going on? Polly wondered.

Why had Alan met Nicky the day before? She had implied it had been an interview. Was he covertly carrying out his own investigations about something? Polly hoped he wasn't doing anything to put either *The Bedfordshire Post* or the Daffodil Dance Group into disrepute. She was unsure if she should tell Phil at this stage, but decided not to until she had further information.

She went to have a chat with John. He was editing some photos on his computer.

She sat opposite him, and he smiled.

"Nice to see you, Polly. What can I do for you?"

"John, what can you tell me about the Daffodil Dance Group? I need to know everything that happened when you went with Alan to see them."

John was a little surprised at her request but explained

about the meeting and how Alan had tried to get a date with Nicky.

Polly then told John about the conversation she'd just had with Nicky and whether he could shed any light on why he would have re-interviewed her the day before.

He couldn't, which was disappointing, and he seemed just as confused.

"Why would he be suggesting that he still works here?" he enquired. He was intrigued, so was happy to go with Polly to see Nicky on Thursday evening.

"I haven't told Phil that Alan saw her yesterday. I wonder if you'd mind not saying anything to him until we know more?"

John didn't like lying to his boss, but he agreed.

Returning to her desk, she decided to ring Harold Pond. She profusely apologised that the article had not appeared. Explaining that Alan no longer worked for the paper and the notes he had left weren't comprehensive, she asked if they could meet to rectify the situation.

"Are you taking me out to lunch too?" Harold asked eagerly. "Your colleague did."

"I am afraid I can't, but I can come to your offices in London, if it is easier for you?"

Reluctantly, Harold agreed. He would have preferred another free lunch, but that sounded out of the question with this reporter.

Next, she tried to ring Helen on the number Alan had written down in his notebook. Blast – the answerphone cut in. She left a voice message, explaining who she was and asking if she would ring her back. She wasn't sure how she was going to handle this one, as there were no leads other than the connection to the Daffodil Dance Group. Perhaps Nicky may be able to shed some light on that.

On Thursday evening, Polly picked up John from home and they drove over to the Scout hut. On the way over, she quizzed John again about the previous interview with Nicky.

He told her about the previous meeting with the group, and how he had taken his own notes as Alan hadn't seemed to be making many. That explained why the article had seemed so thorough, Polly concluded.

He also told her about Alan's approach to Nicky and how he obviously thought he stood a chance with her, which had made John squirm, and how cross Alan had been when she knocked him back.

John was itching to find out why Polly had taken such an interest in the group, but he knew better than to question her. From the stories he had heard about her work in London, he understood she had been a very good journalist in her heyday and would have had to be really tough to get some of the stories she had been involved with. It had always struck him as strange that, with her background, she would leave London and work for a small paper like *The Bedfordshire Post*.

This was also the first time he had worked with her, as she didn't need a photographer for her weekly column. He was keen to see how she would handle clearing up Alan's mess and what her approach would be. He continued telling her more about the dance group, including the fact that, following the article, his granddaughter had joined. He also informed her that there was now a problem with the rehearsal venue, following the discovery of asbestos in the community hall roof, resulting in them needing to find new premises.

Polly and John agreed it was best not to tell Nicky that Alan was no longer working for *The Bedfordshire Post*, as it could cause more problems for the paper. He agreed to follow her lead. He was there to take photographs and not question her motives.

Polly wasn't sure how she was going to handle the interview. She knew she would have to do a fair amount of bluffing, but that was something she could do standing on her head. Her years in London had taught her that.

The group were already into a routine when they arrived. Like John, Polly stood there, unable to take her eyes off the children. They moved perfectly together to the music, and their concentration didn't seem to waver, which was impressive.

Next, she turned her attention to Nicky. She could understand why anyone would be attracted to her. She was slim, pretty, and had an engaging personality.

John's granddaughter saw him and waved, causing Nicky to turn to see who was there. She was pleased to see John again and smiled at him.

Stopping the group for a moment, she came over and greeted the pair of them.

Polly held out her hand.

"Hi, I'm Polly. Lovely to meet you. And you have met John, of course."

He smiled warmly at Nicky. Some of the children waved, remembering him from his previous visit.

Nicky called over to one of the other women, asking

if she could take over from her, before sitting in a corner with Polly and John.

"So, I heard how well you did in the finals. What an amazing achievement! You must be so proud of the kids, and that all your hard work has paid off," Polly gushed.

John had to admire her approach and ability to put Nicky at ease.

"I am so pleased you are here. I thought the original article would be all we needed to get us to the final, but now with the loss of the hall, I am so grateful for *The Bedfordshire Post's* continued support. It really is appreciated."

Polly sat back in the chair, calm and composed.

"Yes, I was really sorry to hear about the hall. I'll be honest with you, I haven't had the opportunity to speak to Alan in much detail about his meeting with you yesterday. As he has a couple of other stories he is working on, I am taking over yours. I don't want to make you repeat everything, but as we both have different styles of working, could you give me a rundown on what you discussed with him yesterday? I want to make sure that I fully understand your current situation to try and make sure you get the help you need."

Nicky went through everything again. She didn't mind. This journalist seemed much more respectful and interested in the group than Alan had.

John walked over to the children, who had now stopped for drinks, and started to take some pictures. He suggested to Nicky's colleague that perhaps the kids could pose with the trophy they had won for coming second in the finals. Soon he was snapping away, and once again, he persuaded Nicky to join the group briefly for another photo. She looked happier than she had during their first meeting, but he could tell that the lack of a permanent venue was weighing heavily on her mind.

While Nicky was involved with the photos, Polly was frantically trying to understand what was going on. Why had Alan wanted to follow this up?

While she was still trying to figure it out, Nicky came back to join her. She seemed more relaxed.

"I am so pleased you have taken over from your colleague. I did think, when I first saw him yesterday, that he had changed, but after a few minutes I could tell he hadn't. He always seems to have an ulterior motive, and I never feel comfortable with him."

Polly decided to push.

"What makes you say that? He didn't come on to you again, did he? Our editor had very strong words with him about his behaviour."

"No, he was OK. It was just he seemed more interested in the donation we had received to enable us to go to the finals rather than our current situation."

"You mean the £8,500 donation?" Polly enquired.

"Yes," replied Nicky, suddenly appearing slightly nervous by the mention of it. "But I am not going to talk about that. I made it very clear to Alan it was an anonymous donation, and I would not reveal the person's identity."

Polly thought it odd that he should be so interested in the donation, but even she had to admit it was a large amount from one person. She then remembered the spidergram in his notebook.

"That's fine," she continued. "The article should be online tomorrow and in the paper version the day after. I really do hope we can help you find another venue. Kids need all the chances in life that they can get, and you should be so proud of what you have achieved, Nicky. You are a remarkable woman."

Nicky smiled, but didn't respond.

With John wrapping up the photos, they were soon in the car again, heading back to the office.

Polly's mind was still whirring. It sounded as though Alan's interest this time had solely been about the donation and who had made it. She wasn't sure how everything tied together, as she only had one strand at present.

She decided to get John's opinion.

"John, what do you think about the huge donation that was made to the group?"

"I don't know. I did wonder why the person hasn't approached them to help fund a new venue. All I know is I hope they get the help they need, as my granddaughter's confidence has grown since she joined, and it would be a shame for them to have gone through all they have to then lose a venue."

"Mmm," said Polly.

The next day, she was on her way to London to meet Harold Pond. Sitting on the London Underground, she reminisced about the mad dashes she had made when she worked in London, using the Underground, buses, and when there was an urgent need, taxis to cover stories at a moment's notice, hoping to be there before the competition. She really didn't miss that and some of the other aspects that went with it, but she did miss the excitement of chasing a good story.

She soon found the offices of Freeland's Fruit & Vegetable Company and asked for Harold Pond at reception.

Harold came down to meet her.

"I was surprised that it wasn't Alan coming to see me," he said. "He took me to lunch last time."

Polly could tell he wasn't happy about the lack of wining and dining this time round and decided to lay on her female charms instead.

"I know. I am so very sorry that your article didn't appear. I think there was a mix up, and Alan has moved onto other projects now. We would still really love to tell your story, so I do appreciate your valuable time."

Harold took her into a small, but still impressive, office, full of period furniture and a couple of big oil paintings of fruit and vegetables in sunnier climes.

"So, let's start at the beginning, Harold. Would you like to fill me in on the article that Alan was working on with you? It sounded very interesting from the notes he left me, but you are the man with the story to tell, and I am really keen to hear what you have to say."

That pleased Harold immensely. This woman was eager to know more about him.

"Well, I was a little surprised when Alan contacted me about wanting to write an article about our company, as sourcing fruit and vegetables in an ethical manner is not something that I thought my local paper would be interested in. Equally, I suppose when you are as successful as me, local people probably do want to hear about the company."

What? Was this some kind of joke? Polly wondered what Alan was working on. What was the angle on this?

She let Harold talk about the company and his role within it for the next forty minutes. She wasn't sure where she was going to go with this story for the paper, but it would probably make a good 'green and environmental' read for their audience. She couldn't afford to make it a long article though. It would have no commercial value for the paper, as his company wasn't paying for the space.

After well over an hour, Polly managed to bring the interview to a close and thanked Harold for his time, apologising once again. Just as she was about to leave, a thought crossed her mind.

"By the way, Harold, are you related to a young lady called Helen Pond?"

Harold looked puzzled.

"No, although it is funny you mention it, as Alan asked me the same thing. I thought it wasn't such a common name, but now I am beginning to wonder." He laughed.

Catching the train back to Bedfordshire, she was happy it wasn't close to rush hour when it would be busy with commuters and school children.

Returning to the office, she started to write up the article about Harold Pond. As she was doing so, Phil came past, and she decided to give him an update.

"Well, that's two people I have had to apologise to about my ex-colleague's behaviour. At least that should placate Harold Pond, and I think Nicky will be pleased with the extra publicity."

She was unsure if she should mention about Alan visiting Nicky a few days before, but decided she ought to tell him in case something else was hiding in the wings.

She could tell Phil was angry.

"Why didn't you let me know what was going on after seeing Nicky? What is he up to? Saying he is working for us when he has resigned! He could land us in so much trouble. I might need to talk to HR to understand what this could mean for us and how we protect the paper."

This was not what Polly had hoped for.

"Look, I know it is a lot to ask, but can you just give me a couple more days before you take any action, Phil? I am really confused, too, but hear me out. He is obviously working on something that he considers to be big. Perhaps we can try and work out what it is. Why would Alan be wasting his time writing about an ethical fruit and veg company? What is the link between Harold and Helen Pond? Is there an actual connection, or is he trying to rule one of them out? Both are mentioned in the notebook, but Harold says he doesn't know anyone called Helen Pond. What about this mystery donation to the Daffodil Dance Group? Harold doesn't seem to have any connection with them, but looking at Helen's Facebook page, she apparently does, but I don't know why."

"So, who is this Helen Pond?" Phil asked.

Polly went onto Facebook and showed him Helen's Facebook page. He looked at Polly.

"I've met her!" he responded, staring at the photo in front of him.

"So, you *do* know her?" Polly asked.

"Well, no, not exactly. Karen and I went out for a meal a few weeks ago and afterwards popped to the pub. Alan was there, and he was with that young lady. He was being cagey and really didn't want to talk to me."

Polly decided to try and placate Phil.

"I have left a voice message for Helen, asking her to contact me so I can try and find out what is going on from her perspective. I just need an angle, and I don't know what that could be yet, but I can wing it. Look, in Alan's notes against Helen's name, he has put 'lottery' and a question mark. We know someone did win the huge rollover a few months ago, and there was no publicity other than an idea it may be someone in this area, but I doubt if it was her. She seems very unassuming. However, it does seem that she may have come into some money, as Alan indicated in his notes that she bought a car, and apparently, he believes she isn't working. If she did make that donation, £8,500 is a lot of money, so where would that money have come from?"

Phil seemed to be getting impatient, but Polly continued anyway.

"As you know, he is still giving people the impression that he is working for *The Bedfordshire Post*, so why would he do that? Who else is he talking to? I think the only way to handle this is to be honest with Helen and see if she will open up. What do you think?"

Phil really wasn't sure. His main concern was to protect the newspaper, but nothing was going to be closed down until they knew what Alan was up to. Without other options, he reluctantly agreed.

"OK, speak with this Helen Pond. I don't think for one minute that she is the lottery winner, it's a ridiculous notion. However, whatever you say to her, I don't want it to result in any complaints about *The Bedfordshire Post*. Also, if you haven't come up with any conclusions within the next two days, I'm having a word with HR, as who knows what damage Alan can cause *The Bedfordshire Post* unless he is stopped."

Polly nodded in agreement. As she had not heard back from Helen, she decided to send her a private Facebook message. It was a little cryptic, but hopefully enough to get her to return her call.

Hi there. You don't know me, but I work at The Bedfordshire Post. *I know you are friends with Alan, but can we talk? It's about the Daffodil Dance Group. Please don't let him know I have contacted you, as I think my chat with you will be in your interest, not his, and I am worried for you. Thanks.*

Below that, she left her mobile number.

It was a risky move. If Helen was very good friends with Alan, Polly was potentially alerting him to the fact that she was aware something was going on. She hoped her instincts were right, and that Helen might be curious about what she had to say.

Later that day, Helen came across the private Facebook message.

Who was this woman called Polly? Why did she want to speak to her about Alan? A shiver went through her. She knew what this was probably about, and it was all due to her jumping in and not thinking before making the donation to the group.

Her phone pinged. It was a text message from Nicky, asking her to give her a ring as soon as possible. Now this was *too* much of a coincidence. Panic swept over her. What should she do? Trembling, she reached for the phone. Who should she speak to first?

She decided to ring Nicky, a known quantity. She dialled the number. Damn! Answerphone!

She left a message, asking Nicky to call her back.

She wondered if she ought to contact Polly in the meantime. She was obviously keen to speak with Helen. But, no, Polly was a journalist from the newspaper. All sorts of thoughts began to race through Helen's mind. She had come so far keeping her anonymity, and now, through one stupid, stupid mistake, she had blown it. George and Ben had warned her about this kind of thing happening.

Her next thought was whether to tell Ben. How could she confess that she had been such an idiot? She would have to tell him about her date with Alan.

She thought back to when she had made the donation. It had been such a difficult time. After losing Ana, she hadn't been thinking straight. While she was still mulling it over in her head, the phone rang.

"Helen? It's Nicky from the Daffodil Dance Group. Thanks for calling me back. I need to talk to you about your donation."

And there it was.

Nicky told Helen everything about how she had accidentally indicated to Alan that it was a woman who had made the donation and how he seemed to know about Helen, as he had even mentioned her by name. He had obviously shared his information, as a second journalist, Polly, had undertaken a follow-up interview with her.

"I am so sorry, I definitely haven't been talking to any journalists about who the donor may be, especially Alan."

Helen took a deep breath and sighed.

"Don't worry, it's not your fault. I do appreciate you letting me know. How are things going?"

Nicky told her that the group had come second in the finals. She decided not to tell Helen about the issues with their venue, as she didn't want her to think she was after another donation.

"You should come down and see the group. You can just say you are a friend of mine, nothing more. It would be lovely for you to see what a difference your donation has made to the group's confidence levels."

Helen thanked Nicky for the call and said she would definitely arrange a visit.

So, what should she do now? She was pleased that Nicky had been so honest with her.

She decided she would have to tell Ben what had happened. She knew it wouldn't be an easy conversation.

"For goodness' sake! What did George and I tell you? If this is to work, you can't afford to make that kind of mistake. Who is this guy? And now you have a second journalist calling you? You need to tell me everything, in as much detail as possible."

She now had to explain about her initial phone call from Alan and their evening out. Ben didn't seem too upset about the fact she had met up with him, which was a relief, although she did point out that they hadn't been seeing each other at the time. He seemed more disappointed in her slip-up with the donation, which made her feel even worse.

"Damage limitation is now important. You don't have to meet this journalist. If you would prefer, you can speak on the phone. She must think she knows something about the donation, as Nicky said that she had mentioned to Alan the donation was made by a woman. I imagine he would have looked up the name of the donor on the GoFundMe website and seen your name, since you didn't make it an anonymous donation."

He pondered for a moment.

"So, what does that mean and what does he know? He is aware that you have a new car as you told him on the date. He is assuming that, somehow, you managed to make a large donation to a dance group. If I were him, I would be wondering how you could afford to do that if you aren't working. He may not have thought about you being the lottery winner, but we can't rule it out.

"OK, let's break it down. We need to come up with a plausible story about how you were able to make the donation and afford a car. We also need to think of what you can say if there is the suggestion you may have won the lottery. A fair leap, but forewarned is forearmed. We just need to make you sound as convincing as possible, to get both this Alan and his colleague, Polly, off your back. I have a lot of work to do with you, to make you sound as though any cover story we come up with is believable. How are you with role play?"

That evening, Ben spent three hours rehearsing a script with her. He pretended to be both Polly and Alan, trying to catch her out. It was easy to do that, and she quickly became confused and upset.

"I can't do this. I'm just going to have to confess," she cried.

"Don't be ridiculous."

He pulled her close to him in a tight hug.

"You *can* do this. You have so much strength. I am being hard on you because they are journalists, and believe me, they won't tread carefully. Learn the script off to a 't' and you might just get away with it. Remember, stick to a basic explanation and don't try and elaborate. Now, let's start again…"

When she went to bed that night, she was still panicking. Could she pull this off? It was all such a mess. Before long, exhaustion took over and she was asleep.

Ben, however, remained awake for most of the night.

Reluctantly, the following morning, Helen called Polly. She got the answerphone, and asked if she could meet up with her the following day. About ten minutes later, Polly returned the call and confirmed she would meet her at a local coffee shop at four o'clock, which gave Ben enough time to conclude his meetings so he could accompany her.

When Ben and Helen arrived, Polly was already there. Seeing Helen scouring the room, she waved, recognising her from her Facebook page.

They made their way over to her. As it was late afternoon, it wasn't too busy.

Helen shook Polly's hand, and looking at Ben, he introduced himself as Helen's partner.

Polly had thought very carefully about how she would approach the interview and tried to make the pair welcome, ordering drinks and making casual conversation. When they seemed settled, she began.

"I know you might find this weird, but I need to talk to you about an ex-employee of *The Bedfordshire Post*, Alan Fletcher. I believe you know him?"

Helen nodded.

"Well, clearing his desk, I found a notebook. In it, he mentions your name, and a donation of £8,500. Do you want to comment?"

Ben was relieved. If that was all the journalist had, Helen could handle this. She just needed to keep her nerve and say exactly what they had rehearsed. He squeezed her hand for reassurance.

"Do you want to explain, Helen?"

She hesitated, before giving the details of the carefully rehearsed speech.

"Yes, it's true that I recently came into money, but it is all very innocent. Alan didn't even ask me about it, which seems strange if it was such a big deal. The money was left to me by my aunt who was something of an eccentric philanthropist. This monetary gift came with very specific instructions. She requested that some of it should be used to help someone else. If you want to check it's true, I did buy a car recently and that is what I used some of my inheritance for. You are also correct that it was me who made the donation to the Daffodil Dance Group. It seemed the kind of thing my aunt would have approved of, as she was a dancer in her younger days. I meant to mark it as an anonymous donation, as I didn't want any recognition for a gift which was really from my aunt. I don't understand what the problem is."

With her years of journalistic experience, Polly didn't believe Helen's answer. She didn't sound convincing, and her response appeared too scripted.

Polly took a moment before replying. She could tell that the delay was making Helen nervous, which was to her advantage.

"The problem is, and I know it might seem like a huge leap, but my ex-colleague Alan seems to believe that you may have won a lot more money than that, maybe even the lottery. I take it you saw the news, that the winner was someone in the area? It was a highly significant win, too. Now, if there is any truth to it, that would be an amazing story for my ex-colleague to get his teeth into."

Ben looked at her and laughed. She had to admit, he had a good poker face.

"Well, that's very fanciful! I think if *I* won the lottery, I wouldn't be spending money on a small dance group, I would be buying an expensive car, not the kind of practical one that Helen bought. I would also be looking at upgrading from a small flat to a much bigger property, treating myself to exotic holidays, splashing the cash. Wouldn't that make more sense? Has Helen done anything like that? If you have done your homework, you would know that's not the case. So I agree, it would be a very imaginative leap."

Polly noticed that Helen wouldn't make eye contact with her. If this was all so innocent, why did she appear so nervous?

Polly responded.

"I do agree, but Alan thinks there could be something to it. What do *you* have to say?"

Helen glanced briefly at Polly, but didn't answer. She looked alarmed, like a rabbit caught in the headlights.

"Why have you got Alan as a friend on Facebook? Did you know he resigned from the paper?" Polly asked.

Helen was surprised to hear that. Trying to remain composed, Ben's advice kept ringing in her ears: stick to a basic explanation and don't try and elaborate.

"I have only met him once. It was for, er, a date." Helen blushed, embarrassed to be talking about it in front of Ben. "He rang me, initially, regarding a survey he was doing for *The Bedfordshire Post*, and he asked me out. I went, but I soon discovered we had nothing in common. He did ring to ask for another date recently, but I told him I wasn't interested."

Polly decided to try a tougher approach. She didn't believe what she was hearing. She knew she would have to use shock tactics.

"Just to warn you, Alan is a really good journalist. He will keep digging until he finds whatever it is you are hiding, and because he has now resigned, he has nothing to lose."

She leant in closer to the couple, speaking quietly.

"Let's just suppose for a minute that you *had* won the lottery. Can you imagine what kind of scoop that would be for a journalist? A national would pay someone like Alan a great deal of money for something like that. Now *I* could do a lot more digging if I wanted, and yes, I might find I am barking up the wrong tree, but if I was a journalist who really wanted to make a name for myself, I would keep looking until I got to the truth. With no job, and knowing Alan as I do, he will be happy to undertake any dubious means to look into your finances, life, friends, anything that could give him a lead to prove he is right. I, on the other hand, am not that kind of journalist. Plus, at my age, I have nothing to prove. Two more years and I want to retire anyway."

She looked at the pair of them to see if there was any reaction. Helen continued to appear nervous, but she couldn't read what Ben was thinking, so she persisted.

"If you had won the lottery and wanted to keep it quiet, that's very difficult to do, and bearing in mind there is a ruthless journalist on your tail, my suggestion would be to seek professional advice to ensure you could cover your tracks. Obviously from my perspective, if there was any truth to that fanciful idea, I would be really interested to know about it and would be willing to make a deal, but not for an immediate article."

She let them digest what she had said before continuing.

"Why would I do that and what's in it for me? Well, it would be amazing to observe someone who had won the lottery, to understand how they manage their win and all the trappings it brings, especially if the intention was to remain anonymous. From a journalistic point of view, perhaps a few years down the line and if it was interesting enough, the story could be turned into a book. Anonymous, of course. *The Life of a Secret Lottery Winner*, or something along those lines. I could be a brilliant ally to have. I can also try and get Alan off the scent, and I think I know how I can do that. Hypothetically speaking, could that work for you, if you knew someone in that position?"

She addressed the question to both of them, although she knew it was Ben who was driving this meeting.

He didn't rush to answer, and his response was measured.

"It's a very fancy idea. Why would it be in your interest to sit on a story for so long if you felt it was true and how could someone know they could trust you? After all, you are a journalist," Ben asked.

She knew she would have to give something in return, and this revelation would be difficult and could backfire if her instincts were wrong, but she had to take the risk.

She took a deep breath.

"I am going to tell you something that I have never told anyone else. You then have something to use against me if you ever wanted to."

She lowered her voice even more, cautiously looking around her before continuing.

"I used to work in the City as a freelance journalist. I was young, ambitious and, to be honest, really good at my job. However, it was very much a man's world back then and really tough. I learnt early on that you had to be as ruthless as them and push and shove to get to the top, which sometimes meant cutting corners. I came across a story that I knew could have massive repercussions in the drug world and would catapult me to the attention of any national I wanted to work for. I found someone who wanted to get out of the drugs game, an informant who was willing to talk, and he knew key players at the top. This informant wanted to take things slowly as his identity was at stake. Keen to make my mark, all I could see was a sensational story, and I didn't want to wait."

She looked down, unable to look at either of them as she reminisced about the terrible tragedy that unfolded.

"I pushed too hard, went too quickly, and spoke to someone at one of the papers about my source. Unfortunately, the person I spoke to was in the pocket of the drugs cartel, and I didn't have a clue. My insensitivity, naivety, and big mouth got my informant, his wife, and two kids killed as they went for a walk in the park. I was immediately put into police protection before the case came up. I was a major witness and could provide a lot of information that would bring down many important people in the underworld, which it did. After the trial, I was given a new identity because I was told there would always be a target on my back. This meant I had to give up my family, friends, my whole life, including my name. Can you imagine living with that? I have had all this on my conscience for the past thirty-two years. My actions had resulted in people being killed, including a wife and children who were totally innocent. I had a breakdown."

Ben could see how much of an effect reliving this event was having on Polly. She was visibly shaking.

"When I started to recover, I worked in a cafe for a long time, feeling I couldn't continue being a journalist when I knew the catastrophic impact it could have on people's lives. However, journalism was in my blood and the only thing I knew. So, after years of counselling to cope with what I'd caused and rebuilding myself, I moved to Bedford and joined *The Bedfordshire Post*, writing nice, feel-good stories. Nothing that would bring me into the spotlight – I would leave those pieces to other journalists. I know the devastating effect of what one sentence or article in a newspaper can do, even long after the story has been told. I can't allow someone else to go through all that if I can stop it. Whether you won the lottery or not, it was a wonderful gesture to make a donation to that small dance group. For some of them, it will be an amazing memory to look back on, others may even become professional dancers because of the experience they have had, while some will have gained confidence, enabling them to go on and achieve remarkable things in their lives. Whatever their paths, your generous gift will have had an everlasting impact on those kids."

She stopped for a while to compose herself. She could see that they both appeared to be listening intently to what she had to say.

"So, if you have come into a great deal of money, I would be intrigued by what motivates you and what you decide to do with it. I don't want someone like Alan getting hold of a story like this; taking something that has given immense pleasure to so many people and twisting it into something ugly that could ruin lives. If you feel my suggestion could be an option later down the line, all I would ask is that you would consider allowing me to tell the story? I understand why you may think you can't trust me, but believe me, I would make a good ally. I've also shared my own story, and apart from you two, *no one* knows about my new identity. If you ever wanted to blackmail me, I am potentially as huge a story for any national as you are, and my life could be at risk if my identity was ever revealed. There are still people out there who want me dead. So, to be honest, I have even more to lose than you do. My name was Stephanie Loadsman before I became Polly Cuthbert. Look me up."

She pulled out a card from her purse.

"Here's my business card. Think about what I've said, just don't leave it too long, for your own sake. Alan is literally on your tail. I can try and make that go away if we move fast, but we would have to be one hundred per cent honest with each other. The sooner I can try and put him back in his box, the better for you. Once he really starts digging, it will be out of my control. I hope to speak to you soon."

With that, she got up and walked to the till. Having paid for the coffees, she smiled at them and was gone.

When Polly had walked out of the cafe, she turned and watched Ben and Helen through the window for a moment, unable tell what they would do. She knew that when someone had relied on her to protect them before, it had gone disastrously wrong. She was sure Helen was hiding a secret, and she didn't want Alan to destroy this poor girl's life. Perhaps any intervention she could undertake would be some form of atonement for her previous actions.

"Wow! She has some nerve!" exclaimed Ben, nervously running his fingers through his hair.

"You sound as though you admire her," Helen replied sullenly.

"Well, she did put up a pretty powerful case for having her on your side. This Alan sounds like a real lowlife. I don't know what you were thinking getting involved with him, but there's no point in me banging on about how naïve you were, it wouldn't achieve anything. Also, I know you weren't thinking straight when you made the donation."

He grabbed her hand in his.

"Equally, it emphasises the point George and I were trying to make about the importance of being discreet and how dangerous it can be if you aren't."

She nodded. "Do you trust her?"

Ben seemed calm, but she was still feeling very shaken from the meeting with Polly.

"I don't know. At the end of the day, she is a journalist. However, if what she has said is true, she would have quite a lot to lose herself if *her* story came out. Perhaps we should look her up?"

Ben went on his phone and looked up Stephanie Loadsman. Yes, there she was, admittedly looking much younger in the photo, but although her appearance had changed as she had put on weight and her hair was a different colour and a shorter style, it was definitely her. It was true, he couldn't find anything about her after the court case. A journalist with morals? With Ben's past experiences of journalists, that did seem strange, but she had obviously been through so much herself and had learnt a terrible lesson. But working with any journalist, whatever their motive, would be a huge gamble. However, he recognised that Alan needed to be dealt with. He turned to Helen, just as a tear began to roll down her face.

"I'm sorry," Helen said.

He hugged her.

"Let's sleep on it tonight. Tomorrow's a new day."

Ben didn't sleep much that night. This was something he had never faced before. All he wanted to do was protect his girlfriend, but he wasn't sure how he could do that with what they were now facing.

Polly arrived in the office early the following morning. She'd also had a sleepless night. Opening up to Ben and Helen had brought back awful memories of a time in her life that she had thought had been buried. She had given up her whole life: family, friends, and even after all these years, she was hesitant about making new connections for fear of her past catching up with her.

She went into Phil's office.

"We need to shut Alan down. He lied to Nicky, saying he was still working for *The Bedfordshire Post*. He's been following his own agenda, whatever that is, and now he is trying to dig up dirt on an innocent young woman."

Polly didn't want to say anything about Helen's story, so played her trump card.

"He could seriously damage *The Bedfordshire Post's* reputation and is a liability. Speak to whoever you need to, but you have to stop him."

23

Six weeks after resigning from *The Bedfordshire Post*, Alan still hadn't found another job. Life was not going well for him. To add insult to injury, speaking to a solicitor, he had discovered that he had no case against his former employer, as he had walked out.

Due to his lack of finances, he had been forced to return home to his parents' house. It really had been a last resort. He knew it wasn't a good look, and he could hardly invite girls back there for a night of passion. His parents, especially his dad, wouldn't be impressed to find a girl coming down the stairs in the morning. He could hear him now: 'we brought you up better than that, son.' He would probably have something to say to the girl he had brought home, too.

His mum was overjoyed to have 'her little boy' back, making him cooked meals every day and washing and ironing his clothes. His dad, on the other hand, was far from happy, as he had changed Alan's bedroom into his beer brewing room, and unfortunately, the aroma permeated into all his clothes, leaving him smelling like he'd had a heavy session in the pub.

His life was a mess and the whole situation made him angry. Very angry. Phil should have been pleased with the way he had been digging into potentially explosive stories. But, no, he was content for *The Bedfordshire Post* to continue to be a small, local paper, selling stories about puppies rescued from a drain or a little girl who raised five hundred pounds for charity.

Once again, his thoughts returned to the donation made to the dance group. He knew there was a story there, and Helen Pond was almost certainly at the centre of it all. If he could just get to the bottom of it, he was sure it was a story that a national would be interested in and he could then ask them for a job.

Like a dog with a bone, he knew he couldn't let it go. It just didn't make sense. Where was her money coming from? How could she afford her car and even her flat, when she was in between jobs?

He had been keeping tabs on her Facebook page, and recently, there had been lots of photos of her and some guy called Ben. He looked a right drip, although from his clothes and the car he was driving, he obviously had money, so maybe it was his money she was spending. But she had been splashing the cash on her car before she met him. So, what was her source of income? How had she come into money? A rich relative? He needed to know, and he still wasn't happy with the way she had brushed him off when they had last spoken. Why would someone like her do that to him?

Alan had tried to ring her a couple of times, but on

each occasion, it went to voice mail. He couldn't believe she would ignore him.

However, currently, there were other things to worry about. His credit card debts were now spiralling out of control. He had also borrowed money from friends, and they were now becoming impatient, asking when they were going to be repaid. He had tried to speak with his dad to see if he would bail him out, but he wasn't prepared to listen to him.

"No one gave me handouts when I was young, and I was married to your mother by your age. You need to take some responsibility for your actions," was his cold response.

Yesterday had been the final straw. A friend had suggested going for a drink, and Alan had been looking forward to it. However, one pint in, and his friend passed on some worrying news. There was a rumour that a girl he had recently dumped was saying she was pregnant and believed Alan to be the father. What? He was shocked. He assumed she had been taking precautions. It was what women did these days, wasn't it? There was no way he wanted to get trapped with a baby, and definitely not with the girl concerned. A baby was certainly not on his agenda.

Things seemed to be going from bad to worse. What could he do?

Then he remembered something. A couple of months before he left *The Bedfordshire Post*, Greg, an old friend of his in Germany, had contacted him, as his paper was looking for journalists to go to various locations worldwide to report on news items, and he believed it would be perfect for Alan. At the time, he hadn't been interested, but now, this could be the solution to his problems. Perhaps this was the breather he needed, and if he was travelling the world, it would also mean he could pick up a girl in every location, without having to worry about any ties.

Helen could wait; she wasn't going anywhere. He had kept his journal, which contained everything he had uncovered so far, so he could always pick up her story at a later date. His own precarious situation needed to be resolved, and quickly. He rang his friend.

"Greg, my friend, how are you doing? Enjoying all the fräulein's and everything else Germany has to offer? Listen, I've been thinking about the vacancy you mentioned as a world correspondent at your newspaper. Is it still available?"

"It is, but I thought you weren't interested."

"Well, I have thought about it and believe it would be a good opportunity for me."

Greg was taken aback. If he remembered correctly, the last conversation they'd had, Alan had implied his current job was much more interesting and highbrow than that of a world correspondent abroad.

"OK. Would you like me to tell you more about what the job entails?"

Alan just wanted things to get moving quickly. *Why is Greg wasting time with details?* he thought.

"No, don't bore me with the specifics, I am sure it will be fine. Just let me know who I need to speak to."

Greg asked him to send through his CV, and he would then get someone from the paper to ring to discuss the vacancy. Alan said he would be available immediately, if that helped.

Greg wondered what the urgency was to get away from the UK, but he didn't query it further. He knew that his friend could be a difficult and miserable individual at times, so he didn't want to make him cross.

Emilia, head of the overseas correspondents' team, rang Alan the following day. She was keen to clarify what the post would entail. Being impatient and eager to leave the UK, he said Greg had filled him in and he was keen to take on a new and exciting opportunity.

After ten minutes, he had her eating out of his hand, and as a result, she was happy for him to join them as soon as possible. When could he fly out? He said he hoped it would be within a week but would let her know as soon as everything was tied up in England. She stated that the paper would pay for his flight and asked if his passport was up to date. He confirmed it was valid for another seven years, so that was one less thing to worry about. He just had to get vaccinations sorted before he went. Greg had agreed that he could initially stay with him for a few nights, if the paper hadn't arranged accommodation in Germany, depending on when his first assignment commenced. He also suggested that Alan could leave his possessions at his while he was away, as each mission was typically six to nine months each, and it seemed a waste to rent somewhere that he wouldn't be using.

Alan was still keen to have some finance in place to help him with his lifestyle if he was jetting to exotic locations. As this would be to help his career, he decided to tackle his dad again to see if he would help. He would need to make it sound as though it was in his dad's interest to loan him the money, and he thought he knew a way of achieving that. He decided he would ask for more than he wanted, recognising his dad would probably agree to pay half of what he asked for, but at least it would get him started. He had a few things he could sell to raise additional funds if he needed to, so he was happy he would be OK until his first pay packet. He rang his dad at work to ask if they could have a discussion about his future over dinner that evening, and although he didn't sound excited about the prospect, he agreed.

During the day, he popped to the supermarket to get his mum some flowers and found some in the reduced section. No point in spending more than he had to. He peeled off the reduced sticker and as he expected, when he gave them to her, she was over the moon. He needed to try and get her on his side.

His mum had cooked a roast dinner, sensing there was going to be something important her son wanted to discuss. Maybe he was thinking of settling down, she wondered.

From Alan's perspective, the only things he would really miss about being at home was his mum's cooking and her washing his clothes.

As usual, they ate in silence, and once the meal was over, his dad, never one to mince his words, said, "Well, lad, what do you want to talk about?"

Alan cleared his throat. He had been preparing for this all day.

"I have been offered a job in Germany. It would take me all over the world, reporting on all the big news stories. The thing is, I would love to go, but I just haven't got the funds."

His dad snorted.

"And it's my problem because…?"

Alan hated eating humble pie and knew he was going to have to put on a really good performance and lie to get what he wanted.

"It's the opportunity of a lifetime. I could even end up on the TV making live broadcasts. Can you imagine seeing your son on the news? Something to brag about to your friends. The thing is, I can't go unless I have the money to finance my flight, accommodation for six months, and general expenses I may incur in the early days. I wondered if you would be able to give me around £5,000?"

His mum took a sharp intake of breath before nervously waiting for her husband's reaction.

His dad didn't even look at him and, for good effect, left a considerable pause before he replied.

"That's a considerable amount of money. When would you pay me back? It would be a loan, nothing more. I am not made of money you know."

Jim, his dad, had never been paternal towards him. He had shown no interest at any stage of his life. Alan didn't even know if he was proud of his achievements.

"I could pay you back as soon as I was settled, which shouldn't be too long. As I will be travelling all over the world, they'll probably give me an additional allowance for living expenses too. Please, I really wouldn't ask if I didn't have to."

With no immediate response, he then played his trump card.

"It would also mean you could have your beer brewing room back."

As he had imagined, it was enough for his dad to reply fairly quickly.

"OK. I'll see if I can transfer the money in the next couple of days. However, we will need to have a strict repayment plan. When are you leaving?"

Alan explained he would need to go back to his friend and start organising flights and arranging accommodation. He wasn't going to tell his dad that those expenses had already been met by the newspaper. To be honest, he was very surprised his dad had agreed to the full amount. He'd worry about repayments at a later stage, as he didn't envisage returning to the UK for a long time.

His mum was desperately trying to hold back the tears.

"Darling, when will we see you again? I'll miss you so much."

She then brightened up.

"Perhaps when you are settled, we can pop over for a long weekend? Germany's not far, is it?"

He didn't reply. The last thing he wanted was his parents turning up and cramping his style.

He thanked his dad for the loan and gave him his bank details.

His thoughts turned briefly to *The Bedfordshire Post*. He hoped the German newspaper wouldn't contact them for a reference. From what Greg had told him, it seemed the paper was desperate for overseas correspondents, so he thought it unlikely.

On the day of his departure, while he was packing, his mum knocked on the bedroom door. As there was no response, she decided to just enter.

"Do you need any help?"

"No, I'm fine."

He didn't even bother to look up.

She sat on his bed. He'd hoped she would just go away, but it was clear she had something she wanted to say. He hoped it would be quick.

"Listen, don't tell your father, but I've been saving some money. I'd hoped to give it to you when you got married, but you obviously need the money now."

She produced a very thick padded envelope from her bag.

"There's a thousand pounds in there. Along with the money from your father, it should help make things a little easier for you in the first few months."

"Thanks. Yes, it will be useful."

She went to give him a hug, but he pulled away.

"I'm sorry, I really do need to pack."

Feeling sad, she reluctantly left the room. As much as she loved her son, she couldn't believe how thoughtless and cold he often acted towards her. Unfortunately, she could see a lot of her husband in him. She really hoped it wasn't how he treated his friends. No, she was sure he wouldn't.

Alan was ecstatic. An extra thousand pounds! His dad had agreed to more than he had hoped for and now his mum had given him additional funds. He would enjoy having some great nights out around the world with all this money. If he didn't come back for a few years, his dad would hopefully have forgotten about the money, or at least the exact figure he'd given him. Life was beginning to look great again.

24

Polly was sitting at her desk when Susie came bounding through to the main office, crying.

"Whatever is the matter?" Polly asked, sitting her down at the desk opposite hers.

"The most awful thing! I've just heard Alan has taken a job in Germany and flew out yesterday! He didn't even let me know. I had hoped that one day, he would realise what a mistake he had made by dumping me. We would start seeing each other again, and longer term, maybe marriage would have been on the cards. I'm heartbroken!"

The howls and tears recommenced. Polly handed her a tissue.

She was always amazed at how dramatic things were with Susie, but she let it go. Also, she had never been able to understand what women saw in Alan. He was selfish, arrogant, and full of himself. But women never stopped fawning over him for some reason.

This development, however, was very unexpected, and she needed to know more.

"I am sure there is someone out there who is even better for you. It's his loss, not yours. So, tell me what you know about this job?"

It was handy, Polly thought, that Susie knew so much about what was happening with him.

When Susie left, Polly went into Phil's office to give him the news. She shut the door, so no one else could hear, and told him what Susie had said.

"Funnily enough," said Phil, "a few days ago I did have a call from a woman at *Der Weltkorrespondent*. She said she had offered Alan a job and wanted a reference. Fortunately, she just asked me to confirm he had worked here and for how long. She didn't ask about his work or behaviour. I don't know what I would have said if she had asked for more details, as I couldn't give him a glowing reference. I must admit, I am surprised he has taken the job. The work sounds both difficult and dangerous. I wouldn't have thought something like that would be his cup of tea. Still, it gets him out of my hair, so what do I care? Thanks for filling me in."

This was great news for Helen. Polly couldn't wait to ring her and bring her up to date.

25

As agreed, *Der Weltkorrespondent* paid for Alan to fly business class to Germany and were even willing to fund his first three months' accommodation up front. *They must really have wanted me*, he thought, as he admired the amount of leg room and the comfortable seat he had on the plane. He had also enjoyed the benefits of lounge access before he had boarded and before long, he would probably be served a choice of first-class food and alcoholic beverages. Hopefully, all his adventures around the world would enable him to travel in this way.

He wondered where his first assignment would be; Thailand, America, maybe even Dubai. This was the start of a whole new life for him. Relaxing, he waited for the remaining passengers to board.

After landing, he picked up his luggage and made his way out to arrivals. The newspaper had arranged for someone to pick him up, and he soon saw a gentleman with a sign bearing his name.

"Hi, I'm Alan," he confirmed.

The driver took his suitcase, and they headed out of the airport to the car.

"I Friedrich. I work as driver for *Der Weltkorrespondent*. Welcome to Germany. I take you to company," he said in broken English.

It was only a short journey to *Der Weltkorrespondent's* offices. Alan was impressed. It was a very modern building and considerably larger than *The Bedfordshire Post* office. *I've really landed on my feet*, he thought.

He walked into reception and said he had an appointment with Emilia.

She came down to meet him. Emilia was older than she sounded on the phone but was still an attractive woman. Taking him upstairs to her office, she gave him some paperwork to complete. Fortunately, it was in English, but he didn't bother reading it, just signing where she indicated.

"So, that's all the paperwork and formalities completed. Now, I am sure you are keen to know where your first assignment will be?"

Alan nodded.

"It is Afghanistan. You will fly out in three days. It will give us enough time to fill you in on all the information you will need and arrange for a float until your first month's wages are paid. Welcome!"

He looked at her incredulously. Surely, she was joking!

"But that's a war zone! Is there nowhere else you can send me?" ·

She laughed.

"You funny Englishman! What do you think a world correspondent does for our paper? You said Greg had told you what the job would involve? We have all your flights, accommodation, and your safety equipment organised. Why do you think we are paying you so much money?"

He felt sick. This was not what he had imagined. He should have asked for more details and not been so arrogant. All he had seen was an escape route.

It would be too late to back out now. He knew the paper had invested a lot of money in him. He would have to undertake this initial assignment and then find an exit strategy. Perhaps he could fake some foreign disease when he was out there if things got too bad. Surely the areas the journalists went to weren't as deadly as they looked on TV, were they? It was all probably just for show. He soon had his answer.

"You will be working with a translator, and luckily, we have found you a new photographer. The last guy we had out there was shot, and although he has recovered, he doesn't want to go there again."

Alan had thought his problems in the UK were bad enough. But this…What was he walking into?

26

Polly rang Helen to give her an update.

Ben was with Helen, so she put Polly on speaker.

He could see the relief on her face as they listened to what Polly had to say about Alan's move abroad.

"So, where does that leave us?" Ben asked.

"Well, as far as Alan's concerned, I don't think he will have the time, energy, or resources, at the moment, to be looking into anything, so unless he comes back to the UK, you can breathe a sigh of relief. I know you don't trust me, but just remember, I have given you great leverage if I backtracked and published anything currently. However, at some stage, I would like to have a longer chat and learn more about you, and whatever your 'situation' is. Let's just leave things for now. Enjoy the break from Alan."

With that, Polly hung up. She thought for a moment. Did she really want to cover whatever this story turned out to be? Possibly, but not now. There was no rush.

Back at Helen's, Ben pulled Helen towards him.

"You have had an amazing stroke of luck. Please, please don't do anything like that again. Speak to me, George, or Kathy if you want to go ahead with anything before the company is set up. My nerves can't take it!" he said, laughing.

It was a relief that she could, at least for the time being, put Alan behind her. She shuddered, thinking about what could have happened. However, she was now in a different position, with the company in the final stages of being established. She vowed not to make any further donations until the trustees were handling things for her. Ben didn't appear too upset about what had occurred, and they could now concentrate on moving forward.

27

Ben had made Helen breakfast, and while eating, they talked about their plans to visit Alice and Dick later that morning. From what they had told her, the renovations were almost complete, and she was keen to see the changes. She also knew Alice would make a fuss of Ben, and when she had rung to make the booking, Alice said she would bake a red velvet cake ready for his arrival.

Purchasing a bench and some trees in memory of Ana was still on her mind. She was keen to go and find the location with Ben.

They took his car. He seemed so nervous about meeting Alice and Dick, although he had seen them briefly at the funeral. He was aware of how important they were in Helen's life and was keen to make a good impression. As a result, not knowing what they would prefer, he had bought two bottles of expensive wine: one white, one red, and a beautiful box of chocolates wrapped in a pink ribbon. Helen had only ever seen chocolates like that on

TV. As they got into the car, she reassured him he really didn't have to try so hard, and she was sure they would love him just as much as she did.

"Do you?" he asked.

"Sorry?" She looked at him, a little confused at what he was asking.

"Do you love me?"

She had always hoped he would say those three words to her first, but it had just slipped out. What the hell.

"Yes, I do," she said slowly. "I know it's early days, but the one thing I have learned from losing Ana is not to waste time and opportunities. If you don't feel the same or it's too early, I understand, but I just can't lie."

Leaning over, he kissed her. He cupped her face in his hands, looked deeply into her eyes, and replied, "I love you too."

The conversation had made her feel light and happy on the way down to Clacton, and the journey gave her the opportunity to tell him more about Alice and Dick and the part they had played in both her and Ana's lives over the years, as well as during Helen's childhood.

Alice hadn't asked too many questions when Helen mentioned Ben was also coming. She did, however, enquire whether they wanted a double, twin, or two single rooms. It was silly to mess around. She confirmed a double would be fine and she would pay on arrival. Alice was insistent she wouldn't accept any money for their stay, but Helen threatened her by saying if she didn't let her pay, they would go to one of their competitors. She eventually agreed, but at a discounted rate, in return for Helen's recent help with the decorating. Jokingly, Helen said it didn't make good business sense, giving out discounts. Alice reminded her the B & B wasn't officially open yet, so from her perspective, the visit was as friends, not as guests.

Ben was horrified Helen had suggested she would pay. Forever the gentleman and to create a good impression with Alice and Dick, as well as payment, he would also treat them all to a meal out during their stay.

As predicted, on their arrival, Alice immediately made a big fuss of Ben. She was gushing all over him like a schoolgirl. While she got to know him, Helen wandered outside to take in the refurbished exterior of the building. It was now a very soft peach colour and looked fresh and inviting. The garden had been tidied, and there was a new bench, hanging baskets by the front door, and a smart new sign above it. It looked really pretty.

When she returned inside, Alice showed her guests to their room, which looked so different from the old ones. Two comfy leather armchairs were placed by the window, and on a little table in between the chairs, a pair of binoculars, plus a book on British birds for those who may want to birdwatch or look at the boats out at sea. Ben was in his element!

Once they had settled in, Alice gave them a tour of the rest of the B & B. Even though it was only a few weeks since her last visit, Helen couldn't believe how much more they had achieved.

With careful planning, they had even managed to create a couple of extra bedrooms by re-organising some of the ground-floor space, resulting in two beautifully decorated, seaside-themed family rooms. The interior was as impressive as the outside; modern and bright, it was a relief to see all the 1960s ornaments were now gone.

You could tell how pleased Alice and Dick were with the results, and they talked excitedly about the future of the B & B. It was lovely to see them so animated.

Apparently, they had already been in contact with a couple of charities to offer reduced prices for their members and were due to receive their first guests from them in a couple of weeks' time.

Alice then asked Dick to bring tea and the red velvet cake she had made the day before into the lounge.

"Er, I think we are out of that, love," Dick said in a very shifty manner.

"Oh no, not again! Don't tell me, you've eaten *all* the cake, have you? Honestly, Dick, you should be the size of a house. I have told you before, the nice cake is for guests, not for you!"

Everyone burst out laughing, and when he realised no one was really angry with him, a very red-faced Dick joined in too.

"Luckily, I made a batch of bread-and-butter pudding this morning, which is still cooling in the oven. You didn't find that too, did you, Dick?"

Mumbling, he confirmed he hadn't, and soon they were tucking into big slices filled with juicy sultanas and topped with a sprinkling of sugar.

When everyone had finished, it was still very early, so Helen suggested taking Ben for a walk around Clacton. This gave her the opportunity to point out all the regular places she used to visit with Ana.

When they arrived at the fish and chip shop by the

beach, she was disappointed to find that in the last few months, it had been changed into an upmarket cafe-style restaurant called The Lounge. Ben suggested they try it, so reluctantly, she let him usher her into the building for a cup of tea. She had to admit, it really was impressive. Ben looked round at the walls in admiration. They were covered in quirky paintings, and it had a 1920s feel. They decided to go back there in the evening for a meal. Although she missed the old fish and chip shop, Helen knew Ana would have liked the new place even more, and it would also have become a regular haunt of theirs. Although she understood she would still reminisce about the times she had spent in Clacton with her parents and then Ana, she would now make new memories with Ben.

Ben said, "Don't be offended, but Clacton is not somewhere I would have thought to go for a break. However, when the sun is shining, I can see the attraction with a view like this." He pointed out of the window towards the beach.

It was great to hear he appreciated the area and could see it in the same way she did.

As the sun was shining, they continued to wander around. They walked to the end of the pier where a few fishermen were hoping to get a catch. They watched for a while, and talking to one of the fishermen, Ben was informed there had been a few small bass caught much earlier in the day but nothing since.

They finally headed back to the B & B for a shower and to get ready for their evening out. Ben went straight upstairs while Helen went to find Alice. She wanted to get her opinion of Ben. As usual, Alice was to be found in the kitchen, hands buried deep in a bowl. She was making some bread.

"I thought I would offer you some home-made bread for breakfast tomorrow. It is also nice to be able to bash at it – it's a good way to take out my frustration," she laughed.

"How are you feeling about the renovations and the new start?" Helen asked, perching on one of the breakfast stools.

Alice broke from the bread-making and, wiping her hands on her apron, came to sit next to Helen.

"Well, I'll be honest, at first, I wasn't sure. We had come into all this money and my initial thought was we should close and buy a small cottage somewhere.

"I mean, Dick and I aren't spring chickens. Did we really want to carry on? I know the letter we received said the money was to renovate the B & B, but who would have known? However, the more Dick and I talked it through, we realised we had to carry on. I mean, could you honestly see Dick and I sitting in a couple of armchairs with newspapers and a cup of tea all day long? It just isn't us. We would still need to be busy doing something, and what would that be? The only thing we have ever known is running this place.

"Also, we would miss having the constant stream of people in our lives. For us, a quiet house would be awful. However, to make life a little easier, we are employing someone part-time to give me a hand with the cleaning and making up the rooms. So, I think we have made the right decision. If we haven't, or when we eventually find it all too much, then we will sell-up, but for the time being, it's business as usual. Having the idea to offer accommodation to people who, under normal circumstances, wouldn't be able to afford a break, well, it makes it even more special."

Deciding to take a risk, she began to press Alice for more information.

"And you have absolutely no idea who could have left you the money?"

Alice thought for a moment.

"Other than Dick's suggestion of it being Sally, the old lady with the cat, I don't know. It was an amazing amount of money and very generous. It's the kind of thing that only happens in films, not to the likes of us. Whoever it was has really made a difference to our lives. Dick won't admit it, but I know he was having sleepless nights about what would happen in the not-too-distant future."

For a moment, Alice seemed to be thinking about how the future could have been, if it wasn't for the unexpected donation, but she quickly snapped out of it.

"Anyway, enough of that. What about this nice young man you have brought with you? I think he is incredibly handsome, and by the car he drives, he must be quite successful! Hang on to him, he seems genuine and kind, and it looks like he has money."

If only Alice knew the truth. But it was something she could never know. It was great they had been able to have an honest conversation about what a difference the money had made. If she had known where the capital had come from, she would never have accepted the money in the first place.

"So, what are your plans for the rest of the weekend?" she asked.

Explaining about the Woodland Estate, she told Alice about wanting to buy trees and a bench in memory of Ana. Alice thought it was a wonderful idea.

"And how are you holding up, love?" she asked, looking at her guest intently.

Trying to fight back the tears, she didn't know how to reply. Losing Ana was still so raw.

Alice hugged her tightly.

"It does get a little easier, but the pain of losing someone special never really goes away," Alice said wisely. "And Ana was a *very* special person. Of course you shouldn't forget her, but equally, she would expect you to move on with your life."

Helen knew Alice was right, but 'moving on' was such an awful expression as it seemed to dismiss all the wonderful times they had shared together in the past. Yes, the loss would get easier, but her life would never be the same without Ana. She was grateful that all her plans were keeping her occupied, and Ben was being as considerate and understanding as he could be.

As she started to go up to the room, Ben was coming down the stairs.

"I thought I had lost you," he said, laughing.

She ushered him back upstairs, and when they were back in the room, she filled him in on the conversation she'd had with Alice.

It was a relief to know the donation to the B & B had gone to plan, but Helen had found it stressful, and concluded, in future, it might be better not knowing how things turned out. Perhaps the best approach would be for the trustees to give her a brief update, as that way, she wouldn't be disappointed. If the trustees felt there was additional information they needed to share, they could enlighten her.

Ben then disappeared into the bathroom to get ready for the evening, and when he came out again, Helen thought he looked *amazing*! He was wearing a navy jumper, white T-shirt underneath, and blue chinos. She knew how lucky she was to have such an incredible man like him in her life.

He waited patiently while she showered and chose a suitable outfit. Wanting to make an impression, she had bought some new clothes for the weekend. This included a beige cashmere jumper (Ana would have approved), brown trousers, and a practical pair of low-heeled brown boots, in case there was walking involved. It wouldn't look good tottering in high heels and ending up with blisters. She had also invested in a long woollen coat, as although the weather was warm during the day, the evenings were still chilly, and as she knew from previous visits, it was often windy by the sea.

Heading out, she was pleased she had the coat – the wind was blowing, so she pulled the collar closer.

Taking her hand, Ben led her into the restaurant.

During the day, it had been reasonably quiet, with mainly older couples enjoying a cream tea or a sandwich. This evening, the clientele was younger and there was much more of a buzz, with everyone chatting excitedly, which meant it was harder to hear each other talk. They managed to grab a table overlooking the sea. It was a lovely setting. Ben went and ordered some drinks while Helen looked at the menu.

The meal was lovely, and after a couple more drinks, they headed out into the cold night air.

Deciding to walk along the seafront, it was quiet and still, apart from the gentle sound of the waves breaking on the beach.

"I think I would really love to buy myself a small cottage by the sea." she murmured.

"Where? In Clacton?"

"Maybe around here, I am not sure. I need to think about it. A little bolthole, for when I just want to get away on my own," she replied.

Realising how selfish that might sound, she elaborated.

"I really want to be with you, but sometimes, it might be nice, just to have my own space for a while. So much has happened. Can you understand?"

He nodded.

They turned back to the B & B and decided on an early night. Helen knew the following day may be difficult, making plans for a place to remember Ana. It was important to find the perfect setting.

28

After a full English breakfast, with Alice giving Ben three sausages instead of the usual two she normally gave to her other guests, Helen and Ben headed off to the Woodland Estate.

Helen struggled to remember where her and Ana had parked in the past as it was a few years since the girls had last visited, but Ben soon found signs to one of the car parks and drove in.

It was so peaceful. The only noise they could hear so early in the morning were the sounds of birds chirping in the trees. Crossing over a little bridge, Ben stopped for a moment, looking upwards and pointing at a bird circling above their heads.

"Look, a red kite," he said.

Helen was very surprised he seemed to know about birds.

He then confessed that in his youth, he used to go out bird spotting with his granddad.

"I can name you a number of different birds, even by their call if I can't see them," he said proudly.

Having looked on the Woodland Estate website, he informed her there was a huge variety of both birds and wildlife, including water voles, otters, and muntjac deer.

They spent an enjoyable couple of hours walking through the woods, the sun casting shadows through the trees. After a while, they found a stream, and Ben laid out the blankets they'd brought with them next to it, together with the picnic Alice had hastily packed earlier.

"So, what do you think? Is it a good idea to buy some woodland in memory of Ana?"

Ben was stretched out on one of the blankets, his eyes closed. He looked totally relaxed.

"It *is* beautiful here and really tranquil. Although I hadn't known her for long, I am sure Ana would be really pleased with this location."

She was so relieved he agreed with her.

She laid down beside him.

"Great, that's settled then. When we have finished here, we can go to the shop near the entrance, and I'll pick up the details to get things moving."

For the first time in her life, Helen felt a sense of purpose and direction. Even though she would have preferred to do everything with Ana by her side, she realised it was possible to achieve anything she wanted with the money. This *could* work.

The afternoon went by quite quickly as they took in the beauty of the woodland, and Ben was eager to point out a stag beetle and the names of a few butterflies that fluttered past. He said he would buy a little nature book for their next visit so they could fully immerse themselves in the fauna and flora.

When they got back to the B & B, Ben suggested to Alice and Dick that to save them having to cook, he'd order a takeaway. Alice agreed and soon they were helping themselves to the different Indian dishes. Dick eagerly tucked in to the spicy food in front of him, and Alice enquired how the day had gone.

Before the couple had a chance to reply, Dick's face had turned bright red. His eyes were watering as he rushed to the sink for a glass of water. The curry was much hotter than he expected.

When he had recovered, Helen began to tell them more about the woodland area, and they were keen to take a drive out and have a look for themselves before they started to get embroiled in the official re-opening of the B & B.

Helen's sleep was badly interrupted that night with dreams of Ana. She knew there was something she still needed to do, so the following morning, she got up early.

Dressing quickly and as quietly as she could, she left a note on the pillow for Ben.

Heading into the kitchen she made a flask of tea, packed it into a carrier bag and closed the front door behind her. Walking towards the beach, she wanted to be on her own to undertake her next task.

Clacton beach early in the morning was usually very empty, and it was no different on this occasion, just a few joggers and dog-walkers.

She headed to the bench where the best friends had fish and chips during their last visit to Clacton. For a while, she sat there, just watching the palm trees swaying in the wind. They seemed totally at odds with Clacton, but with the sea behind them and the sun shining, Ben had recognised with a little imagination, you could be anywhere in the world.

Sitting there, a slight breeze brushed her face.

It was like Ana was with her, touching her cheek with her hand, which she often did when she was concerned about her.

Reaching into her pocket, she withdrew the envelope George had given her. With trembling fingers, she slowly opened it and took out the letter.

Hi Helen,

Well, what a whirlwind! Who would have known what we would face over the last twelve months! Sadness, happiness, and so many other emotions along the way.

I wish I could still be there with you, to continue your wonderful and exciting journey, but unfortunately, it was not meant to be. I am pleased I could share as much of it with you as I have done. It has been the perfect distraction for me, something to focus on rather than thinking about this God-awful disease. I am truly grateful.

You think you are not strong, but you really are much stronger than you give yourself credit for, and if you have Ben helping you along the way (and I hope you do), I know you'll achieve great things.

He can take over from me and support you with your ambitions. Please remember, though, you are more than enough in your own right, and you don't need anyone else to provide that validation.

I am so pleased to have called you my best friend. You have always been my rock, my constant, my support, the one person who I could lay bare all my dreams, hopes, and fears. You are amazing, and in the dark days after my death, don't dwell on your loss, just remember all of our good times together. Things will get better. You have a tremendous opportunity to change lives, so go and do it.

It's been a blast, and my life wouldn't have been half as much fun without you in it.

I love you, and if there is a heaven, I'll make sure I save you a special seat.

See you on the other side, providing I've done enough to get into the 'good' place!

Ana xxx

Though the tears were now coming thick and fast, Helen smiled. Typical Ana, trying to lighten the mood, even in the face of death.

Sitting back, she realised Ana was right. There was no reason to doubt herself. She had great ideas and the money to achieve everything she wanted to do, even though it would be incredibly hard without her best friend. They had already accomplished so much together, and now it was important to continue what had already been started.

Popping the letter back in the envelope, she felt some resistance and, looking inside, noticed some tissue paper in the bottom. Pulling it out and carefully unwrapping it, she discovered Ana's gold bracelet with the circle charm on it with her name and the little rose engraving underneath.

Her mum had bought it for her eighteenth birthday while on a trip to see relatives in Portugal, and she had worn it every day since. Carefully, Helen slipped it onto her own wrist, feeling Ana close to her once again.

Suddenly, her mobile rang and, seeing Ben's number, she picked up.

"Where are you? I woke up and you weren't here. Is everything OK?"

Ben sounded worried.

She explained about the letter from Ana and how she had wanted to read it on her own. He understood completely. Now he was no longer a 'professional' part of her life, they could spend as much time together as they wanted.

She promised she would be back soon.

She was feeling much more confident now, and with the support she had around her used in the right way, the lottery money could help so many people.

Staring at Ana's bracelet, she had a flash of inspiration for the name of the company. She would use her surname (Pond) and Ana's middle name (Rosa), and name the company Ponderosa in memory of her, so she would always be part of Helen's life and journey. With Ponderosa also being the name of a tall North American pine tree, it seemed even more appropriate, as Ana had been tall, graceful, and strong.

It's a shame it's not possible to plant one of those trees in memory of Ana, she thought. From what she understood, Arizona had the world's largest Ponderosa pine forest in the world. As she had been discussing a trip to the Grand Canyon with Ben, perhaps there was the possibility to plant some trees there too.

As she continued to sit on the bench, she observed a little robin. It was tiny, so it was probably still quite young. It looked around expectantly for some crumbs, as well as looking out for any danger. Not far away was a larger robin, and Helen wondered if that was 'Mum'. For a moment, the larger robin seemed to look directly at her, as if to say 'You'll be OK'.

Then, suddenly, both birds spread their wings and were off into the air and, before long, out of sight.

Now, she realised, it was *her* time to fly...

ACKNOWLEDGEMENTS

Thank you to my husband, Clive, for his continued support in all my endeavours, however mad they may seem at the time. His technical skills and common-sense approach have kept me sane while producing my first book!

Also, a big thank you to my son, Thomas, for his help with the front cover and navigating social media.

Special thanks to Lydia, Catherine, Ian, Mike, and Pam for reading the book and giving me honest and constructive feedback.

I am truly blessed to have such wonderful people in my life.

ABOUT THE AUTHOR

Lyn Asquith always dreamed of being an author. Now a retired Human Resources officer, she is fulfilling that wish. Born in Hertfordshire, she spent her childhood holidays in Essex—the nostalgic settings for her debut novel—and still visits often. Now living in Bedfordshire with her family, Lyn fills her free time with singing, travelling, and learning Spanish.